DIR

Grace Thompson was born in Barry, South Glamorgan, and apart from a few childhood years at school in Luton, she has lived in South Wales virtually all her life. She trained as a Nursery Nurse once her two children were at school, and has worked with children in care. Recently she moved from Wales to Chesham in Buckinghamshire to be near her daughter and her two grandsons. She is currently working on a sequel to *Dirty Nelly*.

Dirty Nelly

Grace Thompson

HEADLINE

First published in 1988 by
HEADLINE BOOK PUBLISHING PLC

ISBN 0 7472 3149 4

Typeset on 10/11 pt English Times
by Colset Pte Ltd, Singapore

Printed and bound in Great Britain by
Collins, Glasgow

HEADLINE BOOK PUBLISHING PLC
Headline House
79 Great Titchfield Street
London WIP 7FN

To Bowman, and all our family

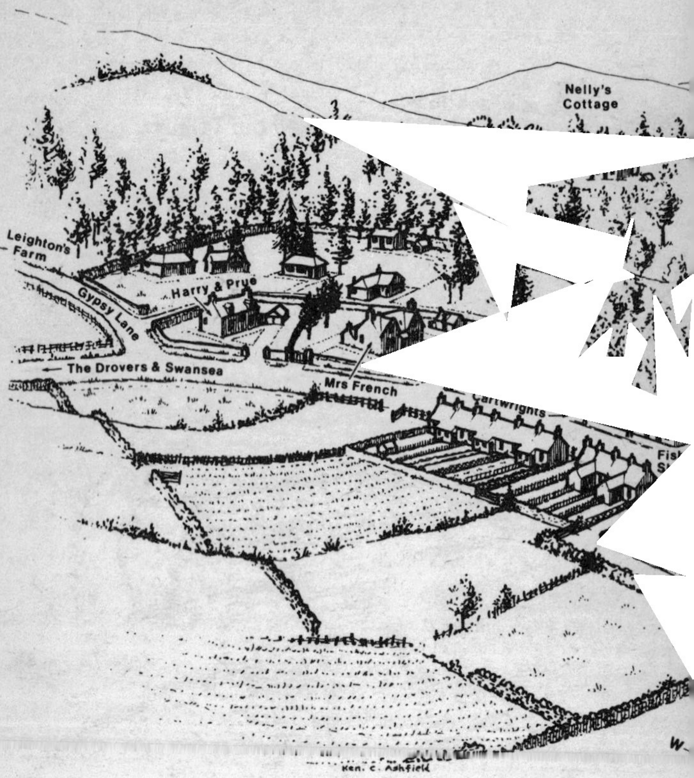

Hen Carw Parc

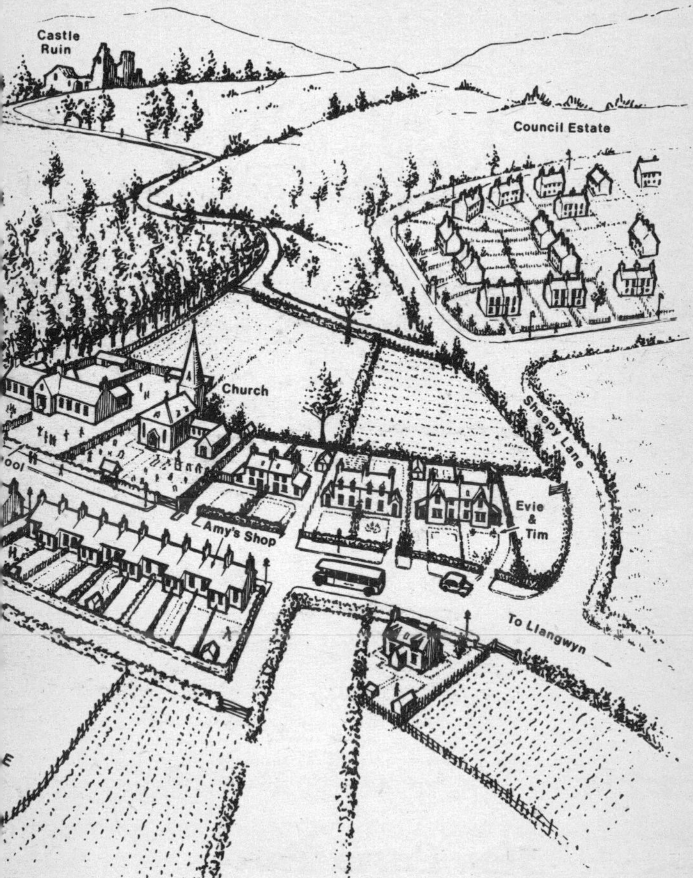
Castle Ruin
Council Estate
Church
Sheepy Lane
Evie & Tim
Amy's Shop
To Llangwyn

Chapter One

Nelly Luke woke early and was immediately wide awake. She was not the sort to lie there wasting time trying to coax back sleep which had fled too far. She slithered out of bed, lowering her feet straight into the furry slippers waiting for them and stretched inelegantly, with arms behind her head, her neck bending to one side and then the other. A loud yawn changed to a laugh as anxious barking from below urged her to hurry.

'All right, Bobby an' Spotty, give us a chance will yer?'

She pulled off the shapeless nightgown that had once been white and pulled a pair of pink, fleecy-lined bloomers on to her ample hips. She added a jumper, lisle stockings held up with bands of elastic, socks, a thin dress without sleeves and finally a loose, navy dress. Still yawning and stretching and talking to the dogs, she went down the curved staircase into her living room.

Opening the door for the impatient dogs she laughed as they pushed against each other in their haste to get out. Looking up at the slowly lightening sky she nodded approval at the weather prospects for the day. 'Rain's stopped,' she said to herself, 'thank Gawd fer that.'

The fire in the oven range looked dead but the removal of ash and some encouragement from a few sticks soon made it glow. She shook the kettle experimentally and, hearing water sloshing about, turned the swivel on which it rested over the heat and sat down to wait patiently for it to boil, a Donald Peers record on her wind-up gramophone.

The dogs were large, long-legged and boisterous. Cross

alsation and Pyrenean mountain dog, Nelly joked when anyone asked. In fact they were part sheepdog and part labrador; the rest was a mystery. They bustled in, leaping on to the chair to lick Nelly, then settled in front of the fire, blocking the heat from her legs and completely covering the rag mat, heads on her feet, their long tails tapping gently to show their pleasure that the night-hours without her were over.

After drinking several cups of tea, Nelly set off for the woods. This was another part of her life from which Spotty and Bobby were excluded. Not having running water in the cottage, the woods were her lavatory and she always spent the necessary moments alone.

It was still barely seven o'clock and the early February morning was chill.

'Come on then, boys.' She set off again, leaving the door open, the kettle re-filled from the tap in the lane and warming over the now bright fire. With the dogs barking their delight she pushed through the garden gate and into the trees.

There was a narrow, unmade track that passed her cottage, that led in one direction to the main road and the village of Hen Carw Parc, and on the other, by a wandering route, past the edge of the council estate and into the town of Llan Gwyn. Few people passed her gate, but those who did invariably called in to share a cup of tea and a bite of food.

She looked up and down the lane in the hope of seeing someone to talk to before heading into the trees towards the old ruin of a castle where the dogs loved to run and hunt rabbits. She took her time, savouring the freshness of the newly washed trees. There was no hurry; Mrs French for whom she 'did' would not expect her until nine o'clock.

The castle was nothing more than a collection of walls gradually disappearing under the insidiously creeping brambles and bracken. She thought of how it had looked two years previously when it was used as a centre for the Festival of Britain celebrations.

Hordes of people from the village and the council estate had appeared with every imaginable tool and hacked away at the invading plants, painted the walls with a wash of white and even put a new roof on the buildings that had once been the castle kitchens, to use as dressing rooms for the players who came to entertain.

Soon they would come again to prepare the place for the Coronation Party planned for the Saturday before June the third. Nelly was excited at the prospect of crowds passing her gate. She smiled as she remembered the school-children as they had sung rousing and patriotic songs and performed a pageant of the history of Wales, supporting large banners that somehow managed to defy the wind that had tried to whip them out of their tiny hands. Soon the preparations would begin again. Committees would be formed and the measuring, and the flag-making and the plans for fancy dress would fill the minds of everyone in the country. Yes, she thought, 1953 would be a year to remember.

She sat on a low wall and watched as the two dogs sniffed and followed trails between the wet bracken and the rocks, along animal paths that told them exciting things they were unable to share with her. Suddenly they lifted their heads and stared towards the repaired kitchen block. Nelly screwed up her brown eyes and followed the direction of their gaze.

She stayed as still as the dogs for several minutes, patient and hopeful of seeing a rabbit or a fox or something rarer. But instead of the good fortune of sighting a wild animal about its business, a man stood up, stared at her for a moment and walked away.

'Bleedin' 'ell, you give me a fright!' she shouted, her cockney accent more pronounced than normal. The man ignored her and walked further into the crumbling buildings as if unaware of her having spoken.

She caught glimpses of him and noticed the collar and tie before he wrapped his scarf more tightly around his face. He wore a brown overcoat which was much too large for him, and the belt, which had been tied instead of slipped through the buckle, dangled until it almost touched the grass. The coat was long and its hem too was lost in the damp grass. A brown trilby sat at an angle on his reddish brown hair.

' 'Ere, you lost or somethin'? Got a cuppa tea back in the 'ouse if you want one,' she coaxed. The man raised his left hand in salute but did not turn or even change his steady pace in acknowledgement.

'The village is the other way. Where you 'eading?' She was standing now and shouting loudly. The dogs, who had been growling low and threateningly, began to bark but they did not leave Nelly to follow the mysterious man, but moved closer to her in a protective way. Nelly shrugged and called the dogs. 'Come on, boys, it's time fer some grub. Then it's off to Mrs French.'

Monica French picked up the clock on her dressing table to dust it. This was one room she preferred to attend to herself. Nelly was careful and rarely broke anything, but Mrs French hated to see Nelly's dirt-grained hands touching her special things. She took note of the time; ten minutes to nine, Nelly would be here soon. She tensed with the expectation of the shouted proclamation from the kitchen door. Nelly could never wait until she came inside before telling her she had arrived. Mrs French wondered, not for the first time, why Nelly's London accent was as strong as when she had arrived in the village, thirteen years before.

In spite of her briefly felt disapproval, Monica French smiled. Nelly was not like the servants she had before the war had changed everything, but she was a good worker, happy to have around, even if she was rather loud.

Replacing the clock with its broderie anglaise face, she picked up the photograph of her daughter, Rosemary. The photograph had been taken in black and white but an artist had added colour, to show the beautiful auburn hair and rosy cheeks of the child. The eyes were brown and Rosemary was smiling happily.

Mrs French sighed. Rosemary had grown up so quickly

and now lived far away from her in Cardiff. It was only on rare occasions that they met. Another photograph standing beside it was of a young man in army uniform, the last one she had taken of her son, Alan.

She picked up the photograph in its brass frame and stared at it. Alan: missing presumed killed, amid the insanity of a war he didn't understand and which he didn't want to fight. The photograph showed him smiling, his arm around his fiancée, Fay Lewis, who was soon to marry another young man. Johnny Cartwright had been fortunate enough to miss the call up, being a few years too young.

She held the photograph to her chest and opened the wardrobe door. Inside was the suit she had bought with clothing coupons scrounged and saved and illegally bought, to wear at Alan and Fay's wedding. They were to have married on Alan's next leave, but he never came home again.

Dare she go and watch Fay and Johnny married? Could she risk upsetting everyone by her presence? What if she were to burst into tears at seeing Alan's girl at the side of Johnny Cartwright, dressed in white and promising to love him and cherish him 'Till death do us part'? Better not to go.

She closed the wardrobe door and then shook her head, angry with herself for her selfishness. Fay had a right to a good and full life. She would invite them both to lunch before the wedding. She began looking through cupboards and drawers. There must be a few things she could spare them from her stored linen, to help them start.

'Mrs French dearie, it's me, I'm 'ere.' Nelly's call broke her mood and she replaced the photograph and started down the stairs, a smile of welcome on her calm face. Brown eyes met brown eyes, one pair composed, the other with a hint of mischief in them. Nelly always looked about to burst into loud laughter, her teeth, exposed by her smile, were crooked. Some, on the left hand side of her mouth were missing altogether, adding to the look of saucy expectation.

'Start upstairs, shall I?' she asked, tying the dogs to a line post.

The church where Fay Lewis and Johnny Cartwright were to be married was at the eastern end of the village. Hen Carw Parc sprawled along the high street, groups of houses and small terraced cottages with gaps in between, where wild flowers gave a riotous display in the months of summer, but were now just yellow areas of fallen grasses. Next to the church was the school and the church hall, the buildings linked together in age and in the stones from which they were built. Passing westwards past the school, a row of cottages came next with a matching row across the road. They were identical, differing only in the curtains that hung in the small windows, showing the individuality of the occupants.

A field then, before the winding, narrow road that led up to Nelly's cottage at the edge of the wood surrounding the old castle ruins. Past the turning, more houses but these were grander and larger. One, the oldest and most imposing, was owned by Mrs French. Behind it, snuggling into the band of trees that followed the road for a while, were the houses more recently built, in what had once been the grounds of Monica French's house.

As Nelly and Mrs French set about the occasional weekday tasks, Fay Lewis walked around the empty church and tried to imagine herself standing there, before the flower-decked altar as the bride of Johnny Cartwright. The sun shone through the plain glass of the window recently replaced after enemy bombs from a bomber way off course had shattered the ancient coloured illustration of the Shepherd with His sheep. It shone on Fay's shining, blonde hair which fell in an under roll to rest on the shoulders of the grey suit she wore. The blue eyes seemed to match exactly the frilled blouse and the smart, lace-trimmed hat, and the high-heeled shoes and the handbag held in her hand. She looked slim, elegant and expensive. That she was successful was obvious, the fact that she was unhappy, less so.

The flowers on the altar had not yet been replaced since the previous Sunday. Daffodils and the slender branches of hazel with the yellow catkins drooped sadly in the large vase. The stems of the daffodils arched low, spilling yellow piles of dust onto the polished surfaces. The smell was cloying and redolent of death. Fay shivered and walked to the doorway and the generative sun.

She looked at the graves; all but a few overgrown and neglected after the winter months, the sun shining on the memorials with their long forgotten names. No grave for Alan. Only a name on a plaque to say he had lived, and been loved. Yet this place had echoed with his laughter. Here they had hunted for wild flowers to arrange for her mother's delight, had listened to birdsong and thrilled to their first kiss.

Memories, she thought. Why are they so painful? They had enjoyed every sun-filled, joyous day, yet it was an agony to remember. Now they were all gone; her mother, killed in a stupid accident, her father dead soon after from the shock of it, the child who was Alan had vanished and the child who was herself was a stranger she had once known.

She thought of the small cottage in which she would soon start her married life with Johnny and his family and stared about her, wishing things could magically return to how they had been. She clenched her fists and pressed her lips together, trying to force herself to forget the doubts and imbibe herself with the excitement of her forthcoming marriage. Wasn't that what every woman wanted, deep down? Marriage, a loving husband and children? Wasn't second best better than nothing? Guilt filled her, and shame, that she should think of Johnny that way. She glanced back through the church door and silently promised to give him all her love, to forget her dreams and begin to build new memories with him at the centre of them, from the moment of their wedding in a little over one week's time.

In a corner of the old building she opened her handbag and began repairing her makeup. Her eyes were critical of the slightly reddened lids, her lips pursed in disapproval of giving way to self-pity.

'Fay? Fay? You there, love?'

She snapped the compact shut and went along the path to where a puzzled Johnny stood, his bus purring quietly beside the hedge of yew.

He was a small man, but he gave her the sensation of being protected. His slim body seemed ready to charge into action on her behalf the moment he was needed. He was quick to rise to anger when someone was unfairly treated and prepared to fight in a good cause. Yet with her he was never anything but gentle. He understood about her difficulty in accepting that Alan had really been killed, during the last days of the war; the lack of a funeral and the necessary grieving that went with it, making the death difficult to accept.

'Johnny!' She pushed her recent unhappiness aside and because of it, her welcome to her fiancé was more demonstrative than usual. Ignoring the solitary face staring out from the bus window, she hugged him, taking care not to smudge her lipstick against his cheek.

'I recognised your car,' he said. 'What are you doing in the church all on your own?' His young face flushed slightly with the pleasure of her greeting.

'I was on my way back from Swansea and I thought I'd pop in and dream a little about next week.' She stared into his eyes, lowering her lashes in a way that was both coy and provocative, an attempt to forget her recent doubts. 'Johnny, I can't wait for us to be married.'

'Well, we didn't, did we?' he chuckled. 'That old castle has seen some sights in its day!'

Fay stiffened and pulled away from him. She could not understand his openness in talking about their private moments. She found it hard to discuss them, and preferred it to happen, then be forgotten until the next time they felt passion overwhelming them.

'You'd better go, that customer of yours will be putting in a complaint.'

'Never. It's my auntie. Old romantic she is; had three husbands she has, and would take a fourth if she was given half a chance!'

He gave her one brief kiss which she turned her face to receive on her cheek, then ran lightly down the path, under the lych-gate and across the road to his cab. He tooted noisily on his horn as the purring became a roar, and the bus disappeared behind the yew trees lining the road.

Getting into her car, Fay again added a touch of powder to her cheeks and turned on the ignition. She was smiling. Johnny's happiness was in no doubt. They would be happy, she would make sure of that. Checking her mirror she pulled out into the road, but she did not increase her speed. A hundred and fifty yards from the church was the house in which she lived. It might be an idea to call and see if anything had arrived by second post. She parked outside the large semi and got out.

Already the house was looking abandoned. The curtains had been taken down from the windows and all the potted plants which had bordered the front path were gone. The marks on the concrete where they had stood added to the air of neglect which the untidy piles of rubbish accentuated. The rubbish consisted mostly of unwanted mats and lino. She was determined to leave the house clean and litter-free for the new tenants, whoever they might be.

Her rent had been paid for the next two weeks and by that time the place would be devoid of everything that would tell of the years she and her parents had lived there. She had an urge to go in at once and begin scrubbing the wooden floors, to wash away her old life and so impose a stronger feeling of the new.

There was one letter; it looked official, probably a bill, she thought. She opened it and read a letter from the owner, reminding her that it was her responsibility to leave the place as she would wish to find it. She tore it angrily and threw it onto the cold ashes of last night's fire.

She went into the kitchen to make herself a cup of tea and found a note pushed through the window. 'Parcel in the shed' it said. The parcel could have waited, but she was expecting supplies of some new 'Bride's Mother' creations. April, May and June were busy times for weddings and she knew they would sell well. She brought the large box into the house.

Fay was a saleswoman who travelled through Glamorganshire, Brecon and even as far as Pembrokeshire, selling hats to small exclusive outlets. She carefully unwrapped the delicate millinery, pausing to admire some and frown at others, then decided to take them all on her last calls of the day.

Dogs barking made her start and when she stepped outside, she found herself staring at Nelly's two dogs.

'Go away! Out of here, get out!'

'Sorry, dearie,' Nelly said, appearing around the corner of the house. 'Thought you 'ad burglars. Couldn't see no car, an' what with you usually bein' out sellin' yer 'ats while the shops is open, well I thought – sorry, love.'

'Hello, Nelly. Thank you for keeping an eye. I'd ask you in for a cup of tea, but I have to get on.'

'Don't worry, dearie, I won't keep yer. It's just that I saw one of them tramps up near the castle and thought 'e might 'ave got desperate and broke in. Furtive 'e looked.'

'I'll make sure I lock up properly.' Fay edged a bit closer to Nelly's plump form, hinting for her to leave, but Nelly stood her ground, it wasn't often she had a chance to talk to Fay.

'Been gatherin' sticks.' Nelly showed her leather-cloth bag with its load of small twigs and pieces of rotting wood. 'Want some, do yer?'

'No thanks, Nelly, you keep it. I'll manage fine until I leave here.'

'Not much more than a week now, is it? Gettin' excited are yer?'

'Yes. But I can't talk about it now, I have to go.'

' 'Course. Work to be done. Tell yer what, call in an' 'ave a cuppa with me, why don't yer?'

Fay inwardly shuddered at the thought of eating or

drinking in the filthy old cottage in the wood, but she smiled politely and said, 'I'll do that, Nelly, when I have some time to spare.'

'Come with Johnny. 'E often comes. 'Is Mum an' me, we've bin friends for years, we 'ave. Little Johnny Cartwright gettin' married, an' to someone as posh as you. Can't 'ardly believe it I can't.'

Pulling the door firmly closed and edging around Nelly with a distasteful frown on her face, Fay walked down the path to the gate. 'Goodbye; see you soon.' She carried the box and put it in the car.

'Tarra, love, an' drive careful.'

In the mirror, Fay could see Nelly standing at the gate, a dog on either side, waving as if she were a mother waving off a schoolgirl. Irritated, Fay drove faster than usual towards her next call.

Once she had passed the turning which led up to the council estate, there were open fields on either side and she pressed hard on the accelerator, knowing it was unlikely she would see anyone on the lonely stretch before the town. It was with a gasp of disbelief that she saw the man step off the grass verge, making her swerve and stop with a squeal of brakes.

She stopped the car and got out, her irritation at Nelly's visit, grasping the excuse to turn to anger. The man stared, pulled his scarf higher on his face and walked away. He slipped through the hedge and began hurrying back up the field he had presumably just left. With an explosive sigh, Fay returned to the car. She was shaken and had to wait a while before driving on. The hedge was thin and bare, lacking the leaves that would make the barrier complete and through it she was able to see him limping across the furrowed field towards the back of her house.

Where could he be going? There was nothing but fields, woodland and eventually hills and sheep in that direction. She guessed he was the mysterious prowler that Nelly had reported and her attitude to the old woman softened. He was acting oddly and she appreciated Nelly's concern.

When she eventually reached Llangwyn, she was thankful

to put aside thoughts of the near-accident and put her mind into her work. She did well, the new spring hats were popular, and she was glad she had bothered to unpack the parcel, even if the delay had meant a few shocks. She was in a happier mood when she set off home.

When she reached the beginning of Hen Carw Parc, she was still feeling a benign affection for Nelly so when she saw her walking along the road with her two dogs in tow on the lengths of rope, she slowed and waved. She waited until the woman and her straining, impatient dogs had passed her drive, then went in and unpacked the car.

As she stepped into the house she felt a chill of fear. There was a draught. Something was not right. She dropped her parcels and ran back outside.

'Nelly!' she called. 'Nelly, can you come here?'

The dogs barked and pulled their owner in answer to the call as if they understood her alarm and wanted no delay in assisting.

'What is it, dearie? Shall I bring the dogs or leave 'em outside. Tie 'em to the gates?'

'You'd better bring them. I think someone's been inside. There's a window open, I think.'

'Let's 'ave a look out the back. Perhaps you forgot to lock the door, in 'urry you were.' Nelly tutted and shook her head in disapproval.

They went around the house and Nelly pointed in triumph. 'There, french winders wide open. Like me, are yer? Want plenty of fresh air? Never shuts me door, I don't.'

'I didn't open it,' Fay said slowly.

' 'Course yer did. Didn't yer?' Nelly said doubtfully.

'Will you come inside with me?'

'Me an' the dogs'll be close behind yer.'

The small procession went through the french windows but not in the order intended. The two dogs pulled Nelly enthusiastically and she shot inside before Fay could pluck up enough courage to climb the shallow steps. Nelly charged through the place and with Fay now close behind her, reported that the house was empty.

'There doesn't seem to be anything disturbed,' Fay said, looking at the pile of boxes neatly piled against the wall of the living room.

'Better tell the police though, you never know.'

'Yes, I'll call in tomorrow, but you're probably right, I didn't lock it properly, the wind must have opened it.'

'Be all right, will yer?' Nelly asked, making for the door. 'I'll stay a while if you like, though it's almost dark and I 'aven't shut me chickens up.'

'No, I'm fine now. Thank you very much for coming in. You're very brave.'

'Only 'cause of the dogs,' Nelly laughed. Her loud laugh made Fay shudder with an irritation that was never far below the surface. Why doesn't she go, she thought, as Nelly chattered on about how glad she was of the dogs' company.

'But you don't need no dogs fer company,' Nelly went on. 'Not now you'll 'ave young Johnny Cartwright.' She waved her hands at the empty room, hesitating only a moment before asking, 'Why are you leaving this 'ouse then? It won't suit you to live in rooms with Johnny's family fer long, not after 'avin' a place like this.'

'The rent is quite expensive, and the furniture was all old and out of fashion. Johnny and I have plans.'

'You want to live in rooms instead of living with old fashioned furniture?' Nelly deliberately misunderstood, knowing Fay would take time to explain and put her right. A good gossip was worth trying to hang on to.

'We want a house of our own; we hope to save enough to buy one of the new houses up to top.' She waved up through the window at the back of the room, to where fields led up past woods to a distant housing estate.

'Them's council,' Nelly said.

'Yes, but new ones are planned, to be sold. Johnny and I are going to save up by living with his mother, and buy one.' She moved closer to Nelly, urging her to go.

'Tara then. Come an' 'ave that cuppa one day, why don't yer?' Nelly slowly moved towards the door, sensing the girl's impatience to be rid of her. 'Come on, boys, time to get 'ome an' see to the 'ens.'

Fay ran around the house once Nelly had gone, checking every window and throwing the bolts on the doors. Then she sat, still shaken by the suspected burglary, and wondered if the house was really empty. What if she had locked the house up and locked herself in, with the intruder?

She grasped the long poker from under the grate and crept upstairs. When she had looked under the remaining furniture, and opened the wardrobes, and searched between the hangers, she sat down and giggled, fear giving a tearful edge to her laughter. She would never be used to living alone. Thank goodness it wouldn't be for much longer. She would soon have Johnny. And his mother. She hoped she would be able to cope.

Chapter Two

Amy Prichard's shop was crowded, even before any customers arrived. Around three sides of the small room, that had once been the parlour of a farm-worker's cottage, were wide counters of mahogany. In front of them were tins of biscuits, each with a glass lid that lifted on a hinge to allow the biscuits, so temptingly arrayed, to be taken out, packed into paper bags and weighed and sold.

Of the area remaining, much of it was filled with sacks of vegetables. Potatoes and carrots and onions were displayed by rolling down the sacks as the contents were sold. Dog biscuits and meal, and food for chickens added to the scents that filled the air. Amy tried sometimes to stand the sacks outside on the narrow pavement, but the village constable insisted the path be kept clear, and no matter how she tried to sweeten him, he remained adamant.

This morning, new supplies had arrived and she was struggling with the half empty sacks of potatoes and carrots to pile them on top of the new, and make room for customers to come in and buy them. She sighed. Somehow she would have to find the money to extend the shop.

She satisfied herself that she had made as much floor space as possible and began tidying the shelves. New tins behind the old, her mind almost unconsciously checking on items she would need to order for the following week. She did not hear Nelly come in.

'Got any of them beans with sausages in have yer?' Nelly asked, sitting on one of the boxes placed to support a crate of cauliflowers.

'Oh, Nelly, don't sit on the caulis,' Amy grumbled.

'I ain't! It's just a box put ready, with nothing on it.'

'Oh, sorry. I haven't brought them through. There's me thinking I'd made some extra space. Watch for me, will you, while I bring them in?'

Nelly watched her go, a plump, very pretty woman, carefully made up, and with her blonde hair fluffed out, and ear-rings, dangling and sparkling, almost reaching the shoulders of the pink overall she wore.

Amy hurried through the cluttered back room, which was a store as well as a living room which she used during the day, settling into one of the large, leather arm-chairs whenever there was a lull. When she struggled back with a large crate of cauliflowers that seemed determined to catch on everything she passed, the shop was full.

'Go on, you.' Nelly waved her hands at the impatient customers. 'Me time's me own. Serve me last, why don't yer?'

Amy quickly dealt with the requests and smiled at the complaints, refused a bit of extra on the rations, used greaseproof to pick up the cheese which was cut with a length of wire, and an old leather glove to pick up the potatoes. She was quick, and neat and soon there were only two people left to serve.

'Mrs French?' she smiled. 'How can I help you this morning?'

'Isn't Nelly before me?'

'Not in any 'urry, dearie. You get what you want.'

'I would like to add to my Friday order. I've invited Fay and Johnny for Sunday lunch and I'll need some extra vegetables.'

As Amy opened her mouth to recommend some of her selection, Nelly said. 'Them caulis look good. Just look at the 'eart. All fancy, like it's been knitted.'

'French they are,' Amy explained. 'Expensive I'm afraid. But in February they aren't that plentiful.'

'I'll have one.'

'It's the war,' Nelly said dolefully. 'All the farms messed

about an' told to grow things then the men took away an' only them bits of girls to see to it all. No wonder we 'ave to buy from the French!'

'They fought a war too, Nelly,' Mrs French laughed.

'Yes, but they didn't win it, did they?'

The logic of that escaped the other two and they smiled at each other, and at Nelly.

The dogs were becoming restless and as Mrs French left, Amy shouted, 'Nelly! Your dogs have peed against the sack of dog biscuits!'

'That reminds me,' Nelly said unconcerned. 'Biscuits is what I want. Got any broken ones or mis-shapes?'

'There's some tins of Marie mis-shapes if you want one.'

'Can't afford a whole *tin*, Amy.'

'I'll put it on your bill and you can pay me something off each week. It's half the price of perfect ones.'

'Smashin', Amy, you're a pal.' Tucking the tin into her large, leather-cloth bag, Nelly trundled off through the village and home.

Amy defied P.C. Harris again and dragged two sacks outside, and balanced the caulis on top. If they were seen they would sell more quickly. At least up high, they would avoid the salutations of any more canine callers.

She stood outside for a moment, looking westward towards the house behind that of Mrs French, to where her sister lived. She could see the landing window where she knew Prue spent a lot of time staring down through the village street, observing all that went on. Key-hole Kate, she had been nicknamed, years ago.

She went back inside and tried again to re-arrange the stock to allow a fraction more floor-space. She would have to do something to make more room, and soon. Harry would do the work, she knew that, but how to set about arranging it? Harry Beynon, Prue's husband, was a builder and had agreed to knock the back room wall down and double the size of the shop, but in the difficult circumstances, it was Prue who she had to ask.

It was Wednesday and half-day closing, so perhaps it

would be an idea to visit her sister. It was weeks since they had met for a chat, although they lived so close. The shop filled again and for the next hour she put the problem out of her mind and coped with the difficulties she hoped to ease.

'Heard about the new Headmaster at the school?' Milly Toogood asked, selecting some carrots. 'Seems it's Nelly's son-in-law. What d'you think of that, then? Nelly's Evie coming back to grace us with her presence!'

'Are you sure? Nelly didn't say anything when she was here. Funny for her not to say,' Amy frowned.

'Funny-osity that one,' Milly Toogood sniffed. 'Londoner come down here to escape the blitz. Why didn't she go back I wonder? Funny-osity,' she repeated. 'Got one of those paper carriers, have you? I hope the string handle's stronger than the last one!'

Amy stifled a sigh and handed the brown paper carrier to Milly, who pulled on the string handle and examined the cardboard strengthener on the top before handing over the money for her purchases.

At one o'clock Amy closed the door and went upstairs to make herself a snack. The children ate at school so she usually made do with a sandwich. She put a piece of bacon, that no one would accept as their ration as it was too fat, into a casserole with some vegetables. Leaving it simmering gently she renewed her make up, fluffed out her hair and left by the back door.

She followed the lane that separated the small gardens from the field behind, and came out almost opposite the lane to Nelly's cottage, crossed the road and headed for the houses behind Mrs French's large house. The houses in what had been Mrs French's grounds had been built by Harry Beynon, Prue's husband, and he had bought one for himself.

'Prue? Are you there? It's me.' Amy waited until she heard her sister invite her in, and wondered why they were always so formal with each other. Among her friends, there were none who expected her to wait to be invited in, yet she knew her sister, her only family apart from her children, would have been strongly disapproving if she had knocked, called and walked in. She thought one day she would curtsey, but decided the sarcasm would be wasted on her stony-faced sister.

Prue was writing a letter when she went into the front room. She did not look up or greet Amy, but continued working until what ever she was doing was completed. A wave of irritation passed through Amy's face. It's as if she's expecting me to apologise for disturbing her, she thought.

'Harry in?' she asked. 'I wanted to talk to him about knocking the two rooms into one and extending the shop. It's far too small.'

'You carry too many lines,' Prue said. 'There's no room for some of the stuff you insist on selling. No profit either. All those cottons and pins and mending wools. How often do you sell any?'

'Not often, but there's many who can't get to town and would be stuck if I didn't stock odds and ends.'

'They'd manage. You don't want to spend out money making the shop bigger if you could cut down on your stocks instead. Besides, Harry's busy now. Bungalows over near Swansea. Out all day he is, working very hard. It would be months before he could consider it.'

'You don't want me to ask him, do you? I'd pay the going rate,' Amy snapped. Then more slowly she added, 'If I speak to the bank manager I'm sure he'll arrange something. The shop does well.'

'It's always Harry you come to when you want help. He's only your brother-in-law. You shouldn't have bought the shop if you can't cope.'

It was on the tip of Amy's tongue to retaliate and walk out but something stopped her. 'Prue, what is it? Is something wrong?'

'I'm forty next week, that's what's wrong.'

'But I'm thirty-seven. So what's so terrible about being forty?'

'The realisation that I won't be a mother. I've been the sensible one, the strong one, yet I end up with nothing. And you have the nerve to come yet again and demand help. I've always helped you, right from when we were children, so why is it that I'm forty and have nothing?'

Amy was shocked. That the declaration that Prue had helped her was blatantly untrue was ignored. It was the expression on her sister's face; cold eyes in the thin and lined face. She looked like an old woman; her hair, usually so carefully set, was pulled back and fixed savagely with three slides at each side, the ends fallen from the roll at the back of her head.

Careful not to sound condescending, Amy said, 'I'll make a cup of tea. Then I thought I'd wash your hair and show you a new style I saw in last week's magazine. It's months since you let me do your hair, and you know how I love doing it.'

'Don't bother. I'm going into town tomorrow, I'll have it done there.'

Amy looked around the over-tidy room with its expensive carpet and furniture. It was tempting to point out to Prue that few people in Hen Carw Parc would consider her life a sad one. The kitchen was full of the latest gadgets and boasted a large fridge and a washing machine. She looked at Prue and smiled.

'I suppose you think I should be grateful,' Prue said.

'You've got Harry, and he's done well.'

'*We've* done well,' Prue corrected. 'I've worked this business up as much as him. Did you know when he started *I* did the buying and the book keeping? *I* employed the labour, *I* sorted out difficult payers. He wouldn't have known what to do, those early years, if it hadn't been for me.'

'I work single-handed in a small shop and live in one room above it with two children.'

'But you have children.'

'But no husband.'

'You chose to live that way!'

'We all have choices, Prue.'

'That isn't true.'

Amy was thankful when the clock struck three and she was able to make her excuses and leave. She guessed that Prue and Harry had had one of their regular rows, and for once was glad her sister was not the sort to confide in her.

She walked through the small group of expensive houses with their winter gardens bravely showing a few snowdrops and crocus, and past the lane to Nelly's cottage. She saw someone coming down and hurried past, not wanting to be stopped by Nelly. It took a moment to realise that the figure was not Nelly, but a slim, heavily limping man. It was a bit early in the year for hikers, but that was probably what he was.

She walked on, past the row of cottages opposite her own, and stood outside the school gates. She was early for meeting Margaret, but she did not feel like going indoors. She needed the cold air and a quiet moment before going home, and Margaret would be pleased to see her waiting.

Her blue eyes were shining, the colour so brilliant that the whites were tinged with blue. She wore her habitual smile but she was dismayed. She regretted asking Prue if Harry would do the work on the shop. Now it would be impossible to ask Harry. She sighed. Life had certainly become complicated once more.

Friday morning was Nelly's second visit to Mrs French, and the night before, she had put her hair into curlers made from pipe cleaners to look a bit tidy, so when she opened the door for the dogs to run out, she was disgusted to see rain.

'Waste of time that was! And uncomfortable. Think I'll get meself a smart cut,' she muttered to the dogs, who went out with the assistance of her foot and returned within seconds. She pulled out a large plastic mac and opened a man's umbrella she had bought in a jumble sale, and went to the woods. Like the dogs, she stayed no longer than she had to.

When she walked down the lane and turned right to Mrs French's house, she still carried the umbrella and the dogs walked sedately beside her, less eager than usual to run ahead.

'You'll have to tie them outside, Nelly.' Mrs French showed disapproval as the dogs looked hopefully at the kitchen door.

'Stick 'em near the door, they won't 'urt.' Ignoring the request for them to stay in the yard, Nelly attached their ropes to the door handle and told them to sit. She took off her mac and the large coat that Mrs French thought smelt only slightly better than the dogs, and began work.

'It's good news about your daughter,' Mrs French said and Nelly stared at her with a frown.

'News about my Evie? What's that then?'

'She's coming back here to live, isn't she? Timothy is to be the new Headmaster of the school.'

'No one told me.' Nelly frowned, then added cheerfully, 'I expect Evie's plannin' a surprise. I won't let on I knows. Don't want to spoil it. Great one for surprises, my Evie.'

'They will be living in the house where Fay now lives. She'll be married by then of course.'

'Fancy. My Evie near enough to call in for a chat. Nice that'll be. An' little Oliver. Eight 'e is now, same age as Amy's Margaret. I ain't seen 'im fer months. Won't know me of course. But –' She laughed her loud laugh, 'but 'e soon will, eh?'

Nelly turned up the front of the apron that Mrs French insisted she wore and fixed it with a pin high enough to stay clean. With a bucket of soapy water she scrubbed the tiles on the kitchen floor, singing loudly as she thought of Evie coming back. As she was putting on her coat to leave, Mrs French said, 'Nelly, that coat, isn't it a bit large? I have one here I was given to see if I could find it a home. It would probably fit you far better.' She brought out a dark grey coat and held it for Nelly to try. Nelly fingered the cloth and sighed.

'Lovely that is, dearie. Good bit of cloth. Sure you don't want it? If someone gave it yer –'

'It was given to me to pass on to someone who needed it,' Mrs French smiled. 'Take it. Evie will be pleased to see you looking smart and' – she hesitated over the word "tidy" and said instead, 'warm'.

'Ta. But I don't think I'll wear it 'ome, it's rainin' and besides, I'm goin' to buy some fish an' chips and that Milly Toogood's daughter would charge me double if I was dressed posh!' Her crooked teeth showed and her laughter filled the kitchen.

When she was outside the back gate and out of sight, Nelly took off her mac and used it to protect the coat she had been given, and with the black umbrella saving her from most of the downpour, she went past the bottom of her lane and over the road to the fish and chip shop opposite the school. She looked along the road, past the school yard, past the church where Fay and Johnny were to marry and beyond, to the semi-detached houses. The one in which Fay lived was the last in the row and she could see Fay's car outside on the verge.

So Evie and Tim and young Oliver were going to live there. She hoped they could manage to live that close and manage not to quarrel too often. She loved them all, 'but,' she muttered, 'my Evie's damned 'ard work. Always was.' She turned and went in to queue for her cod and chips.

The day was so dark, that with the news of Evie's return, a pall of gloom settled on the cottage. The fire would not burn brightly and now and again the smoke blew back and covered the mantelpiece with its dust and smell. Nelly was restless. The door was closed, which was unusual. She read the paper with which her meal had been wrapped, screwing up her eyes in the poor light, unwilling to light her oil lamp so early. She screwed up the greasy paper and threw it onto the fire, enjoying its brief flame, then wandered upstairs.

She took up the grey coat and spread it on the bed to admire, then from under the bed, she dragged a large suitcase. Inside it was another coat, of maroon wool, decorated with a fur collar and with pockets trimmed to match. She unpacked it and put it with the grey one. The suitcase also included some good quality winter dresses. All were too small for her.

'Think I'll go into town soon,' she said aloud. 'Got a nice lot of stuff to sell. Clothes rations might be long forgotten, but there's still a demand for good stuff a bit cheap.'

She re-packed the clothes and stood the suitcases ready for carrying. Her face was sad as she went back down the dark stairs. With Evie coming back she knew she would be in need of a cheering day out once in a while. Perhaps she would save the clothes, which would earn enough to buy a bite of food and a few drinks, for a day when Evie upset her. That day would not be long in coming. She put on her plastic mac again. 'Come on, boys; time for another walk.'

The rain obliterated most of the view, but as she went through the trees, she saw the man again. He was coming away from the castle and Nelly wondered if he was sleeping rough. She called to him, but apart from a brief wave of his left hand, he did not reply. When the weather was better she would look around the ruin, she decided.

She didn't go into the trees but down the road to the village. Opposite Amy's shop in the middle of the row of cottages, she called to see Johnny Cartwright's mother. Nice to pass an hour of the gloomy day in chatter.

Netta Cartwright was small; less than five feet tall and she was round and rosy. Her hair had once been dark but was now perfectly white and was complemented by her pink complexion. Her eyes were dark brown but unlike Nelly's which darted curiously here and there, Netta's were calm and gentle. When she spoke, her voice was little more than a whisper and it seemed impossible, Nelly thought, to imagine her roused to anger.

'I'm so glad you called,' Netta said, when the two women were settled with cups of tea. 'Johnny and I have offered to collect for the children's Coronation Party and it's rather more work than we imagined. Would you be willing to help?'

'Course I will, dearie. When d'you want me to start?'

'There's all the council estate. Thought they'd do their own party we did, but the thought of having a party in the castle has gripped the children and they won't settle for anything else.'

'The more the merrier.'

'We try to go out every Friday, that being the day when we're most likely to get the money,' Netta blushed as she reminded Nelly that some of the local people found it difficult to manage. 'What we don't manage, we do on Saturday mornings. All right with you?'

They discussed times and arrangements for a while and as Nelly stood up to leave, Johnny arrived. He went at once to the neatly set table with its embroidered cloth and helped himself to one of the small cakes Netta had made.

'Hello, Nelly. Glad you've left some cake for me!' He divided a second cake and fed it to the two dogs, and patted his mother on the shoulder. 'Great cook, my Mam. I hope Fay looks after me as well.'

'She will. Lucky boy you are,' Netta chuckled.

Nelly smiled and was warmed by the affection in the room. If only she and Evie could get on as well, she sighed. Johnny and his mother were alike in appearance, Johnny being only slightly taller. His hair was medium brown and so straight it refused to even bend over his head, but stuck out at the side, unwilling to conform. He was very young-looking. The moustache he had grown to try to compensate, looked odd on him; like a boy dressing up as a man. Yet he was mature in every other way, and ready to take on the responsibilities of marriage and a family. Nelly knew he had loved Fay for a long time and was overjoyed when she had finally accepted him.

At first, Netta had been doubtful about the couple, their upbringing had been so different. Fay's family had been wealthy compared to the Cartwright's and it showed in more than the expensive clothes Fay wore, and the large house she had lived in. She knew Johnny would change as he and Fay shared their lives.

Nelly looked out of the door as she started to leave and groaned at the sight of the steady rain. 'I hope this is going to clear for your weddin', young Johnny,' she said. 'Though it doesn't really matter what the weather does on yer weddin' day. You'll only see sunshine, won't yer?'

'Sunshine all the way, Nelly,' he said.

Nelly crossed her fingers.

Fay had felt a need to include Mrs French in her wedding arrangements and had gone to seek her advice about the flowers. It was unnecessary and both women knew it. And both felt the strangeness, even after eight years, of talking about a wedding which did not include Alan.

Fay knew Mrs French had appreciated the gesture and she kissed her as she left, holding her book of wedding details, to go home. It was raining and she bent over against the rain in the futile attempt to make it less of a nuisance.

She lifted her head now and again, and saw someone coming down Nelly's lane. The man stopped when he saw her and she passed him and then glanced back. He was following, but again stopped when she looked back. She stood near the school yard and watched him cross the road and look in the window of Amy's shop, then at the price list on the steamed up windows of the fish and chip shop.

She walked home and put the key into her front door, then, instead of stepping inside, returned to the gate and looked for the man. He had re-crossed the road and was passing her gate. Startled by the unexpected encounter, he looked towards her and at once pulled his scarf tighter about his face.

But he was not fast enough. In the gloom of the rainy evening, eyes that were dark and intense met hers. Her head spun, the strength went from her legs as muscles turned to liquid.

'Alan!' she gasped, before she fainted.

When she opened her eyes she was alone, but she had been laid carefully down in the porch, with the scarf the man had been wearing, folded and placed as a pillow beneath her head. A car passed along the road, somewhere a rook cawed its indifference, and rain continued to patter insistently on the gravel path. She felt as if she had newly woken from a dream. Had she dreamt it? Had she fallen, knocked her head and slept? Alan often filled her dreams, was this simply another?

She slowly rose and taking the scarf, pressed it to her face. The scent of him was strong, enhanced by the moisture.

Unseen by her, the man watched from the hedge which separated her garden from the field. Satisfied she was all right, he walked up the field and into the woods, heading for the castle ruin.

It was soon to be her wedding day, yet all Fay felt at that moment was a cold dread. She was certain it had been Alan she had seen. But if it were him, where had he been? Why hadn't he walked up to the door, knocked and walked in? Why was he wandering around the village in the rain, waiting for a glimpse of her? For surely he was Nelly's mysterious and furtive prowler?

Twice she put on her coat and picked up her car keys, intending to go back to Mrs French. If Alan were alive, she obviously must be told. But each time she resisted, and threw off the coat. What could she say to her? 'Your son is alive but chooses not to see either of us?' Mrs French would think her insane. Perhaps she was. That was a more likely explanation.

For weeks she had dreamed of Alan and, as her wedding to Johnny drew closer, the dreams became more real. They were filled with longing for him, so intense at times that she dreaded to go to bed and face another lonely night of frustration and despair. That must be the truth. She was still grieving for Alan. Johnny's loving was not enough to kill that passion.

She remembered clearly the days after they had been told he was 'Missing, presumed killed'. She had seen him everywhere. In bus queues, in the cinema, in shops and on every street in every town. The approach of her wedding day, when she would be admitting fully that he was gone for ever, had made those days return. Half convinced, she ran a bath and sank into it.

In a few days she would promise to love, honour and obey Johnny. He loved her, and his love would lay Alan's ghost for ever. She began to run over the time-table for the wedding morning in her mind, forcing herself to feel the excitement and importance that was every bride's right.

Chapter Three

On the morning of Fay and Johnny's wedding, Nelly went up to the castle again. She saw a man sitting on a stone that had fallen from the ancient walls, oblivious to the raw cold of the early morning. She saw he was dressed as before, in the over-long brown coat that was too large for his thin frame; the collar was turned up but the scarf was different. In profile she could see little of his features but what she did see made her want to cry. The right side of it was horribly distorted by a scar.

He seemed unaware of her, although she had not walked with any intention of keeping her presence a secret. But now, she moved as carefully as she could around the fallen rocks to where she could see him from the opposite side. She screwed up her eyes and focused on him, then put both hands to her mouth to stifle the gasp that threatened to erupt. 'Alan French,' she whispered in disbelief. 'Bloody 'ell. What do I do now?'

She backed away from him, her heart racing and her mind wrestling with the dilemma. She had seen him several times over a period of weeks, and Mrs French had said nothing. So he had not gone home, but instead had lived up here, far from the village, afraid, she guessed, to show his poor face. Unable to go home without one more look to convince herself it really was Alan, back from the dead, she again moved towards him. He appeared not to have heard her, lost in some sad thoughts of his own, and as she came in sight of him, he stood, and she saw that his cheeks glistened with tears. He walked away from the castle, heading for the fields above Fay's house.

'Gawd 'elp us,' Nelly sighed, 'an' today's Fay and Johnny's weddin'.'

She couldn't go home. After he had disappeared from sight she went to where he had been sitting, and from there into the old castle. In the kitchens she found a rough bed and several overcoats, which had presumably been used as blankets. Sadly, she picked one up, thinking of the young man who had a comfortable home only minutes away but who was unable to go there.

What should she do? Persuade him to see his mother who would surely not be so horrified by his injuries that she wouldn't welcome him back with joy? And Fay. What about her? Would she regret marrying Johnny if, soon after, Alan, her first love, turned up? Nelly sat on a stone and shivered, partly from the cold and partly from the shock and the responsibility of what she had discovered.

She sat for a long time, then decided to see the vicar. Yes, he was the one. He'd know what to do. She walked back to the cottage, and the welcome from the dogs then, putting on her old navy coat, set off for the vicarage.

When she told the Reverend Barclay Bevan, he laughed and told her not to worry.

'You must have been mistaken, Nelly. Especially if the young man was as badly scarred as you say. Leave it with me. I'll go up there and talk to this young man, help him if I can. So many sad cases since the war; the reception centres for these wandering, unhappy men are full night after night you know. Now go home, and forget it. Leave it all to me.'

His cheeks shone, his bald head shone, his small, gold rimmed glasses shone and his teeth shone between full, moist lips. To Nelly he seemed to be surrounded by a halo of brightness. Yes, she could forget it. Barclay Bevan would see to it. Best if she said nothing more. He was right, she must have been mistaken.

She apologised for taking up his valuable time, and they stood at the door for a while, discussing the forthcoming wedding and their hopes it would stay a fine day. Barclay Bevan was taller than Nelly by only a few inches, and was every bit as plump; Tweedledum to her Tweedledee.

Still smiling, and making reassuring noises, he stood on the doorstep and waved her off; then went back to his interrupted breakfast and forgot all about it.

Amy's shop was lacking customers and for once she was glad. There was so much to do. With her daughter Margaret a flower-girl at Fay's wedding, and herself to get ready between customers, the morning was hectic enough. She was glad she had decided to warn everyone that the shop would close at twelve.

The crocheted basket with its arrangement of flowers had arrived early and sat on the sideboard with the head-dress and Amy's hat. Margaret was to wear white, and with her rich red hair, would look beautiful. Amy hugged the girl. 'Now you're sure you know what you have to do, Margaret, darling?'

'Of course, Mam. I've been through it so many times you'd think I was stupid!'

'No one would ever think that,' Amy laughed. 'Sharper than what's good for you sometimes, you are.' She went to the bottom of the stairs and called her son. 'Freddie! Come on; you can't need all this time to pretty yourself up!'

The shop doorbell rang and she went to serve Nelly.

'You're out early, Nelly. And where are the dogs?' For once Nelly seemed quiet and unwilling to chat, for which Amy was grateful. She sold her a packet of confetti and went back to her children.

Amy's sister Prue was walking to the church with Mrs French. Monica French wore a dark red suit, being unable to bring herself to use the outfit she had bought, eight years before, for her son's planned wedding, even though the style did not look dated. Prue apologised for the absence of her husband.

'Harry's working of course,' she said. 'When is he not? He leaves the house before seven and I'm lucky if I see him before seven at night. And even then he brings work home.

I've offered to help, do the books like I did when he started, but he won't hear of it.'

Mrs French nodded and made sounds of agreement, but her mind was not on the conversation. She was thinking about Alan's girl who would soon be Mrs Johnny Cartwright.

The church was half full; many of the villagers, aware that Fay had no family, had come to see her married.

'Snob that she is, she needs someone to sit on her side of the church,' Milly Toogood whispered to her neighbour.

'Decent and respectable, I don't call that snobbish,' Sian Owen retorted. 'There's many could take lessons from her on how to behave. Never hear a word of gossip from her for a start.'

Milly changed pews to sit next to Brenda and Bert Roberts and their children, and whispered about the wicked tongue of that Sian Owen.

Nelly walked into the church alone, and looked for her friend Netta Cartwright. She did not sit next to her; on this day she had better leave the family to their business and sit further away. She settled for a seat halfway back on Johnny's side, but, seeing how empty the pews were on Fay's side, moved over to help balance things.

The grey stone church was filled with flowers, the work of Monica French and the vicar's hard-working wife. Daffodils and primroses in small bunches were made larger and more splendid by the addition of branches of hazel and willow catkins that were just showing the fresh spring green of new leaves. Nelly, to whom wild flowers gave immense pleasure, smiled her delight, her crooked teeth spoiling the symmetry of her round face.

Nelly stood up several times to look at the people gathered and study their various hats. She pulled her own grey velour more firmly on her head and nodded to herself, satisfied she was not the worst dressed there. She had not known what to wear and had no one to ask, so had settled for the grey coat given to her by Mrs French that was too tight to fasten. That, and the grey velour hat with a few *primula wanda* stuck in the brim was the best she could do.

Johnny was sitting in his seat at the front, nervously glancing towards the church door from time to time. Nelly smiled affectionately. Remembered him as a small boy she did. Fancy him being a bridegroom. Her face clouded as she thought of the unhappy man hiding out in the old castle and crossed her fingers. Nodding towards the altar, she whispered, ' 'E ain't never done anyone no 'arm, an' 'e loves Fay an 'ell of a lot. Please, Gawd, let it be all right fer 'im.'

Fay's house was only yards from the church and she had originally wanted to walk there with her bridesmaid and flower-girl. But Johnny had pleaded with her to arrive by car. She had agreed, knowing how much the trimmings as he called them, meant to him. So, rather than have the car crawl the few yards hardly getting out of first gear, she had asked to be driven towards town, then left, up the road towards the council estate, along the lane past Nelly's cottage, and down again to the main road. Another left turn would bring her to the church.

Phil Davies the postman was riding with her to give her away. Phil had been a life-long friend of her parents and was best suited to the pleasant role. He looked at her pale face and wondered what was going on behind the over-bright eyes.

'Don't worry, Fay, bach. It'll all be over before you realise it. Then there'll be only you and your Johnny.' He touched her arm, where the sleeve of her wedding dress ended in a frill of lace above her wrist and was shocked to find it was trembling. He covered her cold hands with his own.

He looked out of the car window and began talking about the crowd waiting to wish her well. 'Crowds there'll be but don't let it worry you, never forget their words, brides don't. And everyone there is your friend and young Johnny's. Lovely start you'll have with so many friends around you.'

She gave a faint cry and he looked at her, then out of the

car window to see the reason. He saw nothing that could possibly frighten her, only a man at the edge of the lane. Perhaps she thought the car would hit him.

Fay had seen the man again, not far from Nelly's gate. He had been startled to see the large and highly polished vehicle cruising almost silently along the narrow lane. His hand came up to cover his face, but this time she was certain. It was Alan.

When they reached the gates of the church, where people filled the pavement and were scattered in groups around the churchyard, she said, 'Take me back home.' The driver stopped suddenly, jerking Fay and a startled Phil forward.

'Come on, love; don't scare me like this. Fail in my duty I will if I don't get you to the church.' Her face was tense, and as the car cruised slowly on and stopped at her house, she got out.

'Wait for us a mo, will you?' Phil said foolishly, as if the grand car were only a casually ordered taxi. He followed Fay into the empty house and sat with her on the stairs. 'Tell me. You can say anything to old Phil now, can't you?'

'I can't marry Johnny. Please, Uncle Phil, go and tell them all, will you?'

After trying his persuasive tongue for what seemed an age, and sending several people who had come to see what was happening away with an impolite remark, Phil admitted defeat.

'Been looking forward to this for months I have, walking down the aisle with you on my arm. That proud I'd be.'

'Sorry, Uncle Phil,' she said, using the name by which she had known him all her life. 'It wouldn't be fair to Johnny, not until –'

'Until what love?' he coaxed.

'Until I'm sure about something,' was all she would say by way of explanation.

Phil left her then, and walked slowly to the church, where the curious and the caring were equally anxious to hear his news. He stood beside Johnny for a moment and Johnny's face stiffened as Phil told him the situation. Then he went to the altar, where the Reverend Barclay Bevan waited patiently. He whispered in the small, rosy faced man's ear and the round face seemed to crumple with dismay.

'Friends,' he announced as Phil slipped once more to Johnny's side. 'It seems there has been a hitch. The wedding has regretfully been cancelled at this time. There will be more news later and I'm sure we will all meet again very soon to unite these two young people in Holy Matrimony. God bless you all.'

Johnny's face was ashen. His mother clutched his arm as he seemed about to fall. Barclay Bevan came to stand protectively at his side and he gestured for the congregation to leave. He stood sentinel-like, guarding Johnny from everyone until the old building was empty, except for himself, Johnny and Netta.

'Would you like me to come with you and talk to Fay?' he asked softly, his eyes moist with sadness.

Johnny shook his head. 'No thanks, Vicar, I'm going home.' He shook off his mother's hand and strode out of the church.

The sunshine was a shock. He had somehow expected the skies to have opened and flooded the village with a dark and heavy storm. People still hovered around the churchyard and outside the lych-gate. Constable Harris stood waiting to control the traffic as the well-wishers filled the pavement and blocked the road with their excited determination to cover the happy pair with confetti. Instead, he hurried them away, as Johnny walked out alone.

Nelly walked back with Netta Cartwright, but didn't speak. At the gate of the small cottage where Johnny had expected to return with his bride, she patted the woman's shoulder and left her. Time for talking is later, she decided silently.

Milly Toogood was whispering to Sian Roberts that it was only to be expected, 'that Fay's got too high an opinion of herself altogether.'

Amy walked across the road to re-open her shop, shepherding her two children in front of her: Margaret disappointed both that her services as a flower-girl had not been needed and that the choir in which she sang had been deprived of its performance; Freddy, thankful that he could take off the hated suit and, in comfortable clothes, go fishing.

In the empty house, Fay sat shivering, and staring into space. It was there that Netta found her an hour later and persuaded her to change out of the beautiful white gown, and eat, and sleep.

'I'm so sorry,' Fay began, but Netta hushed her in her quiet way.

'Plenty of time for talk and explanations later,' she said. 'Now, what you want is sleep.' She wrapped the coat she had brought around the girl's shoulders and led her away.

In the days that followed, that were to have been Fay and Johnny's honeymoon, Fay walked alone in the woods and fields around Hen Carw Parc, searching for Alan. She often passed Nelly's cottage, and sometimes saw Nelly in the woods, gathering firewood, but she never stopped to talk.

Finally, Nelly knew that *she* must. So early one morning when she saw the girl, wearing a blue plastic mac, wandering around the old castle, she called,

'I've seen him too, you know.'

Fay stared at her, and Nelly, holding her skirts high, high-stepping through the wet grass went to join her.

'Yes,' Nelly repeated, 'I've seen 'im. 'Im that's wounded and scarred proper bad. You thought 'e looked like Alan French too, did yer?'

'It *was* him.' Fay's voice was so quiet, Nelly barely heard her.

'Couldn't 'ave bin, dearie,' Nelly scoffed. 'Wouldn't 'ave come 'ome without seein' you an' 'is mum now, would 'e? Not Alan.' She touched Fay's arm and guided her back to the path. 'Come on in and 'ave that cuppa, why don't yer? Kettle's boilin' its 'ead off I bet.' She didn't say any more, but Fay went with her as if relieved to be sharing her grief at last. She had spoken to no one, not even Johnny, since the aborted wedding.

Nelly dragged open the gate and went down the path. At her approach, five hens cluttered their way guiltily from the living room, feathers flying as they made their escape.

She gestured to the big armchair, then took two small loaves out of the fire-oven and, turning them over, tapped them to make sure they were done. At one side of the range, a big iron saucepan simmered gently, sending the delicious smell of a vegetable soup into the cluttered room. At the other side, the kettle was beginning to sing.

Fay sat on the armchair at Nelly's bidding and at once the two dogs came to settle beside her, heads on her lap for her to stroke. The comfort of the untidy room over-came her tension and she relaxed into its friendly warmth. She accepted the cup of tea Nelly made and smiled at the plump face that showed such concern. 'Thank you, Nelly. I feel better already.'

Nelly smiled her relief. 'That's good. Now, let me tell you about the man that's bin wanderin' around like a lost soul. You an' me saw 'im once before, remember? When you thought you'd bin burgled? Well, I seen 'im plenty of times since but 'e'd never stop an' talk. I thought –' she hesitated, glancing at the pale, serious face before her, then went on, 'I thought as 'ow it was young Alan French. Not 'alf like 'im he is, in spite of what you can't see because of that terrible scar. So, I thought an' thought, wonderin' what to do, and 'oo to tell. Then I decided to tell the vicar.

' 'E's the one to deal with lost souls I thought. So I went to see 'im, just before your weddin'. 'E says, Barclay Bevan that is, that 'e'll see to it. 'E promised to find the poor man and 'elp 'im if 'e could. Well, I ain't seen 'im since, so I don't doubt that 'e did what 'e promised. Found the man a place to live an' a job as well per'aps.

'Now if it 'ad bin your Alan, that Barclay Bevan would 'ave known straight off, 'im bein' a reverend an' all. So, I think you an' me was mistook. Wishful thinkin' I bet it was.' She stretched out a hand for the cup, replenished it and sat, smiling, waiting for Fay to speak.

'I was so sure.'

'Me an' all dearie! But we was wrong.'

'Johnny's been so kind. He understood my refusal to believe Alan was dead. All these years he's been such a good friend.'

'Good boy that Johnny. You couldn't do better than marry 'im. 'E couldn't do no better neither,' she added firmly. 'If you love 'im as well as bein' a good friend.'

'I do love him, Nelly, and I know we'd be happy. If only I could really and truly believe that "Missing, presumed killed" means that Alan is dead.'

'It's bin eight years. Too long for carryin' on 'opin', dearie.'

The two women sat in silence for a while, then Nelly stood up and pointed to the new loaves. 'Stay an' 'ave some bread and 'ome-made cheese, why don't yer. Then we'll go down an' see Johnny.'

A week later, Fay married Johnny and settled into the room they had been given in the Cartwrights' cottage opposite Amy's shop.

Although the May morning was chilly, Nelly sat outside her door on the old wooden chair to eat her breakfast. The dogs were watchful, hoping for a share and the chickens chortled around her feet.

The dogs barked and she looked up the path to see Phil Davies leaning over, waving a letter. He shrugged the heavy bag from his shoulder and called. 'Morning, Nelly; got a letter for you. Not a bill either.'

Nelly stood and held up the teapot which had rested on the tray at her feet. 'Got time fer a cuppa, have yer?'

'Sure.' Phil rested the bag against the wall and roughed the dogs' coats, talking to them and enjoying their welcome. Nelly brought a cup and for a while they sat talking about the latest happenings in the village, mostly about the wedding that nearly wasn't.

'Felt sorry for that boy I did,' Phil said, shaking his grey head. 'Sick to his heart he was. What came over Fay I don't know.'

'Just nerves,' Nelly said. 'They're happy enough now.'

'I hope so.' Phil looked doubtful and he rubbed the side of his nose in a way that usually meant he was going to repeat something he had promised not to. Nelly waited hopefully.

'They argue a terrible lot, you know. Hear them we do. Can't help it, us living next door.'

'Smashin',' Nelly said loudly. 'Best part of bein' married, as far as I remember. Specially as they've only got one bed so they can't quarrel fer more than a day! No, they'll be all right, just give 'em a while to sort things out. Different they are, see; even if they do love each other. Got a few things to sort out.' She laughed away the thought of problems between the newlyweds but she frowned anxiously long after Phil had eaten her last cake, and gone.

She made herself another pot of tea and sat, sipping it and staring at the letter, putting off opening it. It was Evie's writing. Telling her about them moving back, at last, she thought with a taste of anger. Everyone in Hen Carw Parc knows except me. When she finally opened it, the letter was brief.

> 'Timothy has been appointed Headmaster of Hen Cawr Parc school, so we will be returning to live in the village before the Spring term commences –'

the letter ran. Nelly laughed and re-read it aloud, making fun of the formal, stilted style. 'Blimey, you'd think she was talkin' to *'er* 'eadmaster the fancy way she writes! Poor Evie. Never could accept she wasn't born posh.' She put the letter in her pocket, locked up the dogs and went to work. Mrs Dorothy Williams today and she wouldn't have the dogs no matter how Nellie pleaded.

Dorothy Williams lived some distance outside the village,on the way to Swansea and Nelly caught a bus. After she had finished cleaning, she usually stopped at The Drovers Arms, for a stout and a packet of crisps, but today she was in a hurry. Carrying a woollen dress that Mrs Williams had no further use for, she caught the bus home.

Most of the afternoon was spent cleaning the cottage. She lifted up the coconut matting, and the heavy rag mat, and scrubbed the flagstone floor. She black-leaded the grate, and whitened the inside of the oven. The rag mat was lifted with great difficulty onto the clothes line and beaten until the garden was lost in a cloud of dust and dog's hair. 'Like a bleedin' eclipse of the sun,' she muttered. 'Still, Evie's sure to check, so I got to get it done.' She took an old distorted tennis racquet and continued her beating.

Hanging on the back of the chicken shed was an oval-shaped galvanised bath. She lifted it down and, dragging it on a length of carpet, brought it into the cottage. Two kettles and the stewpan full of boiling water, plus a lot of cold, carried, bucketful by bucketful from the tap in the lane, gave her a good bath, which she lavishly scented with bath salts. She picked up her book and glasses, and the magazines and papers she had collected with pictures and articles about the forthcoming coronation, and settled herself for a long soak.

On the day Evie, Tim and Oliver were due to arrive, Nelly borrowed the key from Fay, who still held it, and went to light the fire. The day was dull and the sight of a blazing fire would be cheering. Nelly guessed Evie would need something to brighten her mood. Reading between the lines of the stilted letter, Nelly knew her daughter would have preferred to keep the fifty or so miles between herself and her mother.

She was still there when the van arrived with the furniture and she watched as the men laid the carpets in the living room and the two bedrooms that were going to be immediately used. Blue, she noticed for young Oliver, mottled and rather dark. His furniture was dark brown and highly polished. No sign of him being only eight, she thought with disappointment.

The car, with its three occupants came as the last of the furniture was being unloaded. Evie stopped when she saw a red-faced and very tired Nelly waiting for her at the door, then walked to her, put an arm around her and kissed her, pulling away before Nelly could overdo the greeting.

Tim's eyes showed more pleasure and as he walked in and saw the room already looking like home, with the curtains up and the fire burning brightly, he thanked her.

'Mother-in-law, that was very good of you. You must have worked very hard. Thank you.'

'You ain't got a proper kettle so I couldn't 'ave no tea ready. One of them electric ones,' she explained. 'They don't simmer like a proper one. Put it on now, shall I?'

She went into the kitchen and switched on the kettle, nervously straightening an already straight tray. She had only nodded and smiled at Oliver. She felt shy of the small, neatly dressed boy and he obviously wouldn't welcome a display of affection from a woman he could hardly remember. Best I wait, she had decided, when she noticed how he had hung back from her when he had stepped out of the car.

He was thin for his age, she noticed, and dressed as if he'd been prepared for a shop window in one of the big shops in Swansea. A suit. Gawd 'elp us! On a kid like that. And a bow tie! Even his socks, which were ribbed and turned over at the top to show a coloured pattern, were dead straight, the rib in perfect lines. His shoes were polished like Mrs French's windows and his hair was pressed flat against his head, the white parting adding to the severity of his expression.

He stepped hesitantly into the kitchen and she asked, not looking at him, 'Want tea, do yer? Or don't yer mum allow it? Fussy, some mums, aren't they?'

'I would like a cup of tea please, Grandmother. Mother does allow it, but only very weak and with plenty of milk.' The careful little voice chilled her and she doubted if she and this strange child would ever be friends.

'Sit yerself down, dearie an' I'll bring it for yer.'

'No need, Grandmother. I can manage.'

Nelly looked at him. Grandmother. Blimey, that would have to stop.

'Would you like to come an' see the dogs, while yer mum and dad unpack?' she asked. She saw him glance at Evie and then shake his head. Nelly turned to her daughter. ' 'E can come fer a while, can't 'e? Bring 'im back in an hour or so?'

'Not today, Mother. He has unpacking to do too. Perhaps tomorrow.'

Nelly shrugged. 'I'll get out of yer way then.' She picked up the grey coat she had worn for Fay's wedding and had put on hoping to please Evie, but Evie had already turned away and was busily unpacking a tea-chest, handing the china it contained to Oliver. Sadly, Nelly let herself out.

Chapter Four

Wednesday was half-day closing for Amy's shop and in-between customers she got herself ready to go out. She always loved dressing up and spent a while deciding which of her large collection of jewellery she would wear. She settled for diamanté earrings that dangled in three separate chains, and a necklace that filled the wide neckline of the red dress she had chosen. She fluffed out her thick hair and smiled at her reflection in the mirror. Satisfied with what she saw, she winked at herself and taking a light-weight mac and slipping varnished toes into shoes, she set off.

Margaret was playing with Oliver, Nelly's grandson, and Freddy was out, probably fishing. He was almost fifteen, seven years older than his sister, and soon to start work.

She left food out in case he came back before her, and locking the shop and hiding the key where the children could find it, she ran to the main road to catch the bus for Swansea. She alighted at The Drovers.

As she went into the bar and looked across to their usual table, her brother-in-law, Harry Beynon waved and stood up to greet her. He rolled his mischievous blue eyes and looked with exaggerated care around the almost empty room and gave her a kiss on the cheek. When she had taken off her mac and slipped into the seat beside him, he kissed her more affectionately on her full lips.

'Darling,' he said, holding her slightly away from him, 'you look fantastic.' They kissed again before Harry went into the next room to the bar and brought her a drink.

They talked idly for a while, making each other laugh at

things that weren't really funny; happy to be together. Then Amy said, 'Harry, I have decided to get something done about the shop.'

'At last! Trying to persuade you for months I have.'

'I went to see Prue, foolishly, I realise that now. I thought if I asked her to ask you it might be easier.'

'She hasn't said anything to me.'

'No, she wouldn't. Told me I was a scrounger and I shouldn't have bought the shop if I couldn't cope.'

'Prue speaks before she thinks.'

'Prue automatically says no before she thinks, and rarely changes her mind!' She looked at him. 'Will you do it for me, Harry? Could you tell her it was your idea, and nothing to do with me asking?'

'I think we could come to some arrangement.' He winked a bright blue, laughing eye and his hand slowly stroked her arm, sliding up and up until his fingers were caressing her body. 'Where will we go to discuss it?' he whispered.

Amy felt desire ache in her breasts and rise from deep inside her body. Harry's attraction for her grew with age, it did not diminish. She looked at him, her heart beating faster as his hands continued to stroke her skin. His eyes, so blue, were slightly narrowed with laughter which always bubbled below the surface. Enjoyment of life showed in every expression, she had never seen him low, or even angry.

He was short-sighted and wore rimless glasses which he carried easily. They were a part of his image, an advantage others lacked. His face was tanned, even so early in the year as, besides owning a building company, he worked in it, laying bricks as fast and as efficiently as those he employed, which was why he had the respect of men as well as the admiration of women.

His brown hair was thinning but even that did not lessen his powerful magnetism, nor detract from the overwhelming confidence of the man. Amy thought he glowed with health and the joy of life. She smiled at him, her long earrings sparkling. Her eyes glowed and promised him a pleasant hour.

'Where?' he asked quietly.

'Margaret's out to tea with Evie's son, but I'm not sure about Freddy. He's gone fishing somewhere.' She moved so her breast touched his, moving against him, watching the doorway. 'If only we dare –' she said wickedly.

'Amy, you'll be the death of me! Let's get out of here before you frighten the landlord and have us banned!'

He took her hand and leading her to his car, drove off in the direction of Swansea.

'Where are we going?' she asked, still laughing at his alarm. 'Nowhere quieter than The Drovers on a Wednesday afternoon, I bet.'

'No, and how he gets away with staying open I'll never know!'

'Favoured customers only, and they won't talk,' she said. 'Go back, shall we?'

'The office is still on site at Greenways estate. It's well out of sight, so be patient, you wanton woman. We're going there.'

'Why?' she asked innocently.

'To talk about your shop widening, what else?' He glanced at her, laughing softly.

Oliver was unhappy. Besides being the son of the Headmaster, he was shy, and he soon became the butt of the other boys' humour. Sitting in the playground and watching the other boys from his class throwing cigarette cards against the wall, or playing marbles into holes dug in the earth around the trees, he felt completely isolated. Even Margaret Prichard, who was his friend out of school, rarely spoke to him. She was unwilling to step outside the circle of her friends and support him for fear of being cut off from them as well.

Nelly saw him occasionally as she walked the dogs, and guessed what he was suffering. He rarely came to see her, and one day she called at the house and asked him to come and see what she was doing with her broody hen. With little show of enthusiasm he politely accepted her invitation to call.

He came after school, still wearing the suit and bow tie which Evie insisted he 'used up' for play. Nelly opened the side door of the chicken coop and peered inside.

'See that stupid 'en?' She pointed to one of the nest-boxes where one of the Buff Leghorns that was paler than the rest, its wattles pink instead of the bright red of a laying hen, was sitting contentedly. 'Off lay she is. Gorn broody so I'm goin' to give 'er somethin' to do.'

'I don't understand,' Oliver said, bending down to look into the strange-smelling coop with its row of nest-boxes.

'I'm goin' to let 'er do a bit of 'atching. I've bin to see about buyin' day-old chicks - and one night, when it's dark, I'll take out the potatoes she's sitting on, and put some chicks around 'er. She'll think they're 'ers and she'll look after 'em well.'

She explained about giving the hen some potatoes to sit on to deceive her into thinking she had hatched out the chicks when they arrived, and that placing them at night was a precaution against them being pecked.

'We'll collect the chicks tomorrow; I'll ask yer mum if you can stay a bit late, so you can put the chicks into the box. Don't forget to tell yer teacher what you're doing,' she hinted. 'The class will be jealous and want to know more I bet yer.'

The next evening, Oliver's eyes were brighter than Nelly had ever seen them as he picked up the fragile little creatures and carefully placed them one by one into the warm nest box, where the hen immediately lifted herself to make room for them beneath her fluffed-out feathers against her warm breast.

As Nelly had cleverly surmised, things were easier for Oliver, once he had something interesting to talk about, and the teasing stopped, particularly the nick-name of Dirty Nelly's boy, and Smelly Nelly's Ollie. Boys pleaded with him to let them to see the hen and her chicks and he watched their progress with a proprietorial interest.

He began to call sometimes before going to school, knowing she would be up and about earlier than most. And gradually he became less shy with her.

'I was just goin' up to the castle with the dogs. Comin'?' she asked one morning. 'They'll be startin' to get things ready fer the coronation party soon.'

'Yes please, Grandmother.'

Nelly looked at the neatly dressed little boy and sighed, 'Call me Gran, why don't yer?'

'Mother doesn't like it. And – she doesn't like you calling me Ollie either,' he added nervously. 'She told me to tell you.'

'Yes, like that, your mum. Insists 'er name is Evelyn, yet I 'ad 'er christened Evie. That's 'er proper name. She won't 'ave it though. So I got to call you Oliver, 'ave I? Well I will, on one condition.'

Oliver looked at her expectantly.

'On condition you calls me Gran. Only when we're alone though,' she added quickly as he began to disagree. 'Our secret, okay?'

'She says I mustn't say okay either,' he gave a slight grin.

'Well we won't, at least, not when she's listenin'!'

They walked through the trees, Nelly pointing out where she had found a thrush's nest and where she went for the wild flowers that filled the vases, cups and jam-jars in her cottage. 'Stand and listen, and sometimes you can 'ear the baby birds twitterin'.' They stood for a while and she was pleased to see his serious face open in delight as the soft sound reached his ear.

'Can I bring them food sometime?'

' 'Course you can, dearie, but not yet. Best to let them train the youngsters to find their own proper food. When winter comes, then they'll be right glad of some 'elp. I got a robin what comes right into me kitchen, ignorin' the dogs, big soft things they are, and cocks 'is 'ead as if sayin', "come on Nelly, you're late with me breakfast".'

Oliver laughed and for the first time since he had arrived,

Nelly felt able to put an arm around his shoulders and gently hug him. 'You an' me, we'll 'ave some fine old times, won't we?' She winked a brown eye. 'Some we might even tell yer mum about!'

At the castle site the grass had been cut. The bracken, that seemed to disappear temporarily during March and April, was forcing itself up strongly through the ground. A small grass-cutter stood half under the new roof of the kitchens and was covered with a piece of tarpaulin. Rocks had been built into walls and painted white. The ruined buildings had also been given a coat of whitewash and the difference was startling.

'It's a real castle!' Oliver said. 'Almost in your back garden!' Nelly sat while he and the dogs ran in and out of the old ruin, climbing walls and struggling through openings. When he had finished exploring, Nelly thought his clothes were a mess but his face was that of a happy, normal boy.

'I'll walk 'ome with yer, an' explain about yer suit,' she said, half-heartedly brushing the white dust and brown dirt from it.

'It's all right, Gran; it's only my playing suit. I'll be changing to go to school.'

'A suit fer playing! Bloody 'ell! An' I bet yer mum says I mustn't say that neither! Come on, time for a drink of Granny Luke's 'ome made pop, then we'll get you 'ome.'

Nelly glanced into the Castle kitchen, wondering about the man she still thought of as Alan. The bed made from bracken and heather was gone. Thrown out no doubt by the men who had cleaned the place ready for the party.

While Nelly made a cup of tea and poured some lemonade for Oliver, she gave him a comic to read. She watched as he slowly made his way across the page, his finger lingering a long time beneath each word.

'What's that say, Ollie, I can't find me glasses,' she said pointing to a simple headline in a local paper. The boy shrugged and looked away. It was what Nelly had suspected, Oliver's reading was far behind for his age.

Nelly opened Evie's back door and called before walking in. The table was set for breakfast. She waited apprehensively for Evie to react to the state of Oliver's clothes, but Evie just hugged him and said calmly,

'Have you had a good time, Oliver? You went out very early this morning. Go and wash yourself and change ready for school.' She looked at Nelly. 'Will you stay, Mother?' Nelly shook her head. 'Best get back, I've got the dogs tied to yer fence . . .'

'Do you have to bring them? Dirty creatures.'

'They ain't. Evie, is Timmy in? I'll say 'ello before I go.'

'Timothy is upstairs, preparing some time-tables. I'll call him.'

'Evie,' Nelly stopped her before she reached the door. 'Can't you be more, friendly-like? I'm yer mum, and we should be easy with each other. I'll try not to do the things you don't like. I'll even try and call 'im Timothy, but –' Words failed and she shrugged.

Evie did not reply, she went into the hall and called her husband.

'He'll be about ten minutes, Mother.'

'Tell 'im not to 'urry on my account. I'm off. See yer soon, Oliver,' she shouted. She untied the dogs and walked sadly down the path, through the trees behind the house and up the hill towards home.

At the top of the field she saw Fay walking towards her. She thought Fay had seen her, then the shining, blonde head bent quickly as Fay seemed to be searching the ground.

' 'Ello, dearie, lost somethin' 'ave yer? Help you look for a while if you like.'

'Morning Nelly. Yes, I've lost my watch. It's only an old one but I'd like it back.'

'Now if it was a bone, me dogs would 'elp.' Nelly laughed. She began moving the tufts of grass with her feet, peering between the clumps. 'Not lookin' fer Alan, are yer?' she said quietly. 'As if you'd be that stupid,' she laughed. Fay only smiled and went on looking at the ground.

They were silent for a while, then Fay asked, 'Are you

going to the meeting tonight to discuss the coronation party arrangements?'

'No dearie! Committees ain't my style. Besides, I got plans. I'm goin' for a ride into town, buyin' a bottle or two of stout maybe, fer me supper. I might even go to the pictures if there ain't no queue.'

'I give up.' Fay straightened and smiled again. 'Thank you, Nelly. If you would keep looking while you're with the dogs, I'd be grateful.'

'Course I will.'

Nelly frowned as Fay walked down the field to the main road. Fay hadn't been looking for any watch, she was certain of that. So, what had she been doing she didn't want to talk about? Nelly turned and looked in the direction of the castle, and wondered.

Nelly decided against the pictures and took the dogs when she went into town. Mrs Greener's second hand clothes shop was shut when she reached it, but Nelly knocked on the side door. It was opened by the proprietress, who invited her inside, ushering her past the shop to the small back room where most of her transactions took place.

' 'Ello, Mrs Greener, dearie. Nice to see yer again.' Nelly said as her suitcases were unpacked and examined. Mrs Greener accepted the clothing without hesitation or any argument about price. Nelly could be relied on to bring good stuff and never wasted her time on rubbish.

The amount of money was suggested politely while the unbelievably red curls on the seventy year old woman's head bounced approval. A row of large teeth, as blatantly false as the curls were exposed in a friendly smile.

'I'll go and find the cash, dear.' Mrs Greener backed, smiling, out of the door, leaving Nelly in the small, over-filled room with its wardrobes and shelves, and rails of clothes; some draped with cloth of indefinable colour, bleached with age. Mrs Greener was not gone long, but Nelly had time to count the seventeen odd buttons on the floor amid the fluff and dust and assorted strands of cotton.

A wardrobe stood half open, revealing a row of sombre men's suits. The sight made Nelly shiver. There was some thing eerie about the sight. If they could talk, they'd 'ave some stories to tell and I doubt if any would make me laugh, she thought nervously.

'Nelly, dear,' Mrs Greener gushed on her return. 'I'd love to ask you to stay for a drink, but I have guests.' Her rheumy eyes were sad with disappointment.

Nelly shrugged. 'What a shame, dearie. It's ages since we 'ad a chat. Still, I couldn't stay meself, got a friend waitin' in the pub.' She edged thankfully away from the funereal suits with their smell of old flowers, and death.

Mrs Greener closed the door on Nelly almost before she had stepped outside, to prevent the dogs leaving their mark. Both women said an affectionate good-day, neither believing nor offended by the other's lies.

The public house near the second hand clothes shop was run by an elderly man who refused any improvements, being too set in his ways to face the upheaval. The floor in the small bar where Nelly drank was of large paving stones of slate, washed each day with a mop and occasionally spread with sand in the old way, to clean its surface.

Nelly tucked the dogs out of sight under her bench seat and drank two glasses of Guinness and ate three packets of crisps. She did not stay long; she was tired and the drink made her drowsy. Carrying her cases, one inside the other, and with a spare bottle for later, she caught the bus back to Hen Carw Parc.

The bus was full and it warmed her, relaxed her and before she reached her stop near the church, sent her to sleep. Laughter, as a group of young people got off, woke her and looking out of the steamy windows, she saw she had passed her lane and was approaching the Drovers Arms. She shouted for the conductor to stop the bus and struggled down the stairs with the case and the dogs.

As the bus went on its way she hesitated, looking at the welcoming lights of the public house, and at the grass-edged path beside the road home. 'Come on, dogs, we'll 'ave just one before the walk.' Leaving her case just inside the door, she went in, looking hopefully for a familiar face and the prospect of a chat.

She saw Harry Beynon in a corner, talking to a woman. Not Prue, she thought, screwing up her eyes and staring at the blonde head that was definitely not his wife. She moved closer and recognising Amy, waved a greeting and went over.

'Hello, Nelly love,' Amy smiled. 'Can I get you one?' She held up her glass.

'O, ta!' Nelly smiled at Harry, who asked what she would like then went to the bar to get it.

'Coincidence me meeting Harry here,' Amy said when he returned with the gin. 'It isn't certain yet,' Amy said confidentially, 'but I might be getting my shop altered, you know, made bigger, using the back room.'

Nelly made a horrible noise and mimed cutting her throat. 'Cut me throat if I says a word!'

Harry left soon after and after discussing some ideas for the improvements, Amy announced she was catching the bus. Nelly, holding her third gin, waved her goodbye, saying she would prefer the walk.

When Nelly stood up to leave, she felt a trifle unsteady, and outside the cold air increased her tendency to lean sideways. She reached the bus stop, but was afraid she might disgrace herself and be sick, so she set off shakily along the path.

As she neared the village her head began to clear and tiredness overcame her. She sat down to rest on a seat placed by some kind-hearted benefactor, whose name was engraved on a plaque, and closed her eyes.

'Nelly? You all right, love?'

Opening her eyes, Nelly screwed them up and peered into the darkness. 'Amy? Fancy seeing you. Where you bin then? I thought you was catchin' the bus.'

'I met a friend and we were talking,' Amy said, rather too quickly. 'All right, are you?'

'Yes, just a bit tired. You go on, I'll get meself 'ome all right.'

'I'll walk with you as far as your lane. Where have you been, into town is it?'

'Yes, 'ad a bit o' business.'

Amy walked to the lane, then watched while the two great dogs dragged her out of sight. 'Hope she'll be all right,' Amy muttered, but looking up into the blackness of the hedge-lined lane, decided she could not face following her to make sure.

She went home, where Margaret and Freddy were waiting for their supper, wondering if Nelly had been sufficiently convinced by their explanation of her and Harry's meeting. Crossing the road, she shrugged away the slight anxiety. No one took any notice of Nelly. Dirty Nelly they called her, living in a tumbledown cottage that should be condemned, with dogs, chickens and a windup gramophone for company, who would take notice of anything she said?

Early next morning, Nelly, fully recovered, went again to look at the castle site. The bedding was back in the kitchen. She frowned. If it was Alan, why was he living so close to his old home and not going there? Perhaps he's lost his mind, she thought with a start of fear. Poor bloke, 'e'll be wanderin' around like a ghost, 'auntin' the places of 'is child'ood. And what if 'e should bump into Mrs French. What a shock that'd be for them both.

The thought saddened her and needing to do something, however useless, she went back home and collected a small, freshly baked loaf and a piece of cheese from her meagre ration, with a slice of seed cake, and took it to the castle kitchens. As she was putting it on the makeshift bed, something sparkled and she reached out and picked up a small diamanté-adorned lady's watch. 'Messages, eh. Seems I ain't the only one keepin' an eye out for yer, Alan French if that's 'o, you are.' She replaced the watch and went thoughtfully home.

On Saturday mornings, Amy's son Freddy went to work on Prue's garden. After several boys had tried to please her exacting standards and failed, Freddy had offered to help for the few shillings Prue offered and had become quite interested in the flowers he tended.

Prue watched him from the kitchen window, taking a slightly guilty pleasure in the way he lifted the soil on the spade and threw it down as he prepared the holes for some new roses she had bought.

Freddy was big for his age, and strong. His shoulders under the sleeveless vest he wore, rippled as he lifted, turned and dropped the spadefuls of earth, such rhythm in his movements that she felt he could continue all day without tiring. She tapped the glass and showed him a tea cup and he waved and, leaving his work, came to get his drink and the cake she had cut for him.

'Thanks, Auntie Prue. Those roses will look a treat from here, won't they? Better than that old lavender. Had its day that had. Straggly.'

She nodded and watched as he ate hungrily, anxious to get back and finish the planting.

'Coming out to make a ceremony of the planting, Auntie Prue?' he asked when he had finished.

'I'll watch from here,' she said.

As he walked away and bent once more to his work, she felt a surge of excitement pass through her and she turned away from the window. He was a boy, only fifteen, she reminded herself. But his body was that of a man, and had a strange effect on her.

Prue had had no experience of men outside marriage, and little within it. The sensation Freddy had produced frightened her. She was very gruff with him when he came in to be paid, and hardly spoke when he explained about the necessary watering and feeding which he had learnt, he told her, from a library book.

She heard Harry's car and went down from the landing window where she had been watching for his return. In the neat kitchen she began the final touches to the casserole. He was whistling and when the door opened to reveal his cheerful face, her heart leapt. The foolishness with Freddy forgotten, she felt that love for Harry which, even after more than fourteen years, was still as strong as it had always been. She added the mixed cornflour to the meat and vegetables, stirring it in before returning the dish to the oven. She did not greet him with more than a brief nod.

'That smells good, Prue. How long will it be?'

'Only about twenty minutes. You've time to wash.'

'I'll make a start on these straight after.' He patted the files he had brought in with him. 'They'll take me most of the afternoon, then I might go for a pint with some of the boys. Got to keep the workers sweet,' he said.

'I wish you'd let me help with the books, Harry. I keep offering and I wouldn't ask if I didn't want to. After all, it was me who did them in the early years. In fact, I did the lot while you were in the R.A.F. It would give you more time; I mean you'd be home earlier.' She wanted to say 'so we could spend more time together' but the truth stuck in her throat. 'Trying to get a meal ready for you isn't easy you know. If you came home at a set time my work could be better arranged.'

'It's not me you miss then?' he teased.

'Put the bath towel in the linen basket when you've finished with it, not in a heap on the floor.' Prue went over to the table and placed the cruet more precisely, then straightened the knives and forks.

'Won't be long.' He touched her shoulder as he passed, and she heard him dropping his files on his desk, before running, whistling happily up the stairs to the bathroom.

She checked the vegetables and walked idly into his office, looking at the piles of books and files in dismay. Harry would be working late again tonight. Another night when she would be sleeping alone. He slept in the spare room when he came up late, out of consideration for her he said, although she was often awake. She couldn't call him though, that would be too embarrassing. So she was left to sleep alone in the big, cold bed.

'I met Amy the other day,' he said as they ate. 'In The Drovers of all places. I'd called in for a pint on the way home and she was there. Needed a break from the shop and the kids she said.'

'I don't like to see women on their own in public houses.'

'She doesn't do it often, does she?'

'She rang to tell me she'd seen you. Nelly was there too wasn't she? And the worse for wear?'

'Poor old Nelly. Not much of a life, hers. I bought her a gin but I doubt it was the first she had.'

'Fell asleep on the bus she told Amy. Passed her stop and thought she might as well have a few more before walking home. Disgusting.'

'It doesn't happen often. Perhaps she gets a bit lonely. Not many people call, only Johnny Cartwright and his mother, and I expect Johnny is less inclined to go now he's married.'

'Her Evie won't like it. Better class of person altogether, Evie and her husband – Timothy is it?'

'I don't think having Dirty Nelly for a mother fits Evie's ideas about herself!' Harry said, his eyes shining with laughter. 'Just imagine them introducing *her* to the school governors!' He looked at Prue, encouraging her to join in his laughter, but she remained stony-faced as he went on, 'Can't you see it? Nelly with her dogs tied up with old rope and carrying her smelly shopping bag. Smelly Nelly, do meet Mr and Mrs Norwood Bennet Hughes.' He helped himself to the last of the casserole then, still chuckling, went into his office to begin the work waiting for him on his desk.

Prue sat for a while, thinking about Nelly and how embarrassed her daughter would be if she knew. Several times she convinced herself it was her duty to tell her, but stopped as her hand touched the phone, glancing at the office door. Then, taking the phone on its long cord into the kitchen she spoke to Evie.

She commiserated at first, pretending surprise that Evie did not know about her mother's escapades. Then she suggested, oh so tactfully, that it might be kinder if Mrs French did not employ her any longer. 'So she doesn't have the surplus money to spend so unwisely.'

What a relief not to see that disgusting old woman around the Close she thought as she mixed her tea and went to sit down. The best thing all round. Feeling she had done her duty, she drank her tea satisfied.

Monica French was angry. She had refused to listen to Prue's criticism of Nelly, reminding her that Nelly was entitled to spend the money she honestly earned, in what ever way she chose. But when Evelyn had telephoned and added her persuasions, she had reluctantly agreed. She went to sleep far from satisfied that she had done the best thing.

Chapter Five

Coming back from 'doing' for Mrs Dorothy Williams a few days later, Nelly called in for some fish and chips. Sitting outside her door on the old wooden chair, she shared the meal between herself and the two dogs. She patted the dogs from time to time, taking comfort from their friendliness and warmth. Although she mmm'd contentedly as she ate, her brown eyes showed worry.

She did not hear anyone coming until the gate creaked and she looked up as the dogs barked and wagged their tails in welcome.

'Johnny! 'ello dearie. I ain't seen you fer ages. Stop an' 'ave a cuppa why don't yer?' She hugged him then went inside to turn the kettle back over the fire. Taking out another chair, she sat, grinning with pleasure at his visit.

'Tell me 'ow you're gettin' on. Like bein' married, do yer? That Fay spoilin' yer is she?'

'It's great! Spoiling me rotten. Nelly, I'm so lucky to have a wife like Fay. Far smarter than me she is. Don't know how I managed to get her and that's a fact.'

'Go on, you daft 'aporth! Lucky girl is Fay. Good catch you was, young Johnny.' She waited as he sipped his tea, guessing there was something he wanted to talk about. She had known him well, ever since she had first come to live in Hen Carw Parc and could read his every mood. His thin, boyish face was unusually serious. The moustache he grew to make him look more mature, looked out of place on the almost child-like features. His straight hair fell across his eyes but did not hide the sadness in them.

Johnny was a small man and today, he seemed to have shrunk, gone inside himself, had become more of a boy without confidence, whereas, during his engagement to Fay, he had looked older, more buoyant. Now something had sapped his pride. Nelly thought of the watch left by Fay in the hope of it being found by Alan. Surely she hadn't allowed love for a ghost to spoil things? Not with Johnny alive, well and loving her so much?

'Nothin' wrong is there, young Johnny?' she asked hesitantly.

'No. It's just – Well, I want a baby see, and Fay, she wants to go on working. Loves her job she does, and she's good at it. Thinks she'll climb the ladder where her job's concerned. Not like me. I love driving that old bus, and I don't want anything more. Fay's different. Won't stop working and have babies.'

'Don't blame 'er, not for a while anyway!' Nelly spoke firmly. 'You don't want to spend years an' years livin' in yer Mum's place, do yer? Not fair to you, Fay nor yer Mum that ain't. Fay's got ambition, Johnny. Not only fer 'erself. She wants a nice 'ouse like what she was brought up in. Give 'er time to get somewhere nice to live, then whisper in 'er ear, gentle like one night.' She gave him a broad wink.

Johnny laughed. 'Nelly, you're a real romantic!'

'Yes an' who'd 'ave thought it, eh? Don't think I've always bin Dirty Nelly, livin' alone. It's all right, I knows what they calls me. Too well I do.'

'Has anyone been rude to you? Tell me if they have.'

'Only me own daughter. Not much you can do about 'er. Someone told my Evie that I was drunk and incapable on the bus an' in The Drovers. Someone, an' I've a good idea who, told my Evie and Evie asked Mrs French not to employ me no more. There, what d'you think of that, Johnny? Me own daughter gettin' me the sack. Very upset Mrs French was, but I suppose Evie was convincing. But what do I do? Got to earn a bit of money.

'I can't manage without. I've cut down all I can. Live on a knife edge now. I've stopped 'avin' a paper, although I'd love to 'ave the paperboy comin' every mornin'. Cheerful lad 'e is. I do buy a few stamps now an' then. I sends off for things from the paper, so as Phil Davies the postman 'as an excuse to call.'

Johnny put an arm on her shoulders. 'Don't worry, Nelly, I'll have a word with Mrs French. No. Better still. I'll ask Fay to talk to your Evie *and* Mrs French. Better with words and arguments, Fay is. You should hear her in shops. And terrifying she is with waiters.' He smiled proudly. 'Yes, Fay's the one to sort this out.'

'Thanks, Johnny. If I could get me two mornin's back I'd manage fine. Tell yer what, if I don't, I'll try fer a job on yer buses. Bleedin' bumper cars that'd be!'

Her loud laugh rang out and Johnny's joined it. The dogs looked up briefly then settled down again at their feet.

'I'll get Fay to talk to Mrs French, and I'll keep an eye on that nosy Prue Beynon!' Johnny said. 'I'll get her proper one day, see if I don't.'

Prue always got up to cook Harry's breakfast, even when he was working a long way from Hen Cawr Parc and needed to leave very early. This morning she rose at five-thirty as Harry was leaving at six to go to a meeting in Newport. A firm had gone bankrupt owing him several hundred pounds and a meeting had been called to discuss the percentage of his claim.

She sat with him, drinking a cup of tea and watching him eat. He ate fast; enthusiastic in that as in everything, she thought. He looked at her a few times and smiled, the electric light gleaming on his rimless glasses.

'Prue, I've been thinking. Don't you think we should give your sister a hand with that shop? I've been telling her for ages that it's too small. She ought to extend into the back room.'

'The bank will arrange it. She's perfectly capable of sorting out her own problems, Harry. Always lands on her feet, that one.'

'But I can do it so much cheaper. She could have the

materials at cost, find her some slightly damaged stock, you know the sort of thing.'

'And will she give you a share of her profits?'

'Prue, she's your sister.'

'I know, and she's had a hard time bringing up two children without a husband. But it's her life. She chose it.'

'I've got two weeks coming up with nothing much on. It would be useful for me too,' he said. 'I have to keep the men busy, so it would be in my interests to get them some work, even if it didn't pay much. Better that than pay the men for doing bugger all.

'I'll be back from Newport early this afternoon, so what d'you say we go over and talk about it? I'll get some measuring done and start making estimates. You ring Amy and tell her, will you? Best she thinks it's your idea. Tell her you persuaded me, let her know you care, because you do. Old softy you are, Prue Beynon.'

He kissed her lightly on the cheek before leaving and she stifled the smile of pleasure. Unwilling, unable to show how much she cared for him. Afraid always of being made to look foolish. She watched him walk to the car; a jaunty step, a smartly dressed, handsome man, whistling happily as he set off to call for his accountant and drive to Newport.

His mind is free from worries, and that is thanks to me, she thought proudly. I deal with all the trivia and liberate him from unnecessary stress. I'm a good wife, and he knows it.

It was barely six-thirty but she did not go back to bed. There was washing to do, it being Monday, then she would give the kitchen floor a good scrub. Best to wait until lunchtime to ring Amy and tell her of Harry's generous offer.

She still felt a tinge of resentment at the way Harry was so willing to help Amy, but she smiled as she recalled his words. 'Old softy', am I? She would do as he had suggested and tell Amy it was her persuading that had made Harry agree to help her.

Harry returned from Newport early as promised and

Prue and he went to the shop to talk to Amy. Margaret was playing with a toy piano, and Freddy was reading a fishing magazine. Both children leapt up to greet Harry, Margaret climbing onto his lap, Freddy showing him some ideas for the garden in a library book he had borrowed.

Amy kept an eye on the shop while Prue made tea in the inconvenient kitchen, and Harry talked to the children.

'Have you decided what you're going to do when you leave school?' he asked Freddy.

'I've made a few enquiries about working in gardens,' Freddy said. 'I don't like the idea of being indoors all day. A job working with flowers and trees and shrubs, that would suit me fine, Uncle Harry.'

'Nothing settled yet, then?'

'No.'

'How would you like to work for me? One of my boys is leaving and I need someone to help me, both in the office and outside. Outside mostly for a start, as you'll need to know what's what if you're to tell people what you want them to do.' He watched the boy struggling with the idea, guessing that it was the work with growing plants that appealed, not just being outside. 'You could still study gardening. Perhaps one day garden design and building will come together. Anyway, think about it. The job is yours if you want it.'

Amy showed surprise and great delight when Prue explained about Harry helping her with the extension of the shop.

'Harry! That's good of you!'

'Harry's willing to let you have the materials at cost, you being my sister,' Prue said magnanimously.

'Oh, what a relief. I'll see the bank manager on Monday, but I'm sure he'll agree.'

'I'd better get some measuring done,' Harry said, 'then I'll give you some figures to show him.'

'Any time. Any time. Oh Prue, I'm so grateful.'

'The shop's busy now,' Harry said. 'So what if I come on Wednesday afternoon? All right?' He looked at Amy, a silent question in his laughing eyes.

She nodded. 'Lovely. I'll have some coffee and that for you.'

'Can't wait for the – and that –' he whispered as he followed Prue out through the tiny shop. He winked widely and waved goodbye.

Johnny Cartwright was one of those waiting for Amy to serve them, and he overheard enough to guess what Amy was planning. He bought the few items he wanted, then asked, 'Will you be wanting someone to help empty the shop ready for the builders starting?'

'I suppose I will,' Amy said, 'although I hadn't thought that far ahead. Why, Johnny, are you offering?' she asked with a pert look.

'No, not me. But Nelly's looking for some work now –' he almost said 'your sister' but stopped in time '– now someone has told Evie about her getting drunk the night you met her. Stopped her working for Mrs French she has. Damned cheek I call it. Interfering with her mother's life because of some nosy old gossip!'

'What happened?' Amy asked, taking the money for a packet of soap powder from Milly Toogood's granddaughter.

'Someone told Evie her mother was drunk and suggested that Nelly would be better off if she earned less. So Evie told Mrs French not to employ her any longer.'

'Who told Evie?'

'Got an idea, but I'm not saying.'

'I'll go and have a word with Evie! I'll remind her of a few things she might prefer I'd forgotten!' Amy's earrings jangled angrily. 'As soon as the shop closes! I haven't forgotten what she was like before she left home!'

'Ta.' Johnny went out, pleased that someone besides himself cared enough about Nelly to do something. He had already spoken to Fay, who promised to do what she could.

He crossed the road and went into the house, and called his wife's name. There was no reply. He went into the room where he and Fay lived, finding it neat, shining clean, and empty. Where could she be? Aimlessly, he went out again and wandered down past the church, past Evie and Timothy's house, and stood at the edge of the field looking up towards the wood at the top.

Towards evening he often saw rabbits come out to feed. There were none in sight today. Too early perhaps. He continued to watch, then saw a figure appear at the edge of the trees. Johnny stared until recognition came. The solitary walker was Fay. He jumped over the gate and walked to meet her.

'Been for a walk?' he asked, taking her arm. 'Wondered where you'd got to.'

'I've only been out for half an hour,' she snapped.

'All right, girl. I'm not checking up on you, or expecting you to be at my beck and call. Wish I'd known so I could have come with you, that's all.'

'Sorry, Johnny. I'm so restless. I can't stay in that room. I miss having a house to see to, I suppose. There isn't anything for me to do.'

'Fay, love. I think you're right. We shouldn't worry about babies just yet. Best get a house first. I'll take every bit of over-time I'm offered. Do a bit of gardening in my spare time. We'll both concentrate on getting a good bit saved. Best for us, isn't it? Both be happy then, you with a nice house and me with a bit of garden.'

'Johnny!' Fay's eyes shone and she impulsively kissed him, ignoring for once the risk of them being seen. 'You are a wonderful man.'

'No I'm not. I love you, that's all.'

They walked slowly down the field and as they passed Fay's old home, they waved to Evie and Timothy in the garden.

'Hello,' Evie called. 'Would you like to come in and see what we've done to your house?'

Johnny glanced at Fay, who shook her head.

'Another time,' she said. 'Johnny and I have things to discuss.' They walked home, arm in arm, heads together, already planning how to tackle their intensive savings plan.

* * *

Nelly returned from a private visit to the woods and collected the dogs. 'Come on, boys; time for a nice walk before tea.' She reached the gate, dragging it protestingly open across the cinder path, when the dogs began to bark, not warningly, but in excitement. Someone they knew was coming up the lane. Nelly waited, hoping for someone to chat to. Lucky she'd made that bit of cake yesterday. Chopped prunes instead of sultanas, but it went down well. Then her grandson came around the corner.

'Oliver! I'm just goin' fer a walk with Bobby an' Spotty. Want to come?'

'I've brought my library book to show you, Gran,' he said, waving the book for her to see.

'Leave it 'ere, we'll look at it later.'

'Can we go to the castle again, Gran?'

' 'Course we can, dearie. Glad to see you ain't got a suit on today. Shorts an' a shirt's much better for an adventurous boy. Gettin' on all right at school, are yer?'

'Yes, thanks. I went to tea with Margaret yesterday.' He ran on ahead, the dogs jumping about beside him waiting for a game with a stick.

Nelly sat in the sunshine and watched as he clambered in and out of the castle ruin. It was much tidier now the ground had been prepared for the Coronation party. She went to look in the kitchen. The food she had left was gone, but the tattered remains of the wrapping suggested it had been found by a fox rather than a man.

When her eyes had become accustomed to the shadows, she looked for the watch. It too had gone, but in its place was a dried posy. She guessed it had once been red roses, blue cornflowers and white carnations. The colours had all but faded, leaving only a yellowing, decayed hint of their former beauty. She picked it up and shuddered. It smelt only of death.

For a moment she stood, thinking about the watch and the flowers that had replaced it, then she dropped the posy into a dark corner. Best it was never found. A guilty feeling settled on her shoulders as she walked away, but her mouth was set. 'Best it was never found,' she repeated aloud.

Oliver and the dogs were hot and tired when their games were finished.

'Home now, fer some of Grannie Luke's 'ome made pop,' Nelly announced. 'Then we'll look at your library book, shall we, Ollie? – I mean Oliver.' She shared a smile with him and they went back to the cottage.

When Nelly saw the library book he had brought, she was angry. A rare emotion for Nelly, but anger made her want to go at once to Evie and tell her how stupid she was to force a child who could hardly manage a word, to struggle with such an advanced story.

'That's a lovely story, Oliver,' she said, when he had explained how his mother had chosen it for him. 'But it ain't right fer you. Not yet it ain't. What say I read it to yer, then we do some practice with somethin' a bit easier, eh?'

Oliver looked doubtful. 'I need to be able to read some of it,' he said hesitatingly, 'perhaps just a page?'

'When I've read you a story,' Nelly said firmly.

She scrabbled about under the pile of newspapers and magazines Netta Cartwright had given her and found the two library books she had borrowed from the travelling library. 'Look,' she said, showing him the colourful pages, 'these is much more fun.'

Patiently, she coaxed him through the first few pages, and then said, 'Readin's a magic door, Ollie. Once you've opened it, there's nothing in the whole wild world what you can't find out about. Think of that.'

'Some words are easy. But some don't make any sense.' He pointed to the word 'know'. 'How do I learn those?' His thin face looked so serious, Nelly hugged him and laughed.

'You got a boy in your class what's always awkward, Ollie? Always doin' the opposite of what 'e's told?'

'Yes. Arthur Toogood is like that. How did you know?'

'There's always one. Well, some words is like that. Bein' awkward. Not doin' what the rest does. You've only got to recognise the awkward ones, that's all.'

He reached out for the library book again and they read

together for a while. It was a funny story about the misadventures of an absentminded clown. Nelly believed in laughter.

Nelly had another visitor that day. Amy Prichard came to tell her that Mrs French would like her to go to work the following day as usual.

'Thank Gawd fer that!' Nelly laughed. 'Stay fer a cuppa tea, why don't yer?

Chapter Six

Fay was irritated by the way Johnny drove the car. His hand was up under the rim of the steering wheel, gripping it and pulling it around corners in a ponderous way.

'Johnny, this isn't a bus!'

'Sorry, love, but it's the way I always drive. You know that. What if I drove my bus like a car? Terrible accident there'd be if I wasn't in full control.'

Fay sighed and looked away from him, out into the night where the headlights showed the hedges black and looming over them. The evening had not been a success. They had met some friends of hers and all evening she had been critical of him. Saying nothing, the small annoyances had built up until she could contain them no longer. He touched her arm, and looked at her briefly but she pushed him away.

As they passed the field at the side of her old home, she looked past Johnny to where the woods were hidden by the night. Was Alan up there, sleeping out, hiding from her yet staying close in the hope of their meeting?

'Stop the car. I want to go for a walk.'

'Not at this time of night you don't.' She heard the rare edge of steel in his usually gentle voice and reacted more fiercely because of it.

'Stop the car!' She began to struggle to open the door, and bringing the car to a stop, Johnny held her with one strong hand. He managed to prevent her getting out and with the other hand he switched off the ignition and pulled on the hand-brake. He waited until he could speak calmly.

'Fay. What is it, love?' He held her more determinedly as

she tried again to pull free of him. He pushed his face against hers and when an opportunity came, kissed her, forcing her to respond. When he released her she was limp.

'Let me go,' she whispered.

'Never!' He felt fear at the thought of losing her.

They sat for a while, both tense, Johnny ready to stop her if she tried to get out and run through the darkness to the castle where she was convinced her first love waited for her. He tightened his grip on her to prevent her running into the night and away from him.

'Tell me what is it, Fay,' he coaxed. 'Pals we are, as well as lovers. What ever it is you can tell me.'

'Take me home.'

'You won't try to get out? Don't want you hurt. If you want to walk, we'll walk, the two of us, together. Right?'

'I want to go home.'

He drove the short distance and parked the car on the grass verge. He helped her out and, not even bothering to lock the car, held her close as they went inside.

The small cottage was in darkness. A flicker of an almost dead fire the only light.

'Mam and the others are in bed. Stay up and have a cup of tea shall we?' He went into the built-on room that served as a kitchen, and as a bathroom as well. He made tea and took it in.

'House getting you down, is it, love?' He stirred her tea and handed it to her.

'I wish you wouldn't stir my tea. Put a spoon in every saucer.' She spoke dully, as if unaware of the words.

'Sorry. I forget every time.'

They went upstairs to the back bedroom that was theirs, and before he reached for the light, Johnny gave a gasp of pain. His shin had banged the edge of the iron bed-stead.

'Changed the furniture about again, have you?' he said. 'You could have warned me!'

The light revealed that the bed, once central, was now close to the door and a table that was far too large for the crowded room was in a corner behind the wardrobe, two chairs tucked underneath it. A china cabinet was under the window, an armchair close beside it.

'Where did all this stuff come from?' Johnny asked. 'I thought we were saving up?'

'I got them out of store. We need a place where we can have a meal in private. It isn't right to eat with your family all the time.'

'Mam doesn't mind. Likes cooking for us she does.'

'Mam doesn't mind, but I *do*!'

'Hush, love, you'll wake them.'

They undressed, and Fay brushed her long hair. Johnny was in bed for a long time alone, watching her, loving her, and feeling cut off, unwanted, useless.

When she put down the brush, he opened his arms to her and with a sob, she fell into his embrace. He stroked her soft shoulders, kissed her, murmured soothingly, longing to find words to ease her distress. They made love wildly, and for Johnny, with a sensation of being used, of being a substitute for Alan who was dead. It was dawn before they slept and they woke feeling un-rested and unable to look at each other.

Helping Amy clear the shop was like a holiday to Nelly. There were people to talk to, the feeling of being important and needed, plus the food that Amy supplied for herself and the dogs. The work was hard: moving all the stock into boxes, carefully marking them in her large handwriting and stacking them in the store room in the yard. Scrubbing the shelves as they came down, ready to be put back when the work was complete. Making endless cups of tea for Harry's men as they set about knocking the wall down between the shop and the room once used as a dayroom by Amy and her children.

Milly Toogood came regularly to complain about the dust.

'Putting up the decorations for the Coronation we are. And there's you lot making the flag filthy before we've tied the ends!' she shouted.

'Blow on it, yer mouth's big enough,' Nelly retorted.

Nelly still went regularly to her ladies, but every spare moment was spent behind the shop, leaving Amy free to serve customers as best as she could from the store-room, with people coming in and out of the back gate. 'It was an adventure,' Nelly explained to Oliver. 'Somethin' different. Nice to be 'elpin' Amy too. Ain't got no one, Amy ain't. Except Freddy and your friend Margaret.'

One morning when the workmen had reached the stage where rubble, cement and plaster had been finally banished, Nelly was alone. Amy had closed the shop and gone into town to order the new stock for the shelves being refitted in the double-sized shop. The workmen were away on another job. 'Waiting for the plaster to harden,' they explained. The door to the house was off, and Amy had asked Nelly to stay until she got back, to, 'keep an eye'.

Restlessly, Nelly looked around for something to occupy the few hours. The shop was as clean as she could get it. There was nothing to do there. She turned her attention to the small hallway between the shop and the yard. Old oilcloth covered the floor and she knew it was Amy's intention to replace it. Nelly lifted the lino, tearing it where it had become stuck fast to the flagstones beneath. She would surprise Amy and scrub the flags ready for the new lino.

Boxes lined the wall, piled high, and she had to remove these before pulling up the last of the worn out floor-covering. Then she noticed an oblong shape pressed out by something underneath the thin lino. She tore up the last pieces and picked up an envelope.

It was dirty and partly torn open and, from the look of it, an offical form of some kind. With a guilty feeling that did not slow her fingers, Nelly opened it. It was a death certificate of a child, one day old, she noticed, in 1944. She carefully replaced the form in the envelope and rubbed it in the dirt to make it look as if it hadn't been touched, and threw it in the corner with some discarded boxes.

She felt the sadness of the unknown child as if it were a death recently happened. She wondered why Amy with three children, one dead, had never married. Wondered at the secrets that could survive in a small, close-knit village like Hen Carw Parc.

Nelly fetched buckets of water and scrubbed at the floor until the dust and grime of years was banished. She was still at it, flushed and sweating, when Amy returned.

'Nelly, love! What are you doing? You shouldn't be doing that! Look at you, all hot and bothered. Come on and have a cup of tea in my posh new kitchen upstairs. Look, I've brought us a couple of cakes from town.'

'No trouble,' Nelly said, climbing to her feet with the aid of a hand on a doorknob. 'Blimey but it doesn't 'alf make me hip ache though. Sit outside, why don't we?'

They sat discussing the next stage of the work, and casually, Nelly mentioned the letter. 'It's in the corner where me scrubbin' ain't reached yet,' she explained. Amy opened it as Nelly sipped noisily at her tea.

'Did you open it, Nelly?' she asked after a while.

'Ain't got me glasses. Don't need glasses fer scrubbin'. Got any more cake, 'ave yer?'

'– Yes – help yourself. I'll – just put this upstairs.'

'Probably some bill. Can't be nothing important, not after the years it must 'ave bin there.'

Amy did not come back down, and Nelly finished the last of the cake. When the scrubbing was completed to Nelly's satisfaction, she called out, 'I'm off then. See yer tomorrow.'

'Thank you very much, Nelly. Goodbye.'

Nelly untied Bobby and Spotty from the gate and went home.

Amy sat on her bed, staring at the form. Foolish to be upset. It was nine years since it had happened. Yet the baby's face was still as clear in her mind as if only nine minutes had passed.

Few weeks had passed without her thinking of him, imagining him beside her, imagining his progress through his baby years, and his growing up. His first day at school and his first bicycle. She imagined him as a companion for

Margaret and could see clearly his colouring and build, and how he ran strongly and won all the races in the school sports. How he swam like a fish, and beat all the other boys in reading and arithmetic. Her dream child had never died, but only she saw him.

When Nelly had gone, Amy did not move. The children came in, found themselves something to eat and went out again. At seven she rang Harry's office.

'It's me,' she said when Harry answered. 'Can you talk?'

'Trouble with the job?' he asked.

'No. It's personal.' She knew someone was with him when he replied,

'Usual arrangement.' Then he added for the benefit of his audience, 'Cash on completion. All right?'

Amy put down the phone and stared again at the paper in her hand.

At nine she left Margaret and Freddy playing Monopoly with Netta Cartwright and caught the bus to The Drovers. Harry's car was parked outside and she got in. He kissed her and asked what was wrong. For answer, she handed him the death certificate.

'Nelly found this today. I hadn't seen it for years. It – upset me.'

Harry bent towards the car window for light and looked at the form. 'He'd have been eight, or nine now.' He folded the form and handed it back to her.

'But he didn't live, which was convenient, wasn't it? The second one you wouldn't leave Prue for.'

'I couldn't. Not with Prue being your sister. If it hadn't been for that –'

'There would have been some other reason. Don't think I'm stupid, Harry.'

'I love you. How could I think you stupid?'

'All these years, and I'm still your little bit on the side. I must be mad.'

'That was a difficult time for me too. Remember that. You left me, and a year later, Margaret was born. I don't even know who he was, my replacement. But he didn't marry you either, did he?'

'I'm not the sort men marry,' she spoke sadly, her beautiful eyes filling with tears. 'I worked that out long ago.'

Harry started the engine and drove out of the car park. He headed towards Swansea, along the quiet country road, and when he reached a parking place where many people stopped in the summer months to picnic and enjoy the view, he stopped.

'What shall we do? Would you like to eat?'

'Why not?'

He leaned over in an attempt to kiss her but she moved away, staring out of the window at a view it was too dark to see, looking inward at her own thoughts which were even darker. Back through all the years she had loved Harry, forward to more of the same. The years ahead leading nowhere, using up the precious time so there would be little chance of finding a new life for herself. 'Yes. Let's eat, and drink, and try to be merry.'

'Forget it, Amy. It's so long ago.'

'Won't Prue have a meal waiting for you?' she asked, her voice brittle.

'It won't be the first time I've had to eat two dinners,' he laughed. 'Worth it every time you were.'

Amy ate very little although the food in the restaurant they had chosen was good. She picked at the trout, spreading it around her plate, playing with it, her mind still on the sad little form in her handbag.

'Not to your liking?' Harry asked.

'I'm not hungry after all.'

'Nine years, love. How can seeing that certificate upset you so much?' He watched her then added. 'Was he your real love? The father?'

'You were his father!'

'I meant the man you got pregnant by so soon after. Mean more to you than me, does he? Regret not marrying him when you had a chance of persuading him?' Harry's voice grew louder and Amy shushed him and stared around, afraid he had been overheard by other diners.

'Who was he, Amy?' Harry insisted.

'I won't tell you. Not now, not ever.'

'Did you love him?'

'No. But he was caring, and kind.'

'But he didn't marry you.'

'I wouldn't agree.'

'Married already, was he?'

'Yes! And he still cared for his wife. I was his loving, but she was his love.'

'Yet he would have married you?' Disbelief curled Harry's full lips, distorting his features into those of a stranger. He was becoming irritated. He could do without evenings like this. He wanted Amy for sex and fun, not gloom and misery over something that happened so long ago! He sighed his exasperation.

'Yes! He would have married me. If I'd agreed. He was *concerned* about me and about the baby.'

'And I wasn't? Is that what you're saying? That I didn't care about you?'

'You left me alone to face it. And the baby, our baby, he died, didn't he?'

Harry looked at her curiously as a thought filled his mind. 'This man who cared so much, yet didn't marry you. Was that how you got the money for the shop?'

'Damn you! I won't be questioned! You've no right! I'm not tied to you in any way. Had your chance for that twice but you hadn't the guts. Twice you left me to fend for myself. Opt for safety every time you do, Harry Beynon. No guts! Call yourself a man? You, you left me to face it all, twice!'

She stood up and, taking her duster coat from the clothes stand, left the restaurant, her throat tight with her determination not to cry. Harry hurriedly paid the bill and ran after her. She was standing beside the car and when he opened it, she got in without a word.

'Come on, Amy. We needn't quarrel.' He tried to kiss her, and put his arms around her but she fended him off with surprising vehemence.

'Take me home, Harry. You're unfeeling and callous. I hate you for your lack of understanding.'

Something about her fury prevented him from trying again to calm her. Instead he asked coldly,

'True about the shop then, was it? Paid you off, did he, this caring, kind man? You've had more than that from me, Amy. Years of fun and excitement. Yes, that's what you need more than caring and kindness. Sex and fun, and a bit of illicit excitement. Forbidden fruits is what you enjoy, not marriage, or you wouldn't have stayed with me all these years without any persuasion for me to divorce Prue and marry you. The other woman is your role, Amy, not the quiet, *faithful* wife!'

Amy slapped him hard, and he gasped at the pain of it. Then the slaps and punches came fast and he held out his hands to stop them reaching their target. She growled in rage and fury, kicked, and hit out, and grabbed his protective hand and bit it until she tasted the saltiness of his blood.

The one-sided fight went on longer than he expected. Each time he thought she was calming down, anger flooded through her and she attacked him again. It was useless to try and hold her off and finally, out of desperation, he opened the car door and got out. He was panting with the shock of it as he stood in the shadow of the restaurant wall.

The car had been parked in the darkest part of the car-park. He was trying to bandage his bleeding hand with a handkerchief when he heard the car start. Too late, he ran towards it to stop her. The car backed dangerously close to him and roared out into the road. Harry was left, swearing, feeling in his pockets for a coin to ring for a taxi. For a brief moment, his anger was so great he was tempted to ring the police and report his car stolen. But he did not.

The following weeks were miserable for Harry. He missed Amy more than he had imagined. Her light-hearted ways had become dear to him. He wondered if he *could* leave Prue. The upheaval would be enormous and he would have to contend with weeks and months of upsets. Harry was not a man to cope with upsets and he knew it. Perhaps if he waited until Amy had calmed down, they might revert to the pleasant life again.

He tried several times to see her but she refused. On the pretext of examining the work in the shop, he called during the hours when it was open, but she treated him coldly and in a purely businesslike manner, giving no hope of a return to their previous relationship.

After spending a few hours in his office one evening towards the middle of May, on a hard chair reading a boring book about an amateur thief and an unbelievably inept detective, Harry went home early.

'Prue,' he said, 'are you still willing to help with the books? I'm sick of working all the hours I do. If you would help I could be here with you more of the time. Like that would you?'

Prue was pleased. But all she said was, 'If you like. I'll start now, shall I? You'll have to go through them so I follow your methods.'

Having Prue attending to his book-keeping, which she did well, meant Harry could arrive home early each evening without having to explain why he had not done so in the past. But it also meant he had even more time to kill.

He missed Amy terribly and one day, out of desperation to fill the empty hours, he called to see Barclay Bevan and offered his services to assist with the forthcoming Coronation party. His muscle and his lorry were both gratefully accepted.

The houses along the main road were decorated with flags and flowers and a few odd items, like draped curtains in the appropriate colours on Milly Toogood's chimney, and red, white and blue fish on the chip-shop window. Rosettes sprouted on Johnny's bus, the church door and lych gate were both surrounded with flowers and the vicar was not pleased, until he discovered it was his wife's work.

Nelly was not to be outdone. She wound red string and white string around her gate and added some blue sugar bag paper to complete the effect. Her windows were bright, being criss-crossed with twists of crepe paper and a few doilies she had bought in town.

Amy's shop window was like a shield, with crepe paper forming a frame for a large photograph of Queen Elizabeth. Everyone made an effort and the village was a colourful sight.

It was a perfect excuse for Amy to overdo the cheerfulness she had showed to everyone since parting from Harry. She was determinedly happy. She sang as she worked, gathering smiles from all her customers. Nelly was the object of her generosity as Amy sorted out and discarded clothes which she associated with Harry. She also gave her some tins which had been in the shop a long time and showed no signs of becoming suddenly popular.

'Here you are, Nelly, take some of these home with you. Some sound a bit fancy, but they'll probably be all right. Tinned melon. How does that strike you, eh?' She threw the slightly scruffy tin to Nelly who caught it and nodded enthusiastically.

'Bit of rust on the top but I'll open it upside down. Do me a treat that will. Ta, Amy. You're a good sort.'

Amy shuddered dramatically. 'God, that sounds awful! A good sort. It's what you say about someone when there's really nothing good to say!'

'That's not what I meant at all,' Nelly protested. 'Wish I could say my Evie's a good sort. Always on at me she is. Bought me a new dress last week and keeps askin' why I don't wear it. It's pink! I ask yer. When am I goin' to wear a dress what's pink? Feedin' me chickens?'

'Handy if the Queen invites you to the Coronation, Nelly,' Amy laughed, her necklace and earrings sparkling in the sun which shone through the open door.

'Hope this sun keeps shinin',' Nelly said. 'I don't think me suger bags'll stand too much rain.'

Which made Amy laugh even louder as Nelly explained.

A group of people came out of the church hall almost opposite the shop and Amy and Nelly waved to them.

'Bin to another meetin' about the party, they 'ave,' Nelly said. 'Plannin' Committee they calls themselves.'

'Monica French and my sister seem close friends lately. I wonder what they have in common?'

'Not a lot, I should think. Real lady is Mrs French. Ooo, sorry. I didn't mean –'

'I know what you mean, Nelly. My sister has money but she hasn't been brought up to it.'

'Yes. You can certainly put things in the right words. Never could meself. Always comin' out wrong.'

The two women in question came across the road and into the shop. Nelly hurried back into the store room to sort out the last of the stock as she had been instructed.

Later, as she collected her dogs and the bag of tins Amy had given her, Johnny walked through the shop and out into the yard.

'Leave that, Nelly. I'll bring it up for you later. There's more tins in the shop for you. I'll bring those as well.'

'Oo ta, Johnny. Bring 'em up on yer bus, will yer?' she laughed. 'Kind of Amy, ain't it? Amy's a good – Amy's a kind 'earted woman. That's what she is.'

The population of the village was expected to almost double during the day of the party and preparations for the visitors meant that the lane which passed Nelly's cottage was well used. She enjoyed the unusual activity, waving at people as they passed and watching the cars driving to and from the castle with items for the various tents and stalls to be built.

Some of the children called to see the chicks, now spiky with feathers appearing through the soft down. She knew that Oliver was asked to give a regular report on their progress and the small importance was helping him overcome his shyness. Teasing was less now his grandmother was no longer merely Dirty Nelly, but the woman with the chicks.

The sound of a slow, heavy lorry coming up the lane was unusual. She smiled as she thought that it might be Johnny's bus. 'But 'e wouldn't dare,' she whispered to the dogs, her crooked teeth showing in a grin. She hurried up the path to lean on the decorated gate to see a lorry pass.

It was an open-backed lorry with the name of Harry Beynon on its sides. Trestle tables and benches and lots of wooden chairs were stacked on board. Some chairs were folded and arranged in rows. Others were in pairs, seats together and all were tied with ropes.

'Come on, boys,' Nelly called to the dogs, and she set off to follow.

It was the day before the party and Nelly was soon involved with the people already there, carrying an endless variety of items to their selected places. She stayed for the rest of the day, unloading furniture, setting out chairs and moving things here and there as instructions were counteracted and argued about by several of the organisers. Bert Roberts who had been in the army and knew all about giving orders was in charge. 'Or so 'e thinks!' Nelly muttered.

There was a lot of excitement and laughter when Harry Beynon's lorry returned with a piano on the back, being played by Barclay Bevan! He watched as the instrument was off-loaded and placed near the castle walls, where the choir was going to sing.

Several stalls were already completed and Harry's men were finishing off several others. Phil Davies was marking out the lines for the races with a marking trolley borrowed from the cricket ground. Music was issuing from a van, also belonging to Harry's firm. This Nelly went to investigate. She found her son-in-law winding up a gramophone and selecting some music for the following day.

'Why ain't you at school?' she challenged. 'Not mitchin' are yer?'

'Hello, mother-in-law. Have you a favourite dance tune?'

Nelly climbed into the van and searched through the 78s, putting aside several which she wanted to be included.

'Ere, Johnny,' she shouted. 'Come an' choose a smoochy record fer you an' Fay!'

'Don't know why we bothered to hire a loudspeaker!' Bert Roberts said. Nelly grinned her appreciation of the compliment.

'Where's Oliver an' Evie then?' she asked. 'They're missin' all the fun.'

'Oliver is at school. I've popped over in my lunch hour. Evie says he can come early tomorrow. He says you and he have planned to spend the whole day here.'

'That's right. We're 'elpin' with the decorations. Tell 'im to come straight after breakfast.'

'I will. Goodbye, mother-in-law.'

'Timmy,' she said sadly. 'Can't you call me Nelly? Everyone else does.'

'I'll try.'

She watched as he carefully put the records in the van, each pile labelled, neatly arranged for the following day. She felt hot and grubby and thought she would paddle her feet in the stream before going home. But Tim looked the same as always; his straight hair parted and in place, his clothes looking as if they had just been bought and put on.

Timothy was a pale, studious man, hardly raising his voice above a whisper in normal conversation. His face, with its worried look and washed out blue eyes never became animated. It was as if, Nelly thought with a smile, he knew life had some dreadful shock prepared for him and he lived in constant expectation of it.

'Cheer up, Timmy,' she shouted. 'Tomorrow's going ter be a smashing day.'

'Yes.' He didn't look up from his task as he added, 'Goodbye, mother-in-law.'

'Stuffed prune,' Nelly muttered. She looked around her for some more entertaining company.

Timothy watched her go, waving to her friends as she threaded her erratic passage through those busily working. The dogs bounced about her as if they were on elastic. He could understand why Evie was embarrassed by her. Nelly represented everything Evie hated and had run away from home to escape. Yet Nelly was a harmless old soul, and Oliver seemed to have taken to her. She couldn't do him any harm, Evie would see to that. He completed the arrangements of records, each pile neatly labelled, and went back to school.

At the other side of the field, Arthur Toogood, Milly's grandson, slipped out from the place where he had been hiding, hoping the Head hadn't spotted him. He should be at school, but the temptation of seeing the preparations for the party had been too much for him.

'You'll get me hung, young Arthur,' Milly said with a false frown. 'Go on with you; he's gone now.' Milly turned to her companion, Sibyl Tremain, who followed her about a few paces behind. 'Terrible boy he is,' she said proudly. She walked away, Sibyl trotting behind obediently.

Nelly nudged Brenda Roberts and pointed. 'There they go, Mrs Nogood and the pup!' The graphic description made the quiet Brenda chuckle. A shout from the other side of the partly erected tent make them both groan.

'Take up the slack, woman, take up the slack.' Bert Roberts was organising the setting up of the tents in which the raffle prizes were to be displayed.

'All right, Bert; I'm doing my best,' Brenda said. Nelly grimaced, baring her gappy teeth in sympathy, and left them to it.

Phil Davies and Mr Evan, the caretaker of the school staggered up the field carrying boxes and sacks containing decorations made by the school-children. These were seized by Gwen and Emlyn Parry, who began sorting them out into their respective places. Nelly stayed to help, handing up the crowns, and swords, and carefully cut out red dragons to Gwen and her husband who were perched precariously on the planks supported between ladders.

'I hope it doesn't rain tonight,' Nelly shouted and a chorus answered, 'Shut up, Nelly!' and made her laugh.

A lorry whined up the lane and the driver, who Nelly recognised as the man who delivered groceries to Amy's shop, deposited a pile of wooden crates containing pop of assorted colours. Constable Harris waved the helpers back and guided the lorry as it reversed and returned to the lane.

Sian arrived with bags full of bunting which she had made from old dresses and the edges of worn sheets which she and her sisters had dyed in bright colours. Bert and the patient Brenda were now dragging ropes with which they began marking out the space allotted for the races. Prue was there, and she was over-seeing the cleaning of the castle kitchens, and the placing of the trestle-tables ready for the mountains of food to be delivered the following morning.

Everywhere people were laughing. Nelly was so excited she wanted to cry. 'Bloomin' lovely, ain't it, boys,' she said to the dogs, her voice strangely high and squeaky. 'Even grizzle-guts herself,' she nodded towards Prue Beynon, 'even *'er* with a smile – never thought I'd see the day!'

She walked to the stream and kicked off her shoes and sat with her feet in the water, which, coming straight from the hill behind her, was icy cold. She watched the clear ripples in the hope of seeing a darting fish and was lost in a day-dream when the dogs barked and woke her. Someone was coming. She turned, a smile ready to greet whoever it was, and was just in time to see a man hesitate, then run back the way he had come. The dark brown overcoat and the trilby were unmistakable. Alan French or whoever it was who looked like him.

Nelly stood up, wiping her feet half-heartedly on her skirt. She remembered the posy of red, white and blue flowers. It hadn't been a message had it? She clutched her face with horror. Was he telling Fay he would come on the day of the Coronation party?

'Bloody 'ell,' she muttered as she began walking back to the castle site. 'Why can't the dead stay dead an' not come back to upset Johnny an' 'is Fay?'

Chapter Seven

When Nelly woke on the morning of the Coronation party the air was already warm and the day promised to be a good one. She made a trayful of sandwiches as her contribution to the celebrations. She had bought the sliced bread from Amy's shop and considered it hardly fit to give her chickens. When she was finished, she sat and waited for Oliver. When he arrived he was flushed with hurrying, knowing he was later than they had planned.

'Come on, dearie. Waited fer hours I 'ave . Where you bin?' Nelly looked with dismay at the neat little figure, his shirt buttoned up to the neck and the bow tie in place. She pulled it off him and threw it on a chair, opened a few buttons and rolled up his sleeves.

'Sorry I'm late, Gran. Mother insisted I read to her before I came.'

'Don't she think *my* time's important then? Eh? Sittin' 'ere waitin' while she 'as you doin' readin'?' She paused. 'Ow d'yer get on?'

'Not bad, but I still can't remember some words. They won't stay in my head.'

'I ain't surprised with Evie breathin' down yer neck! Make me forget me own name, your mum would! We'll get a bit of readin' done tomorrow, eh? You an' me 'elpin' each other.' She handed him the box of cakes to carry. 'But now, Ollie me boy, we're off to enjoy ourselves. Come on, Bobby an' Spotty.' They set off up the lane, Nelly staggering under the loaded tray which was covered with a snowy white tea-towel lent to her by Amy when she had bought the bread.

The field and the castle had been transformed. The old walls now painted white were draped with streamers. Union Jacks and the Welsh Dragon were flying from every possible corner and even the trees were wound around with ribbons.

Bert Roberts seemed to be still in command. Nelly saw him shouting instructions at some boys struggling to hang some streamers across the kitchens. Cardboard shields, crowns and swords and daggers were displayed all along the castle walls, and as a centrepiece, a large poster of Queen Elizabeth was slowly being hauled into its chosen place, high on the tower walls.

Nelly had been there until late the previous evening, yet the sight made her gasp. 'Look at that, Ollie! What d'you think of that!' She spoke proudly, as if she alone had been responsible for it all.

'Want a 'and, Bertie?' she shouted.

'Don't talk to me when I'm balanced on a ladder! Got no sense?' he grumbled.

Nelly looked at Oliver and pulled a face. 'Sergeant 'e was in the army,' she explained. 'Even got stripes sewn on 'is pyjamas!'

Long trestle tables were already spread with white sheets and decorated with jars containing wooden sticks to which red, white and blue streamers had been fastened, one for each child who had paid for the tea. Also at intervals were paper flowers, also in red, white and blue, made by the school children. Above the tables, bunting swung gently in the breeze.

'It's like magic, Gran.'

'Ain't it just!'

They pushed their way through to the kitchens to deposit their food. Mrs French was cutting sandwiches into small squares, and Evie was helping her. Nelly called to her daughter but only had a slight nod on return. Prue Beynon was chattering away as she arranged the small sandwiches on to plates. Only Mrs French thanked Nelly for her contribution.

Before turning and pushing her way outside, Nelly made another effort to gain a response from Evie. She lifted Oliver up and shouted, ' 'E's all right, Evie. I got 'im. Be all right with me.'

'Mind you behave yourself,' Evie said to her son.

Nelly saw the apologetic expression on Oliver's face as he promised and her jaw tightened. 'Why can't she let the kid 'ave some fun,' she muttered. She shouted again at her daughter. 'He'll 'ave a good time today, don't you worry.'

Evie looked doubtful. Prue looked at Evie with a sympathetic frown. Nelly poked out a tongue.

The people already pouring into the field were mostly strangers. As well as the children from the council estate, where Nelly had got to know a number of families as she did the weekly collections, there were small groups of houses where there were insufficient numbers for their own party. These had joined with Hen Carw Parc. Others further afield had heard about the party held in a castle ruin and begged to be included. All had paid their share and had entered the races and some had promised help with the entertainments.

Many families had brought lunchtime picnics and by midday the field was dotted with knots of people circled around blankets and tablecloths set out on the grass. Wasps and bees hummed around jampots. Ants were shaken from skirts and shoes. Grubby fingers reached out for food, then scratched at the irritations caused by the gnats which swarmed around the diners, depositing jam on hot faces.

Children threw off cardigans and shoes and socks, the unwanted clothing folded across the parents' arms. Youngsters ran barefoot around the stalls, pleading for pennies for the side-shows which hoped to raise money for the N.S.P.C.C. Even fathers loosened their ties and rolled up shirt-sleeves, admitting the sun-warmed air to cool their white skin.

A stall had been placed at the edge of the field, and its shelves filled with old, unwanted china. Mostly the white crockery which had had to suffice during the years of shortages and which was now thankfully discarded.

For a penny, you could pelt it with wooden balls, to 'Ease your Frustrations', the banner said. Nelly read it out to Oliver, carefully, syllable by syllable so he could read it too.

'Could do with a few penn'orth of that every time I sees yer mum,' Nelly whispered. 'Rubs me up somethin' awful she does.'

'What's frustrations, Gran?'

'When you gets mad with something – or someone – and there's no way of changin' things. Inside yer, there's a pot boilin' over, and peltin' a ball or two, an' smashin' a few dishes is supposed to 'elp. 'Ave a go, why don't yer?'

She handed him some money and urged him towards the stall. He hesitantly took the balls offered, and stood, wavering between dropping them on the grass and handing them to Nelly.

'Go on! Don't stand there like two penn'orth of Gawd-'elp-us!' She took one of the balls and threw it at the stall, succeeding in breaking a plate. 'See? Now you 'ave a go. Go on, get mad. Throw as if you really means it!'

Oliver threw one self-consciously, but the second reached the shelves and then the balls flew fast and china shattered and fell to the ground. The staff holder laughed and collected the largest pieces to replace on the shelves.

'Needed that did you, boy?'

'Frustration ain't just fer the old uns,' Nelly laughed her loud laugh and led Oliver away. 'Come over 'ere, young Ollie, there's something else you got to try.' She pushed her way through the increasingly thick crowd, dragging Oliver behind her.

Near the entrance, where people were still queueing to pay, or showing their tickets to get in, were some stocks. Phil Davies the postman was firmly fastened in. At his side was Johnny Cartwright, urging people to pay threepence to throw a wet sponge at the prisoner. Buckets of cold water stood temptingly around. Johnny held out large coloured sponges, asking customers to take one and punish Phil for being stupid enough to volunteer.

When things were slack, Johnny himself would pelt the laughing, soaked victim to encourage others to take part.

'If you miss,' Johnny warned, 'I might pick up the sponge and throw it at you!'

'Got to 'ave a go at this!' Nelly paid and collected her dripping sponge and threw it, not at Phil, who was tensed waiting for the missile, but at the unsuspecting Johnny. The crowd roared with laughter. Oliver was shocked and put both hands to his face, before realising that it had been taken in good part and he could safely join in the laughter.

It soon became difficult to get to the stalls, but Nelly managed to buy Oliver a turn on the swings, a ride on a pony, a toffee apple and some candy-floss and an ice-cream already melting from a makeshift fridge.

In the kitchens, the platefuls of sandwiches and cakes were covered with damp tea-towels, waiting for the time to call the children to eat. A flask of tea was being shared between Evie, Prue and Mrs French.

'I do agree with you, Prue.' Mrs French nodded agreement as Prue explained how she had persuaded Harry to let her help. 'I supported Richard whenever I could. He had a full and useful life but he couldn't have done as much without my assistance.'

'You're talking about outside interests,' Prue disagreed. 'I'm talking about Harry's work. By doing the books for him, he can spend more time at home, which is what he wants.'

'Richard wasn't exactly an absentee husband,' Mrs French admonished gently. 'He and I did things together. He sang in the choir and I went along too. I organised concerts, with others too, of course. And I helped out in the music shops when someone was ill. I miss him and I miss the involvement. He was such a considerate husband.'

'Yes,' Prue said, misunderstanding. 'Harry's considerate too. Never bothers me much with – you know.' Mrs French stifled a smile and glanced at Evie, who also seemed amused.

'Always done my duty, mind,' Prue whispered confidentially. 'He's never had cause to complain.'

Monica French took out a lace-trimmed handkerchief and hid her laughter in a fit of coughing.

Prue also looked away. How often had she told that lie? Pretended to be satisfied with the little attention Harry gave her? She gazed across to where a group of youngsters gathered around the piano. Children. Everyone had children, except her. Night after night she waited for him, and night after night she slept alone, and unfulfilled.

It wasn't proper to admit to wanting a man so much, she knew that, but how she envied Amy. Even her brief affairs had been full of love, and had resulted in Freddy and Margaret. She watched the girl touching the keys of the piano, tall, graceful and with such a sweet singing voice. An interest in the piano too it seemed.

If she had been mine, how much more she would achieve. I'd send her to Mrs French for lessons. Very musical, Mrs French. She might be famous one day with the right encouragement. Yet it was Amy, sinful Amy, who had Freddy and Margaret.

Netta Cartwright walked past with a still soaked Johnny and waved at them. Prue stared after them with disapproval on her thin face.

'Those Cartwrights have got above themselves since Johnny married someone with a bit of style,' she said. 'I can't think what Fay saw in him. Not that she's anything special. Worked in a chemist's, her father did.'

'He was a pharmacist.'

'Three times I've called, asking if Fay would like to join our sewing bee, to make things for charity, but she's never in. When she does her housework and cooking I can't think. Probably leaves it all to Netta. She's soft enough to let her get away with it.'

'I think I'll go outside to see what's happening,' Mrs French said. 'Coming, Evelyn?'

The two women went out into the sun, each sighing relief at the temporary escape from Prue Beynon's tongue.

* * *

At two o'clock Timothy Chartridge blew his whistle and voices called for entrants for the first race. With the assistance of Harry Beynon and Bert Roberts, Timothy managed to get the children lined up in ages, and, as each race was won, to hand the winners a rosette made by Prue's sewing bee, and a book about the royal family.

Nelly sprawled on the grass, having found a place near the finishing line, and laughed uproariously at the antics of the sackrace, and the three-legged race. When entrants were invited for the adults' races, she at once volunteered.

'Stay there; won't be long,' she called to Oliver, and sticking a lump of home-made toffee in his hand, she hurried to the starting post.

Her shoes were loose, the laces having been taken out as her feet grew hot and tired. She tripped several times and finally fell, near the finish and rolled in the now dusty grass. She made the most of the humour of the situation and relished the laughter that rang out as she exposed her pink bloomers, which reached her fat knees.

Evie, who had looked to see the cause of the laughter, turned away in disgust. Mrs French patted her arm.

'Don't be upset, dear. Nelly's a character and much loved and tolerated. You won't change her. No one thinks the worse of you because of her. Laugh with the rest if you can, it's far the best way to deal with it.'

'Would you find it easy to laugh if it was your mother sprawled there attracting such remarks?' Evie said bitterly. 'And as for not changing things. I wouldn't be too sure of that!'

More laughter rang out and Evie was persuaded to look. To her relief it was not Nelly this time. Her mother was not the only one to show more than she should that day.

Amy had closed the shop and had arrived at the field intending to stroll around and talk to a few people, then go home again. She was in no mood to enjoy herself although none would have guessed it.

She had dressed unsuitably in a new turquoise outfit with

a straight, mid-calf length skirt and a short jacket; tight at the waist and full at the back in a sort of bustle. Seeing Nelly enjoying herself, she lifted her skirt high above her knees so she could run, and came down the field after the rest of the competitors, showing the tops of her nylons and the pink straps of her suspenders. She tripped over Nelly's sprawled feet and collapsed, laughing, beside her.

She and Nelly helped each other up and they walked back to the start, still laughing. Nelly's crooked teeth were well displayed, and Amy's long earrings sparkled and her blonde hair shimmered as she shook her head to free it of the dried grass that had found its way among the curls. The upswept style fell about her neck.

'I'd have worn something more suitable if I'd known I was part of the cabaret!' Amy laughed.

'Borrowed a pair of mine, would yer?'

Nelly pushed her way back to where Oliver waited, acknowledging the pats on her shoulders with a wide grin.

While the tables were being filled with food and drinks, the children were organised into a group for singing. There was a natural amphitheatre against the mound below the castle walls, and it was here that Timothy gathered the choir. The piano was standing in the shade of a tree, and the vicar was strumming a few chords to set the mood.

Barclay Bevan was dressed in black, but he had discarded his surplice and wore only black trousers and a black shirt with the white dog collar. He was very hot and envied the children running about so free from the restrictions of his formal clothes. His face shone redly and his fingers threatened to slip on the keys. As Timothy raised his arms to gather the children for their first song, he quickly wiped his hands on his plump thighs, poised his fingers above the keys, raised his eyes to Timothy and with a benign expression, awaited his instructions.

The rest of the throng sat where they could, mothers waving to their offspring, friends shouting and keeping places for each other, impatient for the singing to begin.

Nelly watched as Oliver left her to take his place near his father. He looked rather pale and Nelly thought he was unhappy performing, even as one of a crowd. She didn't wave.

Timothy's voice swelled from its usual whisper as he addressed the children. His features lost their habitual frown and he became animated, more alive. His job was his life; there was little room in his heart for anything else.

This day of celebration was acceptable as a useful addition to the school year. Many lessons had been built around the Coronation and the fete day would be the basis of many more. Timothy saw everything through the eyes of a teacher. His son was just another pupil and not a very bright one at that.

After a few popular choruses to settle the children, Margaret Prichard, Amy's eight-year old daughter, sang a solo. Her pure young voice made even the liveliest child fall silent. Nelly gulped at a lump in her throat, and was not the only one to wipe away a tear of pleasure. Margaret wore a long, pale green dress and she swung gently from side to side as she sang. Her red hair was long, and had been released from the ribbons which had held it in plaits, to fall about her shoulders like a shawl of gold.

While the children ate sandwiches, crisps and jellies and cakes, the adults attended them, while hoping there would be something left for themselves. Nelly wandered around, enjoying the crowd and full of a feeling of excitement. She saw Johnny and the vicar struggling up the field with the tea urn.

'I ain't seen Fay yet? She comin'?' she shouted.

'When she's finished work. She always has a few calls on a Saturday morning,' Johnny explained.

The queue for tea was long and Nelly thought she would go home and make her own. She was just pushing through the hedge at the edge of the lane when she saw the stranger.

In spite of the day being sunny and warm, he was wearing a coat, with the collar turned up around his face. He was walking away from her, his limp very pronounced, his head bent down as if to hide his face. Nelly followed him.

The noise from the castle was loud, even at this distance. Music from Tim's gramophone plus the chatter and shrieks from the children. He did not look back, but headed for the trees not far from the cottage. Nelly moved from tree to tree, a bubble of excitement rising as she imagined herself playing detective. Then her mood fell to dismay. Ahead of them she saw a solitary figure. 'Fay,' she whispered.

Standing out of sight behind a hawthorn, she watched anxiously as the two people met. The man looked at Fay, then began to run away from her. Fay followed and the two figures were swallowed up in the greenery.

Nelly went to the cottage to make her cup of tea, but grew cold as she sat, staring up the garden to the wood, wondering what would happen next. That withered posy in red, white and blue, the colours of today. Had it been a message for Fay and Alan to meet?

Fay called Alan's name and begged him to stop. Why was he running? His posy had told her he would be here and she had been longing for the hours to pass. He stumbled on a tree root and she lessened the gap between them. 'Alan. Please wait,' she begged. But whatever his intentions for the day had been, something had changed his mind. He paused at the edge of the stream where it had widened, and giving a brief glance back, he jumped over, scrambling as he missed the further bank, then he managed to gain the firm ground and soon disappeared among the trees. Fay called his name for an age, then slowly walked to the castle grounds.

Nelly walked back to the field and looked for Oliver. Just as they met up, and he began to tell her of what he had been doing since she left him, music blared out and Timothy announced a surprise item. He pointed towards the highest part of the old walls, and as the record was hushed, singing could be heard. In procession, walking down between the ruined stonework, came a band of minstrels in mediaeval costumes. They carried a few instruments, including guitars and accordians, which were hardly in keeping with the costumes but no one seemed to care. They all wore masks.

Using the ancient ramparts for a stage they sang and played a number of songs, and even did a simple dance. People in the audience that had quickly gathered listened, watched, and tried to recognise the people behind the disguise.

'Harry Beynon,' Nelly pointed. 'That's easy, 'im bein' so tall. An' Emlyn and Gwen Parry. Megan, Bronwen and Sian from next door to you, Ollie. Coo, ain't that Mrs French? Fancy! And that's young Johnny. I wonder where Fay is!'

'Fay wouldn't join him, more's the pity,' Netta Cartwright said. 'It's nice to do things together sometimes.'

Nelly glanced at her friend, aware of a hint of dismay in the gently spoken words.

'Don't want to live in each other's pockets, they don't. Not kids today.'

'No, they say they want more variety in their lives.' Still the lack of conviction.

'Seen Fay 'ave yer?' Nelly asked. 'Thought I saw 'er a few minutes ago. Johnny said she's comin' later. Work 'as to come first.'

'I'm just going to the kitchens; they might have seen her. I do hope she doesn't miss all the excitement.'

Nelly shook her head. 'No fear of that,' she said emphatically. Netta gave Oliver a few pence for ice-cream and left them.

Nelly stood up and looked around for Fay's blonde head. Fay was tall, several inches taller than Johnny, and she should be easy to see, if she were here.

The minstrels finished their singing and came down to find a partner each to start the dancing. Nelly saw Fay and Johnny as people moved to the area near the gramophone and began to dance. Johnny was obviously trying to comfort his wife, pressing a handkerchief to her face to wipe away her tears. Nelly did nothing. Best to let them sort it out themselves, although she longed to go and invite them to go to the cottage and talk in private.

'There seems to be trouble within the happy throng.' A voice at her side made Nelly jump with guilt at having been caught watching the couple in a private moment.

' 'Ello, Mrs French, dearie. 'Avin' a good time are yer? Wasn't it you singin' with them minstrels? Fancy you dressin' up an' all!'

'It was my idea. We had the costumes from when Richard and I ran a concert party during the war. I thought it would be fun.'

'It was that all right. Smashin'. Enjoyin' it are yer?'

'Very much. But not everyone is, it seems.' She gestured to Fay and Johnny.

'Early days yet. There's always a bit of sortin' to do when you're newly married, ain't there?'

'Perhaps. Although I don't remember having such problems. Nelly – she can't be still grieving for my son, can she? I know that sounds silly, but she has visited me quite a lot lately.'

'It's eight years now since he – went missin'. Time to forget I'd 'ave thought. For a young girl I mean, not fer a mother of course,' she added quickly. Mrs French patted Nelly's arm affectionately. 'I know what you mean.' She smiled at the rosy-cheeked woman and asked, 'Your marriage wasn't a very long one, was it? You never talk about – See? I don't even know your husband's name.'

'Norman,' Nelly supplied. 'Norman Birkett.'

'Birkett? But I thought – I've always called you Nelly Luke.'

' 'E passed on so quick after we was wed, it never stuck, the new name I mean. Nelly Luke I've stayed.'

Mrs French saw a momentary flash of unease in Nelly's eyes. She had upset her by reminding her of her loneliness perhaps.

Then Nelly added, 'Never did feel like no Mrs Norman Birkett. Nelly Luke people calls me.' Again that shifty, sideways glance.

Monica French felt embarrassment flood her face. Nelly had never been married! Nelly now looked completely unconcerned, waving at Milly Toogood who was aiming balls at the old china on the Frustration stall. Monica hurriedly changed the subject.

'Look, Nelly; isn't that Harry Beynon, still in his mask? He seems to be heading this way. Perhaps he's going to ask you to dance.'

Harry carried a glass of beer and beneath his mask, his lips were open in a smile.

'Hello, Monica. Here, Nelly, this is for you, compliments of Johnny.' He handed Nelly the foaming glass. 'Sorry I haven't anything for you,' he smiled at Monica. 'There's only beer and I didn't think you'd want that.'

'No, no, don't worry. I rarely drink,' laughed Mrs French, 'but I shall enjoy watching Nelly drink hers.'

Harry didn't stay, but went back to where the older people were dancing to records played by Timothy.

' 'Andsome devil, ain't 'e?'Nelly said. 'With that mask, 'e looks like some pirate. Flashin' eyes and long 'air down 'is back – to make up for the bald bit on top I expect. It's a wonder Prue don't make 'im 'ave it cut though. That fussy about neatness she is. 'Er's looks like it's been glued down.' She laughed loudly and Mrs French looked around, hoping no one had overheard, chuckling, in spite of disapproving of Nelly's outspokenness.

Mrs French left her then to go and find some friends. Nelly stood happily watching the dancers and drinking her beer. She saw Harry go to Amy, and from the gestures, guessed he was asking her to dance with him. Amy refused and pushed him angrily away. He laughed, and with an arm around her shoulders, half lifted her towards the rest of the dancers.

They danced together, but even from a distance, Nelly could see they were quarrelling. She wondered if there had been a disagreement about how much the work on the shop had cost, but the disagreement didn't look like a business problem. More like lovers, she thought with a jolt.

Fay and Johnny were dancing, their heads together, hers bent slightly to compensate for her extra inches. They looked like lovers too, Nelly thought with a relieved sigh. Perhaps Fay had accepted that Johnny was her love. Instinctively she glanced towards the edge of the trees, now in shadow as the day was ending. She wondered with a shiver if the stranger, whether he be Alan or not, was watching, and she moved further into the crowd.

Later, Johnny brought her another beer. 'None for sale,' he explained. 'Just some brought for the boys. One for you though, even if you aren't one of the boys, eh?'

'Ta ever so.' She began drinking at once. 'Enjoyin' yerselves, are yer? You an' Fay?'

'It's great fun. We ought to do it more often. Daft really, waiting for the Queen to give us an excuse. Plenty of other ideas I'm sure, if we set about it.'

'What about my birthday for a start?' she laughed. 'Go on you, back to that wife of yours.'

Later still, when she had returned the glasses to the kitchens, Phil Davies gave her a drink, and so did Timothy, much to her surprise, although he added a warning not to mention it to Evelyn.

'Where's Oliver?' Nelly wanted to know. 'Ain't seen 'im for a while.'

'Try the swings. They're free now it's almost dark. He was there with some of his school friends when I saw him last.'

Nelly pushed her way through the laughing crowds, her gait a little unsteady, to the swings. As she came in sight of Evie and Prue, she hesitated, and stumbled. At once, Prue said loudly,

'Here's your mother, Evelyn dear, in need of some help again by the look of her.'

'Old cow,' Nelly muttered, and trying to walk upright and confident, succeeded in appearing more drunk than she actually was.

' 'Ere Ollie, 'ave a sweet.' She pulled out from her pocket a bag of sweets and offered the bag to Oliver, who took one quickly, before Evie could prevent him, and popped it into his mouth.

'He's had more than enough for one day. And so have you!' Evie said. 'Go home, Mother. Go home!'

'No fear. I ain't missin' any of this!'

A bonfire was lit and in its glow, Nelly beamed with pleasure at the assorted faces. Children, red and grubby, many falling asleep in their mothers' arms, on their fathers' shoulders, or sprawled in untidy heaps on the grass. Evie's face showed anger. Oliver's was anxious and pale. Prue, she noticed curiously was intently staring into the crowd, oblivious to everything except the object of her gaze. Nelly moved slightly to see what was taking Prue's attention, making her eyes stare so concentratedly. Harry, she saw, was dancing with Amy, who still looked to be an unwilling partner.

Nelly glanced back at Prue, the coldness of her stare quite alarming. ' 'Ere, Evie, 'old this.' She pressed her empty glass into Evie's hand and went to where the dancers were performing a slow waltz. Pushing Amy aside, she said loudly, 'What about a dance fer me then, eh?'

Amy ran off and after staring after her for a moment, Harry took Nelly in his arms and began dancing. 'Blimey, I only comes up to yer chest!' she exclaimed.

'Pity it's not the other way around!' Harry laughed. He looked down at her for a moment, surprised at the lightness of her steps. 'Why did you suddenly want to dance with me, Nelly?'

'Your Prue didn't like it – you an' Amy. It ain't my business, but this ain't the place to mend quarrels.' Harry laughed again. 'You don't miss much do you, Nelly Luke?'

'Not if I can 'elp it! Got another beer, 'ave yer? Besides,' she went on, 'I don't like your missus. Now if it was my Mrs French or someone like that –'

With a replenished glass, Nelly went back to Evie.

'Where's Ollie?' she asked.

'Oliver,' Evie said with feeling, 'is being sick.'

The crowds were thinning. People, especially those with

small children, were filtering home. There were still a few dancers and small huddles of people, sitting chatting, and kissing, and talking love talk among the shadows. Occasionally laughter rang out, and a few screams as teasing continued among the young and the not so young. Young Margaret stood near the piano staring at the keys as if wanting to try and pick out a tune. But she didn't touch it, just looked.

Fay saw Mrs French standing alone, and knew she must talk to her now, while she had the nerve. Tomorrow would be harder.

'Mrs French, I know this will be a shock, but he's alive. Alan is alive. I've seen him. He's here, now.' The words came out jerkily and unconvincing.

For a moment Mrs French stared at the girl as if she were seeing a ghost. 'Fay, dear. What are you saying? Is this a joke?'

'Alan is not dead.'

Monica stared around her, trying to see through the encroaching darkness, searching for his face among the crowd. Her son alive? After eight years? 'Where is he?' she asked with a choking cry. 'Where?'

Johnny ran up and looked angrily at Fay. 'Fay. You promised.'

'I know I did, Johnny, but she has a right to know. She's his mother.'

Tears glistened in Mrs French's eyes and she asked Johnny shakily, 'What has happened, Johnny?'

'Fay thinks she has seen Alan.'

'I have! He left me a message!'

Johnny looked at Mrs French and shook his head sadly.

'Fay!' the older woman said. 'How could you upset me so? It's wicked to say such a thing. Wicked.' She touched her eyes with a handkerchief. 'If he were alive he would have come home.'

Fay looked from one to the other. 'Alan is alive I tell you. Not dead. Wandering around, afraid to come home.' She gave a short scream of frustration and ran off. Johnny hesitated, wondering if he should leave Mrs French after such a shock.

'Go after her, Johnny,' she said. 'She needs you.'

'What can I say to her?' he asked. 'How can I compete with a ghost?'

Harry danced with his wife and Amy danced with Freddy. Then they changed partners, but Amy pulled away from Harry and accepted a dance from a man who was vaguely familiar.

'Remember me?' he said.

Amy frowned then remembered. 'You're the man who delivers to the shop.'

'That's me; Victor Honeyman. Look different without my brown overalls, do I?'

Harry stood watching, beside Prue.

'Time they stopped,' Prue said. 'People want to pack up and go home. It's been a long day for those who did all the work. Selfish, some people.'

'Amy's enjoying herself. She doesn't get out much, what with the shop and the kids.'

They looked at Amy who was dancing as enthusiastically as when she began, hours ago. When she didn't have a partner she danced alone, her jewellery flashing, her face flushed and full of excitement.

Amy sensed that the fun of the occasion now came from her. Partners were drawn to her like a magnet. Victor danced time and again, unwilling to leave her for a moment. The mood had emanated from her need to expend energy and she knew that when she stopped the mood would change and everyone would go home. She reached into her reserve and went on, pulling others into her energy source, as wildly excited as herself.

Timothy put on a slow waltz and announced that it was the last record.

'Dance, Prue?' Harry said.

She turned to face him without verbal agreement, and they joined the others in the brief finale.

'I'll be a bit late,' Harry said as they walked away from

the music. 'I've got to make sure my wooden planks are safely stacked away. We're leaving the piano until tomorrow. I've arranged with some of the boys to come about ten o'clock.'

'I'll go with Mrs French then.' She walked off without another word, unable to show her pleasure at his asking her to dance, and his attentiveness during the latter part of the evening. She wondered if, tonight, she might not sleep alone.

The last of the crowd dispersed, leaving only a few men to gather up the remaining furniture. Most had been taken back to the church hall earlier in the evening and the cups and plates were stacked back in their accustomed places in the wooden boxes beside the trestle tables and folding chairs.

Harry's lorry was half-filled with the stacked chairs, and as Harry was piling more with the rest he saw two figures waiting beside the ashes of the bonfire. 'Freddy? Margaret?' he called. 'Want a lift home on the lorry?'

'Yes please,' Margaret said. She ran and lifted up her arms to him to be helped up. 'Wait for Mammy, she's talking to someone. She won't be long though.'

Harry lifted her up into the cab and gestured to Freddy to help him finish loading the last of the wood and the remaining chairs.

'Thought any more about working for me?' Harry asked the boy.

'Yes. I'd like to, Uncle Harry, but Mam isn't too sure. She wants me to stay on a bit, get a few exams.' He threw some planks easily onto the lorry. 'Perhaps you can talk her round for me? I'd rather start work see, get a bit of money. Fed up with school, I am.'

'Go and call your mother, boy, I'll perhaps have a word with her. Now it's time for us all to go home.'

With Freddy on the back of the lorry and Margaret inside the cab, Harry knew Amy could hardly refuse to ride with him. He said nothing as he helped her up beside him, and she took Margaret on her knee and they went down the lane past Nelly's cottage in silence.

The field settled back into its customary silence, but it was a long time before the last light went out in the village. Nelly's oil-lamp flickered and went out as she slept in the big armchair, too tired to undress and go to bed.

In the flattened grass around the castle, wind disturbed the rubbish, and swayed the trees. The movement increased as a man stepped out of the trees and wandered around the site. In the amphitheatre where the children had sung the piano stood, covered by sacks and a tarpaulin.

Quietly the covers were lifted. The figure stretched out his left hand and, with a foot pressing the soft pedal, began to play. The ghostly music drifted through the trees and filled the air with plantive melodies until dawn rose and the man closed the lid and walked away.

Chapter Eight

Nelly was chopping wood in the garden when Oliver called some days after the party. She was talking to herself, and he hesitated at the gate, intending to go away if she was not alone.

'Come out of it, you stupid axe,' Nelly was grumbling. 'What's wrong with this wood today, eh Bobby?' The dog sniffed her face, his long tail wagging with pleasure at being noticed, and Spotty strolled over, hoping to be included. 'Just get this lot in the oven to warm, then we'll go up the castle field to see what's left, shall we?'

As she turned to push the door wider, the dogs began to bark; soft, welcoming barks and she looked up the path to the gate. 'Someone comin'? Blimey they're early. Thought everyone'd be sleepin' except me!'

'Gran? Hi, it's me!'

' 'Ello me,' Nelly chuckled, 'thought it was Oliver for a minute.'

'Have you got any toffee left, Gran?' Oliver asked as he pushed open the stiff gate. He pulled a face as it scraped across the ash path.

' 'Course I 'ave. Got some comics too, but don't tell yer mother.'

Oliver picked up an armful of sticks and carried them to the door. He struggled to open it wider so he could get in with his arms full. 'This door's stuck again, Gran.'

'I'll do it. Stand back, Ollie. You 'ave to give it a right good kick.' She lunged at the door with her foot and the door scraped back across the flagstones. Nelly gave a sigh of satisfaction. 'Matches the gate it does. I like things to match,' she laughed.

Oliver picked up the comic and turned the pages. 'Will you help me read it, Gran?'

'Just let me get my sticks in the oven. There. Now I'll get us a drink and we'll sit an' enjoy ourselves. Find the page why don't yer?'

'Gran, how can W-H-E-N spell when? Reading doesn't make any sense.'

'Now yer askin', young Ollie. I don't suppose anyone knows the real answer. What you 'ave to do is learn it. Remember it. Then, after a while you forgets 'ow daft it is. You second name's another daft word. Malcolm, ain't it? You learnt to write an' say that, didn't you? Well, there's nothin' stoppin' you learnin' a few more daft words.'

'It's an awful lot of work.'

'Not fer a clever boy like you it ain't.'

'I'm not clever. I'm slow. Dad says that.'

'An' 'im an headmaster? Should know better 'e should!'

'Do you want any messages run, Gran? After school I mean, not now, I have to go soon.'

Nelly sat down and looked up at the ceiling. 'Ah – um – yes. You can tell the butler 'e can 'ave the day off an' tell cook we'll want dinner at eight.'

They both laughed at the silly joke then settled down to share the delights of the comic.

'Are you sure you don't want anything?' he asked later, as he set off home.

'No thanks, dearie, only a paper. I'll take the dogs and see if Amy's got one left. I want to read all about the arrangements for the Coronation. I'll hear it on the radio down with Netta Cartwright, but it ain't the same as pictures.'

'Why don't you come and watch it on our television? Mother did invite you.'

'Don't like spendin' too much time with yer mum, specially not since the party. Told me off she did for you bein' sick. We always did end up arguin'. I'd only spoil the day for yer. She's me only daughter but we ain't got much in common. 'Ere, there is somethin' you can do for me Ollie. 'Elp me pick an 'orse fer the Derby.'

'Mr Evans the caretaker says this is the year for Gordon Richards to win.'

'Well, 'e might be right, but I think I'll go through the runners in my usual educated way, with a pin.' She laughed, showing her crooked teeth in a way that Oliver had come to enjoy.

'Will you 'elp then, or not?' She pushed the paper, folded to the correct page, closer to him. 'Last night's this is; gives all the stuff we need to know.'

'You haven't lost your glasses again, have you, Gran?' Oliver sounded anxious. He was worried that Nelly was getting forgetful; his mother had once said this was a 'bad sign'.

' 'Course I ain't! Just can't think where I put 'em. Here, look at the names and read 'em out, will yer?'

'It says something about the Queen's horse.' He began to struggle with the words, and Nelly waited patiently then said,

'Don't bother about *every* word, Ollie, just go through an' see what it's about.' She hummed softly to herself as he studied the paper.

'What's rumour?'

'That's an easy one. You must 'ave 'eard plenty of rumours about me since you was back. Rumour says I'm a dirty, useless old drunk.'

'Rumours aren't true then?'

'That's right. They're what some people want to believe. Started by jealous people, spiteful people. Go on, what does it say?'

Oliver pointed at the words and read, 'There's a rumour that the queen's horse Au –'

'Aureole,' Nelly supplied.

'That Aureole is lame.'

'Shame. Be nice fer 'er to win in the same week she's crowned.'

'Why do you say, shame? If it's only a rumour –'

'Shall I back it then?'

'What about Pinza? That's Gordon Richard's mount.'

' 'E's tried twenty-seven times. Why should the twenty-eighth be any different?' She gave a loud burp.

'There's a horse running called Windy?' he grinned.

'You cheeky young devil! Who's ridin' that then?' After a careful study, Oliver announced that the horse was being riden by F. Barlow.

Nelly ruffled the boy's hair and smiled. 'You're such a good boy, Ollie and such a 'elp now you can read.' She shushed his protests. 'Not perfect, I'll give yer that. But you can read the paper and comics, and get the information we need an' what's readin' for, if not that?' She brushed the wood-dust from his coat and ushered him out. 'Go on, or you'll be late and that'll mean a row fer both of us.'

Oliver stopped when he reached the gate. 'Gran, why do they make rumours about you?'

'Jealous of me an' me 'andsome grandson.'

'Mr Evans says you're the happiest person he knows, so perhaps they are jealous.'

'Don't let it worry you, young Ollie. Let the chickens out before you go, will yer?'

She watched him walk past the garden towards home and shivered slightly at the thought that Evie might move away again and take Oliver with her. 'Best thing what's happened to me in years,' she said to the dogs. Perhaps she *could* try to behave as Evie wanted; if she could only work out how. She prepared the hens' mash, included some egg shells she had broken into small pieces after drying them in the oven over night, and put it in their feeding trough.

Still thinking of Oliver she pulled on her old navy coat, fastened the wide over-lap with a safety pin and set off for work. Her face was creased with laughter as she remembered Oliver mentioning the horse called Windy. Coming on a treat 'e was. If it meant a bit of cheek, well it was worth it.

* * *

Evie was looking out of the back window, across the neat garden and up into the field.

'Where is he?' she asked her husband. 'He'll be late for school. Fine that looks, the Head's son late again. He loses track of time when he's with her.'

The phone went and she spoke briefly for a few moments and replaced the receiver.

'Who was that?' Timothy asked.

'Prue. Thought I might like to know that Nelly has just fallen over. Pulled both sides of a lamp post by the dogs.'

Timothy tried not to smile at the picture the words described. 'Is she hurt?'

'Nelly. Nelly. Nelly! That's all I hear. When people stop to talk to me, it's never to ask how we are, it's always to give me the latest gossip about Nelly!'

'You're exaggerating, Evelyn. She isn't that bad. If you refused to listen – she is your mother and entitled to your support.'

'I don't need reminding she's my mother! Timothy, she was drinking again last night. Very unsteady on her feet apparently.'

'Don't let it worry you. There's nothing we can do, just keep an eye on her, see she doesn't come to any harm.'

Evie bit the skin around her thumb nail. 'That's exactly what I want to do. Instead of making excuses for her, I – I want you to persuade her to come and live here, with us.'

'What? That's ridiculous! You'd never stand it and neither would I! It's impossible and you know it.'

'There's the back bedroom. I'd make sure she stayed in it except when she came out with me.'

'She would never stand it.'

Evie looked away from him, out of the window. 'When she became too unhappy, we could suggest she went into a home.'

'Evelyn. That would be wrong for her.'

'There's a nice place just twenty miles from here and –'

'She'd hate it. No!'

'She needs proper looking after. She wanders the streets,

hardly able to stand, let alone walk, and cook and look after herself.'

'Evelyn, I love you but I won't do this. You'd bring her here and hide her away. She's unconventional I agree, but you'd kill her if you took away her away from that cottage of hers.'

Evie began to cry, still looking up across the field for a sight of Oliver, until the scene swam and she had to find a handkerchief to wipe away the tears. 'You don't understand.'

'I do, darling. But can't you understand her a little?'

'I saw Mrs French yesterday. She hasn't seen the new dress I bought her. She's probably sold it. Yes, that's what she does. Sells clothes to buy drink. People think I don't care.'

'Nelly's well known and well loved. No one would think the way she chooses to live is your fault. We've only been back a matter of weeks. She's happy. I think she probably eats well; she grows a lot of her own food, keeps chickens that run in the wood, she heats the cottage on wood that she also has free. She lives like a –'

'Like a gypsy!' Evie ended bitterly. 'A gypsy like my father!'

'Forget it. It's what you are now that matters.'

'If you don't let me do something about her, we'll have to leave here. Move right away.'

'We can't. You know we can't.' Timothy walked up and down the room, anxiously glancing at his watch. He had to go, but how could he leave her like this? 'I should have listened to you and refused the position of Head here. I didn't dream you would be so upset by living near her.'

'Why do you think I left home at sixteen? To get away from her. Every minute of the day I'm wondering what she's doing, where she is.'

'Right now she's on her way to work, as I should be! Here's Oliver. I'll meet him and take him straight to school.'

'He's probably untidy. Send him to me first.'

'All right.'

'On her way to work, being dragged along by those filthy dogs to do housework for my friends!'

Nelly limped to Mrs French's back door, stopping occasionally to rub her knee which she had hurt when the dogs had pulled her over. Bobby cocked his leg near the gatepost and she moved to hide him from the view from the kitchen window. Mrs French didn't like her bringing the dogs and she'd complain if she saw them 'messing' as she called it.

'Yoohoo,' Nelly shouted as she opened the door before tying the dogs to the fence. As she walked into the kitchen she added, 'It's me, dearie. All right fer me to start upstairs?'

'Good morning, Nelly.' Mrs French came down the stairs a duster in her hand. 'Nelly, you're limping. What have you done?'

'My dogs it was. Saw a cat an' chased it, one each side of a lamp post an' me 'oldin' their leads. Smack I went, then fell over as one of them stopped sudden.'

'Is it painful? Would you rather leave things for today?' Mrs French hid a smile.

'It'll hurt whether I complain or not, so what's the point makin' a song an' dance about it? Go straight up, shall I?'

'Nelly, while you're here, will you look for my purse? I've mislaid it. I hope it's somewhere in the house.'

'Oh Lor'. Much in it, is there?'

'About two pounds. But it's the keys I'm worried about. If I don't find them I'll have to have all the locks changed.'

'Blow the keys, it would be me two pounds I'd be worryin' about,' Nelly muttered as she climbed the stairs with the box of cleaning materials. She never locked her cottage door. It didn't fit well enough to allow the key to turn and even if it did she would rarely bother.

As Nelly was taking her money and putting on her coat to leave, the gate was partly opened, then closed hurriedly as the dogs began to bark furiously. Mrs French looked nervously at Nelly.

'Who can that be?'

'Expectin' anyone are yer?'

'Only Mrs Beynon for coffee. But she always comes by the front door.'

'Yes, she would! Hang on to the dogs, I'll go.' Nelly opened the gate and saw a poorly-dressed man backing away, his eyes watching at ground level for the dogs. He was bearded and about sixty, Nelly guessed. His pink skin showed through the white and grey beard, as did pink lips and faded, greeny-blue eyes.

He carried a small haversack on his shoulders and from his appearance, Nelly guessed he was a tramp. His clothes, although clean, were frayed and ill-fitting. Underneath the repaired and patched jacket, she saw several layers of shirts and at least two jumpers.

Nelly turned back to Mrs French and in a whisper, that carried as well as a paperboy's shout, said, 'It's one of them tramps. Got any cake, 'ave yer?'

'Yes.' Mrs French backed into her kitchen and handed her a tin. 'Give him this, but tell him not to come here again.'

'Bobby an' Spotty won't 'urt yer,' Nelly reassured the man. 'Want somethin' to eat, do yer? Bit of cake, will that do?'

When the tramp spoke, his voice was soft, modulated and it took Nelly by surprise. 'Are you Mrs French?' he asked. Nelly laughed. 'Blimey no! I'm 'er daily 'elp. D'you want to see her then?'

'No,' he still had an eye on the dogs, straining to investigate. 'It's just this.' He held out a purse. 'Rather foolish to have a name and an address with keys to the house, isn't it?'

Nelly was staring at him. 'You talk posh for a – gentleman of the road.'

He shrugged deprecatingly and offered her the purse.

' 'Ere, Mrs French, 'e's found yer purse. The two pound's still there.'

'That's very good of him.' Mrs French didn't come any closer. 'Give him the money for his trouble, will you Nelly, and thank him.'

'What, all of it?'

The tramp moved so he could see through the gate and he waved politely at Mrs French, who was standing gripping the rope leads. 'Thank you, ma-am,' he said.

'Don't mind 'er. Scared of strangers, she is,' Nelly said in one of her hoarse whispers as she closed the gate behind him. 'Good luck, mate.'

Nelly took the leads and prepared to go, but Mrs French called her back.

'I have a coat here that might suit you. It's thinner than the one you're wearing, better for this warm weather.' She went inside and returned with a green tweed coat which she held up for Nelly to see. 'It came with some other unwanted clothing for the jumble, but as it's a good quality I thought –'

Nelly held the coat against her, her dirt-grained fingers stroked the green velvet collar and she mmm'd and aahh'd with pleasure. She knew it wouldn't fasten around her ample figure but she could slip it on, and show off to Evie and Tim.

'Very smart. My Evie would approve of this.'

'Yes,' Mrs French said at once. 'She would be so pleased to see you dressed less –' she searched for a word that wouldn't offend 'less – casually. Very dress-conscious, your Evie.'

'Ta, dearie. You're good to me. Proper lady you are.' Mrs French smiled. 'Just see that you wear it – to please Evie.'

Nelly stroked the coat again. 'Green's me favourite colour an' perhaps I'll get used to showin' a bit more leg, eh?' She laughed her harsh laugh and went through the high gate, almost running as she tried to keep up with the enthusiastic dogs. Once the gate was shut and she was out of sight, she stopped, and rubbed her leg, and walking more slowly, went home.

Prue finished polishing the brass pokers and placed them in the tiled grate. Taking off the gloves she wore for dirty work, she washed them, hung them out to dry then went into Harry's office. She was having a late coffee with Monica French to discuss some ideas for the next social evening, but there was time to do some work on the books first.

Although Harry had been home most evenings since she had taken on the task, there was no change in the amount of time he gave her, she thought with a tightening of her lips. She would go to bed alone and lie waiting, hoping he would come to her, willing him to want her as he had done when they had been first married. Her thoughts increased her desire, but every night she slept alone, asleep long before Harry turned off the lights and climbed the stairs to sleep in the back bedroom.

Before she began work, she made a list for shopping. She would buy something specially good for his dinner. He loved his food and something with onions always made him feel content. Her mother had told her that years ago.

'Forget fancy undies and scent,' she had said firmly, 'fried onions is the thing for putting a man in a good mood.' Prue smiled at the memory, but it was worth a try.

She worked steadily at the books for an hour, then something puzzled her. The copper pipe used in a house improvement did not have an invoice. She searched but it was not there. She made a note to remind her to ask Harry about it, and went on. But the item continued to make her curious, she half-remembered something similar with plasterboards, and she began to look through other jobs, starting from the invoices, in case the pipe had been entered in another place by mistake. Instead, she found more sheets on which goods had been used, but not entered in as being bought.

Carefully she went through the invoices and noted the purchases of copper tube and fittings, and plaster boards. There were too few for the work being done. She sat and thought for a while, then tackled the mystery another way. The work Harry had done for Amy would be a simple one to check. She had helped with the estimate and had suggested a few ideas herself, like the new sink-unit. Plumbing goods had been used for the extended heating too, both in the shop and upstairs.

Getting the relevant files, she found the pages referring to the shop and to her surprise and growing alarm, saw it entered as a small repair job. There was nothing about the materials supplied, except for a few bags of cement and plaster and the items associated with them.

She sat looking around her at the rows of box-files and paper files and envelope files which lined the walls in front of her. Harry had covered the expense of Amy's work, but what else besides? Her mouth curled with resentment when she thought of her sister. Why did everyone want to help Amy? She's an immoral woman, Prue thought, her jaw tightening. Two children, no hint of who had been the father. Dressing like a sixteen-year-old, all that sparkling jewellery, obviously common, yet Harry had taken a risk and altered the books to give her the work for virtually nothing.

She left the books where they were and walked upstairs. From the landing window she saw Nelly leaving, limping she guessed from her fall earlier. She saw there was a green coat across her arm. More excuses to go into town and buy drink. She thought it very wrong of Monica; perhaps she ought to have a word with Evie about it.

She touched up her makeup and prepared to go to Monica's. She had never felt less like going out. She wanted to tear down the files and go through them with her accountant's eye, search them for what else she didn't know about Harry. To think he could be dishonest. And to help Amy of all people.

She drank a glass of cold water, trying to calm herself. Should she talk to Harry? Tell him what she knew? She shook her head as she washed the glass and replaced it on the cupboard shelf. Best to do nothing hasty. Tomorrow, while Harry was out, she would do a bit more digging in the files including the ones Harry kept locked away. She had a key, not used for years, but it was still tucked away with the other keys of the house cupboards and drawers.

Stepping out through the front door, she looked back, then went inside again, and tidied all the papers before going to talk to Mrs French.

* * *

Nelly bought fish and chips on the way home and sat outside eating them out of the paper, sharing them with the dogs, and the hens, and the robin who ignored the dogs and hopped along to share her feast. The gate creaked and they all looked up, and Nelly groaned with dismay.

' 'Ello, Evie. Never expected you today.'

'Mother, why are you sitting on the ground?'

'Can't eat standin' up; that wouldn't be proper,' Nelly grinned.

Evie dragged the gate closed and came to examine the grease-stained paper. 'What is it?'

'A feast, dearie. Fish an' chips an' a slice of 'ome made bread. No butter 'cos me ration's finished. A glass of stout to wash it all down and I wouldn't call the king me uncle. I'd 'ave waited if I'd known you'd come.'

'I've eaten, thank you, Mother. I know better than to expect a decent meal here.'

Nelly opened her mouth to reply but she burped instead and covered her mouth with her hand.

'Mother!'

'I wish you'd call me Mum like you used to. I suppose "Mother" is modern. Can't take to nothin' modern I can't.' She mmm'd her way through the last mouthful. 'Lovely that was. Come fer anything special, 'ave yer?'

'Yes. Timothy and I – we aren't too happy about the way you live. He thinks you should move from this place and come and live with us.'

Nelly fell back onto the ground and roared with laughter.

'Drive you both to drink in a week!' She felt in her pocket for a handkerchief, couldn't find one and wiped her eyes on her sleeve.

Evie remained cool, ignoring the display. 'At least for a while. Until we can decide what is best for you.' The laughter drained from Nelly's face. 'Evie I –'

'Timothy is willing for you to have the back bedroom all to yourself. It's completely furnished so there's no need to bring anything. You'll be cared for properly. You'll be ill if you stay here.'

'I couldn't be 'appy away from this place. An' as fer bein' ill, well, 'eaven knows when I last saw a doctor. Not since you 'ad measles. An' then I gave 'im some of me ginger wine fer 'is stomach and 'e didn't make no charge.'

Her hand went involuntarily to her painful hip. Netta Cartwright thought it might be arthritis, but Nelly had no intention of seeing the doctor. She didn't believe in doctors.

'This place,' Evie went on. 'Just look at it!'

Nelly stared sadly at her daughter, wondering how she could have lived for a while in a beautiful place like the cottage, and turn out the way she did. 'Smashin' it is.'

'It's a mess, mother. And you *don't* have proper meals. You spend too much on drink for there to be enough for good food. You fell this morning on your way to Mrs French.'

'How did you know that?' Nelly thought for a moment, then said triumphantly. 'That nosy bleedin' parker Prue Beynon – may her nose drop off!'

'And your clothes. Just look at that coat you've thrown on the ground! It's a disgrace.'

'Keeps me best fer goin' out. Not fer work,' she said reasonably.

'What happened to the dress I bought you?'

'Up in me trunk with me best coat,' Nelly said. 'Want to see me best coat? I'm wearing them both when I go down to Netta's to listen to the Coronation.'

Nelly stood up trying not to show how painful her leg had become. It had been a mistake to sit on the floor; the stiffness was worse now. As long as Evie didn't notice. No point givin' her more excuse to come and interfere.

She went into the cottage confident that Evie would not follow. On the rare occasions Evie had entered, she had stood as near the door as possible, obviously wanting to leave as soon as she could. Nelly slipped on the coat Mrs French had given her and went out again with a smile and a haughty expression. The result was comic but Evie did not smile.

Nelly thought of the scrawny scrap that had been Evie,

full of cheek, and a confidence far beyond her years. And how, after just one year in Hen Carw Parc, she had blossomed and filled out and had become even more ladylike.

'Did my best for yer,' she shouted after Evie's retreating figure. 'Got you out of that awful room and brought you to this place, didn't I?'

'Yes.' Evie stopped and glared back at her mother. 'Then you spoilt it, by coming here yourself!'

'Evie!'

'Happy it was, without you dragging me down.'

'So was my life 'appy 'til you came, so piss off back to London why don't yer, and take that Tedious Timothy with yer.' Nelly's voice rose until she was shouting 'Young Ollie's the only one with any laughter in 'im, an' you an' Tedious Timothy'll soon 'ave him as stiff an' unbendin' as a rusty bed-spring!'

'You leave Oliver alone! I don't want him influenced by someone like you. Dirty Nelly. Yes, I know what they call you.' Evie's voice had sharpened to match Nelly's.

Nelly allowed a silence to develop, then said softly, 'Oo, Evie, you don't 'alf sound common.' Evie ran up the path and along the lane, and as she disappeared from sight, Nelly's fat shoulders began to shake with sobs.

Evie walked home, thinking of the homes her mother had provided for her. First the dark, damp room high above the London streets, which meant a climb up sixty stairs and along corridors where paint peeled in strips off mildewed walls. Where every drop of water had to be carried up and, when dirty, carried down again to be emptied away down the drain in the communal yard.

When the war had begun, it was an escape for Evie. She, like all her friends, had been evacuated to places where they would be safe from the bombing. That first year in Hen Carw Parc, Old Deer Park, was perfect. She had been able to invent a previous life, and beautiful parents.

Then Nelly had decided that if her daughter needed a place of safety, then so did she. Arriving in the village and renting that tumbledown hovel had ruined everything. As soon as she could, Evie had left home and went again to live in London.

Working in a cafe where the students from the nearby college frequently ate, she had met Timothy. They had been attracted at once and as soon as he had qualified, they had married. He had changed schools several times and somehow, had gradually moved nearer to Wales. Most of the schools were large and she had not expected Timothy to even consider a tiny village school.

Now, because of his insistence on taking the position of Headmaster in Hen Carw Parc, she was stuck with the daily horror of having Nelly and her exploits on her doorstep. Why hadn't she held firm and insisted Timothy had refused the promotion? No money was worth having Nelly call her 'daughter'.

Chapter Nine

Timothy watched his wife walk past the school on the way home and felt uneasy. She had been to see Nelly and he wondered what had happened. It was lunchtime and he thought he might go home and find out. But he was delayed, first by a parent calling, then the telephone and eventually he abandoned the idea. Bad news will keep, he decided.

When the children began to gather back in the playground for afternoon school he was still looking out of the window. He saw a knot of boys near the wall and noticed that Oliver was amongst them. He was curious. Pieces of paper were being surreptitiously handed to the boy and he seemed to be explaining something before handing them back.

He was pleased that Oliver was more popular, but his curiosity made him call the caretaker.

'Those boys, what are they doing, do you know? My son seems to be in demand. Some new game, is it?'

Mr Evans looked uneasy. 'Not sure, sir.' Timothy looked at the grey-haired man and shook his head.

'I think you do. Come on, I'm not going to murder them. What are they up to?'

'Well you'd better come around here and have a listen.' He led the headmaster through a gate and along the walls until they were close to where the boys stood.

'My dad wants to know if this is right; fourteen shillings and sixpence,' one of the boys was saying.

'Tell me the prices again,' Oliver asked.

'What are they doing?' Timothy whispered.

'Young Oliver is checking the betting slips for the boys' dads, sir.'

When the two men walked back into the school building, Timothy looked puzzled.

'How can he? He must be making it all up. He's slow at maths and can't add two and two and be certain it's four.'

'Tell him it's a two to one winner at a stake of sixpence and he'll work it out like a shot, sir. Hundred to eight, odds on, he knows the lot, as long as it's racing.'

Timothy walked through the milling children, ducking flying balls and flaying skipping ropes and children involved with whips and tops and all the other games of skill the playground nurtured. He beckoned his son.

'Oliver, where did you learn to work out complicated sums like that?'

Oliver shook his head. 'I don't want to say, father.'

'Mr Evans told me you have found mistakes on some of the betting slips you've been shown. It's very clever. You've had difficulties with sums, and if someone has found a way of helping you, I'd like to know.'

Still Oliver said nothing. He hung his head and his pale face turned a bright pink.

'Was it one of the teachers? Or Mr Evans?' Timothy coaxed.

'It was Gran.'

'Your Grandmother?'

'She's always losing her glasses – but that isn't a bad sign –' he added quickly. 'I help her to pick out her bets. She only does threepenny bets. Nothing wrong with that is there, Father?'

'No, nothing wrong. Does she win often?'

'No. She goes on hunches and names she likes, rather than on form. Although I read out the tipsters column when I can.' He was relaxed now he was reassured that he hadn't got Nelly into more trouble. 'Like the Derby,' he went on. 'She wouldn't back the Queen's horse because it was lame. Rumours aren't true are they? Like some of the things people say about Gran, calling her Dirty Nelly and that.'

'You found the piece about the Queen's horse in the paper?'

'I only read bits of it. I suggested Gordon Richards' mount and it won, but she didn't back that either. She said he'd tried for twenty-seven years and couldn't win on his twenty-eighth try.'

'Which horse did she back in the Derby?'

The blush came back to Oliver's face as he said, '– er – Windy.'

'Why Windy?'

Oliver began to giggle. 'I don't know, Father.'

Timothy began to smile and Oliver's giggles increased.

'I think you do, young man!'

When Oliver had gone to his class, Timothy began to laugh. If Oliver had been present when Nelly was eating, there was little doubt where the idea of backing Windy had come from. Laughter spluttered on and off all afternoon. Timothy was embarrassed by it, but every time the thought came back it burst out again. Like a schoolboy, he thought guiltily, an immature schoolboy, but the humour of it stayed with him for the rest of the day.

Amy managed to close the shop in time to catch the bus into town. It was tempting to look at the shops and perhaps buy a new dress; she fancied the sailor style in navy and white that had been advertised in the local newspaper at two pounds ten shillings, but seeing the queue already forming outside the cinema, she joined it and leaned against the wall to wait patiently until the doors opened and they were allowed to file in.

She did not see Harry's car drive past, slow down and stop, so she was surprised when he touched her arm and came to stand beside her.

'Harry! What are you doing here? You aren't taking the day off to see a film, are you?'

'I could do –'

'Don't!' She turned away, but she was shaking inside at

the feel of his arm against hers. She tried to move away but he wouldn't allow it and the queue held her captive. She imagined that her heart-beat would be felt by him, that he would know how much she wanted him.

'Come for a drive instead,' he whispered against her ear, bending down to make sure he was not over-heard.

'No Harry. No more. I've finished with long journeys that never take me anywhere. Go away, please.'

The queue began to move and she thankfully darted into a space between two women who were obviously friends. Harry stood close behind her, pressing himself against her. He leaned forward, breathing on her neck. 'Just to talk, Amy, love. I promise only to talk. About your Freddy. About him working for me? Like the idea do you?'

She tried to move away from him and was challenged by several people in front of her who turned and glared, accusing her of trying to take their place.

'Please go,' she whispered. 'Leave me alone.'

Then he did, and she felt the loss like a blast of cold air in the summer sunshine.

When Amy came out the sun had gone and it was raining. She bent forward and began running for the bus. Harry was waiting at the corner and he took her arm and guided her away from the bus stop and to his car.

'You can't refuse a lift home, not in this weather.'

'Straight home,' she said.

'And I'll make sure I don't leave the keys in the car this time,' he grinned and Amy found herself responding to his obvious pleasure at having her beside him again.

'I hope you're not expecting me to say I'm sorry. I'm not.'

'I bet you felt mean though, making me walk, and wonder all the time where you'd left the car.'

'I didn't. Satisfying it was. I enjoyed it.'

'I didn't, Amy, and I haven't enjoyed a moment since. Missed you terribly I have. There's no fun in my life now. Can't we go back to how it was? It was good. You enjoyed it too didn't you?'

'I'm thirty-seven and going nowhere.'

'Where d'you want to go? I'll take you!'

'You aren't free to make any promises.'

'But what if I were? What then?'

'Ask me again, when it's happened! Take me home, Harry.'

He drove silently for a while then slowed down and stopped in a quiet, tree-lined part of the road.

'No, Harry. I mean it. Stop here and I'll get out and walk. Rain or no rain. I mean it!'

'Just talk for a moment. Look, I'll put my hands in my pockets, right?'

'There's nothing to say.' She sat rigidly staring at the rain-streaked window, her face sad, but her mouth determined.

'Amy,' he said sadly. His arm moved around the back of her seat, the promise to keep his hands away from her forgotten. Amy pretended not to notice, but her heart was beating fiercely. The air in the small car filled with urgent awareness. His fingers touched her nape, felt the fine hairs, the soft skin.

She moved, and at once his other arm wrapped around her, but she was reaching for the door and she turned her head to protest as she felt him hold her back. They met more positively than either had intended, and the joy of the contact could not be halted and she was in his arms, their lips meeting in a painful yet sweet moment, burning them with the intensity of the longed-for kiss.

When he spoke, his voice was gruff with emotion.

'Where shall we go?'

'Home.' She touched his mouth with a finger to hush his protest. 'I have to pick up Margaret from Evie's. I can't be late. I'll – I'll need Evie's help again, won't I?'

'Half an hour?'

'No, Harry.'

'Then stay here, please. Just a minute or so.'

'What were you doing in town?'

'Waiting for you. I saw what time the pictures finished and I waited.'

'Have you eaten?' Stupid question. An attempt to take the steam out of the situation. What did she care whether or not he had eaten? But she couldn't say what she wanted to say, so she went on with the trivialities. 'Your meal will be spoilt. You've been home regularly lately.'

'I love you.'

'What are we going to do?'

'Where shall we go?'

'I can't, Harry.' She was almost at the point of tears.

'Tomorrow?'

'Yes. Tomorrow. To talk.' She pulled further away from him, stared out at the rain again. 'Take me home.'

Slowly he released her but then he glanced at her and she turned to meet his gaze and the tears glistened and he gave a groan and reached for her. This time she did not try to escape.

When Harry reached home, Prue wanted to talk about the discrepancies in his books, but he shrugged her aside. He was breathing heavily, and Prue took it for anger.

'Is anything wrong?'

'Nothing. I'm tired, that's all.'

He was irritated by her and he looked at her tall, thin face with its constant air of disapproval, and wondered why he was here with Prue, when every part of him wanted to be with her sister. Why should he go on wasting the days, and weeks, and years with a woman he didn't love, while only a few minutes away, there was Amy.

'Your dinner is spoilt,' Prue said calmly. 'Shall I do some eggs? I bought them from Nelly Luke. She's filthy but I'm sure the eggs will be all right.' She went to the stove and began attending to his supper. The meal she had cooked earlier lay on the table, dried and ruined, a silent reproof. He left the room, saying, 'I don't want anything,' and went into the office and closed the door.

'But it's early – I thought we'd –'

Fear clutched at Prue's stomach. For the first time she suspected that there was a woman in his life. His face was flushed and she was almost certain that the redness was enhanced by the slightest touch of lipstick. It was something she had always dreaded. Harry was so attractive to women. They all succumbed to his natural charm and the sparkle in those blue eyes of his. He always attracted the attention of women. Attractive women, she thought sadly. A good wife she was, without a doubt, but an attractive woman she was not.

She had always disapproved of Amy, but now, she wished she were more like her. Amy knew how to attract men, knew how to make the best of herself. Her sister had always had so little, but she had a flair for making the best of herself, a way of dressing that made her noticed, a jaunty way of walking that showed her happy acceptance and joy of life.

Prue made a cup of tea and stared into space, facing the knowledge that she had always been jealous of Amy. That her disapproval of her was a cover for the envy she had always felt. But now, she would turn to her and ask for her help. Amy would know what I have to do to keep Harry. If only I can pluck up the courage to tell her.

Harry was still in his office and she went out of the house and crept around the side to look in through a gap in the blinds to see what he was doing. He was sitting at his desk, his chin on his hands, unmoving, his eyes clouded with unhappiness. She picked a duster off the line, her excuse if she had been seen, and went back inside.

Fay and Johnny were both up early. Johnny was due to take a bus out at five-forty, and Fay was travelling to Pembroke to begin a new area. She knew she was being irritable and unfair, and tried to stop. But even the way he held his knife and fork seemed to be a challenge.

'Johnny, why do you hold your knife that way? It isn't a pen!' She snatched the offending knife from between his fore-finger and thumb, smearing egg-yolk across his hand, and replaced it, slapping it on his palm and folding his hand around it.

'Sorry, love. I forget. Habit of years, see.' He always accepted her criticisms without rancour, angry with himself for not knowing the right way, rather than with her for pointing them out.

'Sorry, Johnny,' she said, still angry. 'But I do hate it when you won't learn.'

'Got a long drive today; shall we eat out this evening? Save you cooking? We haven't been anywhere for ages. Do us both good.'

'We can't waste the money.'

'Yes we can. I've got some overtime this week, and life shouldn't be nothing but work, should it? Come on, love, let me have my own way sometimes.'

'Where shall we go?'

'Nothing too fancy. What about the Swan Inn in LlanGwyn?' He touched her hands, made her look at him and was frightened to see the unhappiness there. 'Promise I won't hold my knife wrong. All right?' He was relieved to see her smile.

'All right, Johnny. Book for eight. I don't think I'll be home much earlier. In fact, if I'm not home by the time we should leave, you go and I'll meet you there at eight.'

'That's a long day, love. I hope you won't have to do it very often.'

'It's a new area. I simply don't know.'

When Johnny had gone, she stared out of the small kitchen window into the yard, with its dustbins, coal-shed and assorted buckets and bowls. On the side of the shed was an old galvanised bath that had once been filled twice a week for the family to bath. How she missed the bathroom from her old home, where Evie and Timothy now lived. Perhaps, if this new area was a success, they would soon be able to find the deposit for a house and move on. Far from this place she hoped fervently.

Yet, she thought as she looked up, above the buckets and the dustbins and the galvanised bath, to the woods she could just see, if Alan were out there, how could she even think of moving away? She shivered. She felt trapped.

Fay looked at her watch, bought to replace the one she had left at the castle, she had half an hour before she must leave. She hadn't been up there for days and she must keep the promise she had made to herself, not to give up hope of finding Alan again. Changing into casual shoes, and throwing a coat over her shoulders, she left the house.

She picked her way through the seldom-used path behind the row of cottages and up through the woodland, where puddles tried to block her progress. Her feet slid in the sticky surface and she cursed as mud stained her stockings. Now she would have to change them.

Making her way to the castle site, she was aware of the silence. Few birds sang. It was as if a thousand eyes had seen her coming and were watching, waiting for her to go back and leave them in peace to get on with their lives.

At the castle, the grass looked oddly tidy. Still short and marked in white lines from the day of the party. Soon the straight lines would waver and vanish, and the softer curves of nature would return. Fay went slowly towards the kitchens. If anyone was sleeping here, that was the most likely place, she decided, even in weather as warm as today.

She stepped away from the outer wallls and as she looked towards the whitewashed, repaired kitchens, a figure appeared, stared briefly then ran away from her. Fay followed. Determined once and for all to see the man, convince herself that she was mistaken, that his likeness to Alan was nothing more than her final grieving.

The man obviously knew the place well because he ran to a wall, climbed it with ease and jumped down on the other side. She ignored the confining straight skirt she wore and went after him. He had paused, convinced she could not follow and stood for a moment longer, surprised as she appeared at the top of the wall and jumped down beside him.

He ran again but Fay, determined, kept up with him. She noticed he was limping and once, when he leapt over a straggle of rocks, saw him stumble. She felt no pity to make her slow up, her expression was one of great determination as she closed in on him. He tripped again, she heard an explosive curse and she was behind him, reaching out, touching his coat, pulling him, making him stop.

'Leave me alone,' the man said in a low growl. 'Go away.' Her heart beating wildly, her cheeks burning with the rhythm, her neck feeling as if it were about to burst, Fay faced him.

'Alan. It is you! Alan. Oh, Alan.' Tears filled her eyes and her throat was so tight she could no longer speak. They looked at each other, her face flushed with running, his partly in shadow, half hidden by the scarf he had hurriedly pulled up.

'Go away,' he said again.

Fay stared at him. His eyes, the only part of his face clearly visible, were bright. She saw flight threatening and took a firmer hold of his coat. 'Alan. Why didn't you come home?'

He stared at her as if about to speak but in the end, said nothing. Fay tensed herself for the moment when he would run. He tried to pull free and she gripped more tightly. He began to hit her hands with his left hand, raining blows that grew more and more violent. She ignored them and hung onto his coat. Her fingers were white with the effort but she only moved them to change her grip when his coat seemed likely to come off and be abandoned, allowing him to escape from her. 'Alan,' she kept repeating. 'Alan. Alan.' It was as if she expected the sound of his name would wipe out eight years like a bad dream. 'Alan.'

She felt him relax, the blows to her hands ceased, but she still gripped him tightly. Then he spoke and all doubts faded and she wanted to cry.

'Fay,' he whispered.

'Eight years. Why didn't you come back to me?'

'The Alan you knew is dead. I have nothing to give you.'

'I should have been given the chance to disagree.'

'Shall we sit down?' he asked. Fay looked doubtful. She was still gripping his coat, afraid he would run. 'I won't run. For a while anyway,' he said, guessing her thoughts.

'You've watched me, stayed where you could see me. Why?'

'There was nowhere else to go when I eventually came out of hospital.'

'Why didn't you tell us you were safe?'

'I couldn't. I'm not the Alan French you knew, Fay. If I had come back to you it would have only meant facing the loss of you soon after.'

He held the scarf up to hide the right side of his face and gently, Fay pulled it away. She had difficulty holding back the gasp of horror when she saw his face. It was terribly disfigured, the eyes untouched, but below them, nothing but shiny new skin over a shapeless mound of flesh. She managed to say calmly,

'If it's only the scar, I think you underestimate our love, your mother's and mine. It's shocking at first, but don't you think we would soon forget it? It doesn't alter our feelings for you.' Even as she spoke, her words concentrating on reassuring him and hopefully persuading him to go home, she felt the chill of guilt run through her. She wasn't his to return to. She belonged to Johnny now.

'It isn't the scar, I forget about it myself at times. I caused the death of my men. The knowledge gives me nightmares. I wake up screaming if I sleep under a roof. I was careless, and the enemy knew we were there. They moved in while I was changing the guard and I had relaxed the rigid discipline, even allowed the men to feed two hungry dogs. We were spotted as if we were amateurs playing games. I wake up full of blind hatred, wanting to kill.' Fay could see his body shaking as he spoke.

'How could I bring that home to those I love?' he asked.

'How do you live?' she asked, trying to bring his mind back from the nightmares.

'I work. I have a job in a library. A back-room boy of course. I have a room too, but I find it hard to sleep indoors, even after eight years.' He was trembling and Fay knew instinctively that this was not the time for more questioning.

'Come home,' she said. 'Your mother is alone now. Your father died six years ago and your sister lives the other side of Cardiff. Come back with me and see her.'

'I can't.' He began to get agitated and he looked around as if enemies unseen were surrounding him. 'I have to go.'

He suddenly ran from her and she stood up and shouted, 'Alan. Meet me again, please Alan. Please.'

When she was alone, she was shaking and had to sit down. It was easy to believe the whole thing was a dream, something she had wished herself into experiencing.

She made her way back through the ruin to the kitchen. On the floor was a bed made from branches, criss-crossed and covered with mosses and bracken. A blanket was thrown across it and on the floor beside it was a thermos flask and a packet of sandwiches. She covered the bed with the blanket, tucking it neatly in around the sides, finding strange comfort in doing something to help him.

She returned from a rather unsuccessful day and sat on the wall all evening, waiting for him, but he did not appear. In Llangwyn, Johnny stood outside The Swan, waiting for his wife, who never came.

Every morning from then on, Fay walked up to the castle. She sometimes saw Nelly, and once they talked for a while about the flowers that filled the woods with colour, the patches of rosebay willow herb that grew in the clearings, the cow-parsley around the edges, and meadow sweet adding scent to the summer air.

Nelly knew Fay was unhappy, and understood why. She longed to help the obsessed girl and could not find the words. What a muddle; Johnny in love with a girl who was in love with a ghost.

While the weather was warm and dry, Nelly often went to the wood to attend to her early morning functions before getting dressed. One day she was digging up a few early potatoes, still in her night-dress, the hens clucking around her in the hope of a worm or two, the dogs watching her from their usual place near the door. From inside the cottage the sound of music came from her old windup gramophone which she left her digging at intervals to re-wind.

A growl warned Nelly someone was coming, but she made no attempt to go inside, but stood, one foot on the fork, waiting for her visitor to arrive. She groaned when she saw Evie.

' 'Ello, Evie. You're early this mornin'. Come fer a cuppa tea 'ave yer?'

Evie dragged open the gate and demanded, 'Mother! What are you doing?'

'Diggin' some 'taters for me dinner. What do'you think!'

'In your nightdress?'

'Oo fancy! I fergot!'

'I'm going to see the doctor.'

'Not expectin' again, are yer? That'd be nice.'

'No I'm not. I'm seeing the doctor about you! I think he'll agree with me, that you are in need of proper care.'

'In need of care? Me? You do talk barmy sometimes, Evie.'

'Your drinking. Your general behaviour. It's – disgusting. Wandering about in your nightdress!'

'As if I'd get up to any mischief with a fella just because I'm wearin' a nightdress! You wear a pair of knickers and a bra that 'ardly 'ides your udders when you go bathin'!'

'*Mother*!'

'Mother!' Nelly mocked.

'I want to care for you, properly.'

A fat lot she cares, Nelly thought, picking up the last of the small potatoes. All those years when she was away with never a call to see if I was all right. *Alive* even. Just a card and a posh present on me birthday. A 'uge, expensive card too. That's a right giveaway that is. Cares? That's a laugh that is.

She threw the potato plant tops onto the compost heap, watched for a moment as the mother hen and the growing chicks ran to see if it was something edible, then turned to her daughter, a sad look on her brown face.

'Sorry if I messes up yer posh act, Evie. I don't wish you

no 'arm, 'onest I don't. But why did you come back?'

'To look after you.'

'Pull the other one,' Nelly shouted. 'You don't give a monkey's arse!'

'Mother!'

'Well you don't! Be honest, why don't yer?'

When Evie had hurriedly left, Nelly washed herself in a bowl on the kitchen table, packed her suitcase and went for the bus. At the gate, she stopped. 'There's that big ugly clock Evie bought me fer Christmas,' she said to the dogs. 'Never did like it. I wonder if I can manage that as well?' She put the dogs on their rope leads, and struggled back up the path with the clock. There were some stones on the path, a result of her earlier digging and she slipped and fell, the clock under her leg and for a time she lay there, while the dogs barked their concern.

She stood up, and tested her leg, then kicked the clock and set off once again for the bus. She had hardly reached the first bend in the lane when she met the tramp.

'Ello. Ain't you the tramp that found my Mrs French's purse?'

'Yes. Hello again. Does this lane lead anywhere, or just serve the cottage?'

Nelly thankfully put down the clock and the cases. 'You can cut through the woods if you're wantin' the council 'ouses. Or go back down to the road to Llangwyn. Where you makin' for?'

'Somewhere to buy a bite to eat and a drink. A friendly pub will do.'

Nelly's eyes were studying his clothes as he talked. They were ill-matched, ill-fitting, but clean. Most surprising of all, his shoes were perfectly polished black leather.

'There's The Crown, or The Lamb and Flag,' she said. 'But they're a long way off. Tell you what, 'ave a cuppa an' a bite with me why don't yer? I can easily get the next bus.'

'I couldn't –'

' 'Course you could. If you carry me cases to the bus stop I'll cook you a great big fryup. 'Ow's that?'

The tramp looked doubtful. 'If you're sure –'

'I'm sure. Fact is, without 'elp I'd 'ave thrown this 'orrible clock in the ditch before I got to the bus.'

'Where are you going with all this, on holiday?'

Nelly roared with laughter at the idea. The tramp smiled widely, enjoying her honest enjoyment, showing clean, white teeth.

'Me? On 'oliday?' She put on a posh voice and said, 'Oh no, my good man, I couldn't possibly manage on the forty-pounds allowance!'

She laughed again then explained. 'No, takin' this lot into town to sell, if I can drag it as far as the second hand shop. I'll leave it all 'ere fer now. No one'll disturb it.' She walked back and dragged open the gate and the tramp followed her down the path.

She chatted away to him as she prepared his meal, but he said very little. After he had eaten he washed his plate and cup in water he poured from the big kettle on the hob, dried them and replaced them on the shelf. He thanked her, and asked what time the bus left.

Nelly looked at the alarm clock on the shelf, its glass broken and the figures almost unreadably faint. 'Ten minutes,' she announced. 'Just time to walk down in comfort. Sure you don't mind givin' me a 'and?' She found that her leg, where she had fallen onto the clock, was bruised and painful.

' 'Urt me leg,' she explained, 'but it ain't goin' to spoil me plans.'

He insisted on carrying both cases, and having the clock under his arm, while Nelly staggered along beside him with the dogs pulling with their usual enthusiasm. He stood with her at the kerb, shabby but somehow respectable. She could imagine him, better dressed, being accepted even by Evie. Though she'd probably make him shave off his smashin' beard, Nelly thought with a sigh. Always 'ad to spoil things Evie did.

Much later that day, Nelly had spent most of the money given to her by Mrs Greener. She was hot and flushed as she and the dogs left their third public house and headed for the bus stop. She wanted to get home before the pictures finished and the buses were full to overflowing. It was difficult for the dogs when the buses were full.

The cases were one inside the other, and they weren't heavy, but they constantly bumped against her legs as she walked. The dogs crossed in front of her and tangled their long leads around her feet. The evening was dull and it was beginning to rain. Her leg hurt and she wished she was home.

The bus was approaching, she could see it as it came down the hill towards the main road where she was waiting. She dropped the cases and leaned against the post. Searching through her purse she found her return ticket and put it in her teeth, ready for when she got on. She would have a snooze once she and the dogs were settled. If there was a seat. The conductor would tell her when she was home.

She saw a car coming, in front of the bus. She screwed up her eyes and peered at it through the rain, then jumped away from the post in panic. Evie's car! Crawling along the kerb, looking for her. Someone must have told her about the trip to town.

She dragged the dogs away from the kerb; the cases caught in her damp coat and almost pulled her over but she got them all out of sight behind the wall of the pub and waited anxiously for the car to pass. It stopped, and she could imagine Evie's face peering through the rain-spotted windows, looking for her.

'The bus,' she pleaded, her eyes raised to heaven. 'Please Gawd, don't let me miss the bus.' But the bus overtook the now slowly moving car, and disappeared into the mist.

Chapter Ten

Nelly picked up the suitcase, gathered the dogs on to a short lead and began walking. 'That Evie,' she grumbled, 'trust 'er to go an' spoil me night out.' She was tired; the drinks she had consumed and carrying the heavy cases made her ache with the need to sit down.

Eventually she stopped where the pavement had changed to a wide grass verge and leaned against the trunk of a tree. She took the laces out of her shoes, closed her eyes and although it was not the most comfortable of places, she slept.

The dogs' low growls woke her and she sat up, startled.

'What's that? 'oo is it?'

'Sorry if I woke you.'

Nelly looked first at the shoes, still shining in spite of the rain, and up, past the grubby riding mac, up into the bearded face of the tramp, over which was a battered sun-hat.

'Oh, it's you. 'Ello. Sorry about the dogs barkin' but there's somethin' about you people. Dogs always bark at tramps. You give me a bit of a fright too, appearin' sudden like that.'

'Why? You've seen me twice before.'

'I thought you was Tim. 'E's me son in law. 'E an' Evie, they want to lock me up.' She struggled to stand. 'Want somethin' did yer?'

'No. I just wondered if you were all right, seeing you sitting there in the rain.'

'I'm fine. I'm walkin' because Evie an' Timmy made us

miss the bus. I just stopped fer a rest.' She looked at him. 'Where you goin' then?'

'I'm heading for the brickworks at The Cymer.'

'For work or a sleep?'

The tramp laughed. 'You ask a lot of questions.'

'You can always walk on if you don't want to answer.'

'For sleep. I don't need to work for a while.'

'I work regular. But not much. I cleans a couple of 'ouses, includin' Mrs French's – 'er what you met.'

'That doesn't bring in much money, does it?'

Nelly shrugged. 'Enough. An' 'oo wants more than that?'

'I find work for a few weeks, then I travel.'

'Sleepin' out all the time?' Nelly shuddered. 'Wouldn't fancy that meself. Not in winter anyway.'

'I get a bed sometimes, and there are a few Reception Shelters still, where I can get a meal and a bed. I stay a night or two when I need to dry my clothes or when I'm cold. But I can usually find a spot somewhere out of the draught.

'There are lots of houses, empty and boarded up, especially in the towns. Bombed out buildings will be with us for a few years yet. It's eight years since the war ended but there's so much to clear and re-build. Yes, it's easy to find a bed and a corner where no one will see you.'

'Wouldn't fancy that much neither! Blimey, I'd 'ave bleedin' nightmares!'

The tramp nodded, his face wise and almost priestlike, Nelly thought, in the half light, which hid the shabbiness.

'House people are afraid of the dark. It's because they aren't used to the night noises, even a well known place sounds different at night. And imagination fills the dark with things that aren't there. Eveything is the same at night, it's like snapping out the light in your room. Put it on again and nothing has changed.' He smiled showing his even, white teeth. 'I think trouble sleeps at night. I like the dark.'

Nelly stood with him, staring into the rain, uncaring of her wet clothes. 'You runnin' away from someone too?' she asked softly. 'Like me, an' Evie an' Timmy?'

'Hiding from past mistakes perhaps,' he said. 'Who is Timmy?'

Nelly picked up her suitcase and handed it to him. They began to stroll along the verge towards Hen Carw Parc.

'Evie's me daughter an' Timmy's 'er 'usband. Headmaster 'e is. It was all right when they lived far away, but now they live on me doorstep an' Tim – or Evie really – is ashamed of me. That's it. Ashamed!' She paused for a moment then repeated, 'Ashamed. Dirty Nelly they calls me, you know. I 'ates sayin' it, but I shame them.'

'Surely not.'

'They want me to go and live with 'em. Leave me cottage what they calls a slum. Give away me dogs an' me chickens and live in their back bedroom, kept out of sight.' She sobbed and he put a hand on her shoulder, squeezing the sodden coat.

'Why should they want to do that?' He encouraged her to talk, sensing in her the need to get it said.

'Put me in a 'ome as soon as they can. They only pretend to want me in their posh 'ouse. Lock me away. They'll remember me birthday and bring great big useless presents – like that 'orrible clock – do all the right things an' everyone'll say 'ow good they are.' She sobbed again. 'They'll never see 'ow it's cruel.'

'Evie's children will probably grow up to be just like you, appreciating the really good things of life. That would serve her right, wouldn't it?'

Nelly sniffed away her tears and tried to wipe her face on her sleeve, but that was wet from the rain so she felt even wetter.

'I'd better be off,' she said. 'Thanks fer talkin' to me. It's good talkin' to a stranger sometimes, *an*' you've made me forget me achin' legs.'

'I've enjoyed your company. Thank you.' He hesitated as she began to walk away, then called, 'Do you have anyone waiting for you?'

'Not so far as I know. Unless Evie's called. She don't like findin' me out. Suspicious she is.'

'If Evie expects obedience, she's got the wrong mother. It's only half past nine; come on, I'll treat you to a good night out. I still have the money Mrs French gave me and a bit besides. You'll forget Evie and Tim for a couple of hours. What do you say?'

Nelly's eyes widened. 'Ooo, no. I couldn't.'

'And when you do think of them again, you'll decide to stand on your own two feet.' The tramp seemed not to have heard her refusal. 'I'll carry the case. Do you play darts? I haven't played for years, but it's a night for re-learning isn't it?'

'I couldn't,' Nelly repeated, staring at him, at the rain pouring down from his hat and dripping off his beard.

The tramp drooped his shoulders and lowered his head, all enthusiasm gone. A river of water poured from his brim onto Nelly's suitcase like a tiny drum beat. 'Oh, I see. Silly of me to think you would.'

'It's not because you're a tramp, you daft 'aporth! I couldn't let you spend yer savin's on me! *That's* why I said no.'

'Please. I'll make sure I put aside the cost of a room.'

'No I – yes I could! Mister Man, whatever your name is, I'll be pleased to come with yer. Fancy me on a date,' she chuckled. 'First since Gawd knows when.'

They hid the cases in a bush and walked back to the pub that Nelly had just left. After a while they became aware of voices lowered, faces staring at them, disapproval in the air. 'Come on,' Nelly said, kicking the dogs into action, 'I know a better place than this.'

At the second place they were not allowed to play darts. Regulars only, they were told, and when Nelly began to protest loudly, the landlord asked them to leave.

'Come on,' the tramp said, 'it's best we don't incite trouble.'

'Blimey,' Nelly said when they were once again out in the rain, 'you don't 'alf talk posh. More like Mrs French than a 'omeless gentleman of the road.'

The fresh air made Nelly feel giddy. She tried to count the

number of gins she had had, but although she frowned with concentration, the numbers became jumbled and she gave up. They set off back along the road to find the suitcases, the dogs pulling ahead. Nelly was glad to lean on the tramp's arm to keep her feet in a straight line.

'Sorry it wasn't more successful,' the tramp said. 'I hope I didn't embarrass you?'

' 'Course not!' She laughed slightly hysterically and added, between gales of laughter, 'But just imagine what my Evie'd say! 'Er mum bein' chucked out of a pub!'

They tried one more public house on Nelly's insistence, although the tramp thought she had had enough to drink. This time they were allowed to stay. Although Nelly was now incapable of throwing a dart without endangering all present, they sat and watched others, and sang a few songs, and came out decidedly more merry and with the sensation of parting with friends.

The rain had ceased, there was thin cloud, but behind it a moon shone weakly, appearing occasionally in the changing sky. They gathered the case and walked slowly on, arm in arm, talking about the evening and at the friendliness of most of the people they had met.

'Phew, it was 'ot in there,' Nelly said. 'Me coat was steamin' like it was on fire.'

'It's a beautiful night, so sweet-scented and warm now the rain has stopped.'

'And the moon's tryin' to shine for us. Fancy that.'

'I'll walk you home, it's on my way.'

'Ta. That'd be nice.' Nelly began to hum one of the tunes they had sung, and the tramp whistled an accompaniment. Cars passed at intervals and added a shushing sound in the wet road, but apart from those things, the night was still and silent. When they came to a part of the road where there was no pavement, the tramp warned Nelly to keep close in.

'These cars come a bit close, especially where the road bends. Shorten the leads and put the dogs on the inside. We don't want them hurt.'

Clumsily, Nelly did what he suggested, but bending over

made her giddy and she had to stand a while before walking on.

They strolled up the lane, Nelly still humming a tune. 'It's bin a lovely evenin',' she said as she stopped and leaned over a fence to look into the field. 'It ended nice, you walkin' me 'ome. Tell yer what! Stay the night why don't yer?'

The tramp shook his head. 'Thank you, but no. I must move on.'

'I won't keep yer. You can sleep on me armchair by the fire an' get up in the mornin' an' make yerself a cuppa an' go off whenever you like.'

'It's kind of you, Nelly. Really kind. But there's no need.'

'I can't say it proper, like you or Mrs French could, but you've given me a right royal time, even if we was thrown out of a pub.' She laughed her loud laugh at the memory. 'It'd be a sort of thanks, if you'd stay. That armchair is real comfy.' She stood, leaning on the fence, looking at him, enjoying his company, not wanting him to go. 'I've slept there a few times meself, when I've bin too drowsy to get up an' go to bed.'

'Like in the frosty cold, when the fire roars and glows red, and the wind howls and you're warm and safe inside?'

'Yes,' she smiled as she remembered. 'The dogs at me foot, the kettle singin'. It's as if movin' would –'

'Break the spell?'

'Yes.'

'I'd like to accept your invitation, but –'

'Good. I'm glad.' She touched his arm. 'Listen, you can 'ear the stream!' Her face held a reverent expression, she was in awe of the wonders of the night. She spoke in a barely heard whisper. 'It's that quiet, you could 'ear a sparrow fart.'

The tramp chuckled softly. 'Do you think they do?'

'Everyone does, except Evie of course!'

They walked on, the dogs pulling now, impatient to get home. As they reached the gate, Nelly stopped. The oil-lamp was lit, its light shining through the open door and reflecting on the wet ground. She dragged the gate open and at the same time a voice called,

'Is that you, mother?'

'Bloody 'ell. It's Evie!' Nelly gasped.

From behind them, Tim said, 'Mother-in-law, where have you been?'

'Yes, it's me, your mum, 'oo else did you expect?' In an effort to sound sharp, Nelly stumbled over the word.

'Mother! You are drunk!' Evie ran up the path as Tim came through the gate. 'And who is that with you? The man who was thrown out of a public house an hour ago I suppose.'

'We wasn't thrown out, was we, George? We was refused entry,' she laughed.

Timothy sounded ominously calm. 'Where have you been, mother-in-law?'

'Drinkin' an' playin' darts and 'avin' a sing-song, with me friend George. Call me Nelly, why don't yer?'

'You'd better come back with us for tonight. We'll sort it out in the morning,' Timothy said.

'No thanks, dearie. George 'as seen me safe 'ome. I'll be perfectly all right. Goodnight.' She spoke the words slowly, sounding every letter. 'Don't worry about me.'

'Don't worry?' Evie snapped. 'We've been searching for you all evening. What's in that case?'

'A case,' Nelly giggled. 'An' a couple of bottles for tomorrer.'

'Come on, mother-in-law.' Tim tried to take her arm. 'You,' he said to the tramp, 'I think you had better disappear before I report the presence of a vagrant.'

' 'E talks posh too, George, just like you,' Nelly said. 'And I'm not goin' with you two neither. Standin' on me own two feet I am.'

'You're too drink-filled to do that!' retorted Evie sharply.

'Come and take her other arm, Evelyn.'

Nelly began to struggle and shout abuse as they forced

her to go with them. She clung to the gate, which finally gave up and down it went, taking Nelly and Evie with it.

'Now look what you done. Vandals!' Nelly shouted as she struggled to get up.

'We know best, mother,' Evie said firmly gripping her mother's plump arm. 'It's painfully obvious you can't be left.'

Nelly was suddenly defeated. She was too tired to argue.

'All right. I'm comin', but only for tonight. Let me give George 'is change back. Asked me to mind it for 'im 'e did.' She walked to where the tramp had stood watching, wanting to interfere but knowing his intervention would only make things worse. ' 'Ere,' she said, pretending to give him a few coins. 'Stay the night like I promised. There's some fat bacon in the larder what I got off ration, 'elp yerself.' She turned back to Evie and shouted at the top of her voice, '*An* I'm takin' me dogs!'

The tramp held her arm for a moment. 'I'll stay, and thank you,' he whispered, 'but tell me, why did you call me George?'

'Never got round to findin' out yer real name, couldn't tell *them* that! You look like a George. What is yer name?'

He chuckled. 'George will do. Goodnight, Nelly.'

In the room above the shop, Amy's children were playing Monopoly and arguing about the unfairness of charging the rent for a newly acquired hotel, when the doorbell announced a visitor. Amy glanced at the clock; seven-thirty. She sighed and put the dishes from the remains of their meal into the sink and called, 'Go on, one of you answer that. It's probably one of your friends.'

'Oh Mam,' Margaret protested. 'If I go, Freddy will cheat!'

'All right, take the rest of the dishes off the table. *Both* of you!'

She went downstairs and opened the door to see her sister, sheltering under an umbrella against the heavy rain.

'Prue, I didn't expect to see you. Come in.' Prue always

rang to arrange a visit, reminding her more casual sister that it 'wasn't done' to call unannounced.

'Can we have a word in private?' Prue asked, shaking her umbrella before closing the door.

'The kids are here.' Amy shrugged. 'If it's that private we could sit in the store-room. Although it's lovely having so much extra room in the shop, I do miss the room behind. My snug, I called it. Handy when the kids had friends in.' She was nervous, talking fast, afraid of what Prue wanted to say. She looked at her sister, but could read nothing from her expression.

'Couldn't the children come down to the store-room for a while?' Prue asked.

'I can't ask them to do that. Playing Monopoly they are. And why should they be disturbed? Come up and say "hello", then we'll bring a cup of tea down. We can light the electric fire, it's quite cosy really.'

It was clear to Amy that something was worrying Prue and she dreaded to be told what it was. She watched as Prue sat upright on the edge of a chair, and only answered in monosyllables when Margaret or Freddy spoke to her. Yet she seemed in no hurry to go downstairs to explain her problem. She took her time over drinking her tea, which Amy had suggested taking with them, and asked for a second cup and Amy knew it was an excuse to delay.

As fear that it was Harry and herself who were the subject of the forthcoming talk faded, Amy began to feel irritated and finally took the unfinished drink and said firmly, 'Come on, time's passing. I'll have to be getting these two to bed soon.' She went to the door and stood, waiting for Prue to join her.

'Get them to bed? They're big enough to do that for themselves I'd have thought.'

'Yes, well, I like to be involved. Come on.'

Everything about Prue was thin, Amy thought as she sat waiting for her sister to speak. Thin hair, thin face, thin nose, body and feet, and thin hands which fidgeted now as she tried to find the words to begin. When she did speak, the words were a shock that made Amy's head reel.

'You think Harry's being unfaithful?' Amy gasped.

'I'm not sure, but something about him the other night when he came home all upset and irritable, it set me wondering. I thought about the hours he works – boasted about that I have. And about the times I haven't been able to reach him at his office when he said he'd been there. Little things that never worried me before. But now I've started thinking –'

Her voice trailed off and Amy tried to gather her wits sufficiently to say something. Anything to break the silence that was agitating the air with accusations. She felt sick.

'What are you going to do?' she asked.

'I think I've been a good wife. He's never had to look for a clean shirt, or wait for a meal. The house is well kept.' She was silent for a moment, and Amy began to shake, afraid of what was coming. Dreading the charge she could not deny.

'I helped build up his business you know. I was more than a secretary. I ran the business during the war, when he was in the R.A.F. He's got no complaints.' She stared into space for a while, memories tormenting her, forcing herself to go on. 'I know he – doesn't want me –' She turned her face away, her voice dropping to a whisper. 'You know – like that.' She could not say the words.

But Amy could. 'You mean you don't sleep together . . . have intercourse.' She could not stop the feeling of relief and selfish pleasure at the knowledge that she wasn't sharing Harry with his wife. 'How long since you did?' she asked, again for selfish reasons.

'It's never been much of a thing. Harry doesn't bother me much. Never has. I thought he was just not interested. Not every man is, you know,' she added defiantly, 'in spite of what you hear.'

'What are you going to do?' Amy asked and a wave of pity came over her as she looked at the stiff, unbending woman she was cheating in the most cruel way. 'Prue, can't you talk to him?'

'I want to change.'

'What do you mean?'

'I want to throw away all my sensible clothes. Have my hair styled properly. Change myself so he'll see me as something more than a good reliable housekeeper.' She looked at Amy, a straight, unwavering stare that unnerved Amy and made her shake. What was coming next? Was it accusation she saw now in those cold blue eyes? She held her breath and wilted under their glare.

'I want you to help me keep him,' Prue said. Amy jumped up and walked to the door to stare unseeing, out into the rain. What irony, she thought. I can't help her and I can't refuse either. She *must* talk to Harry.

'You introduced us,' Prue went on. 'It's the only good thing that's ever happened to me. I worked for him, became his secretary, while you and he were going out together, remember?'

I remember every moment, Amy thought. I remember telling him I was pregnant and pleading with him to marry me. I remember him refusing, and telling me to get rid of the child. I remember going away and wanting never to see him again. And loving him, wanting him, and coming back to ask him to change his mind. And finding him married, to you.

'– then you went away to Yorkshire for a time and Harry and I found we had a lot in common. We got married just before you came back with the baby and pretended you'd adopted it.' Even at such a time, Prue could not keep the disapproval from her voice.

'No one believed me for long, did they?' Amy said. Thanks to you, she thought. No one loved gossip more than Prue, her tongue couldn't be stopped, even when it was her sister who suffered from it.

'Prue, can't we talk about this some other time. I have to get Margaret to bed. Stay up 'til midnight she would if I let her.'

Prue stood up, angry with herself for saying so much.

'Don't worry. I won't bother you with my problems again.' She picked up her umbrella and shook it open.

'Don't be like that, Prue. Of course I want to help. Just

let me get Margaret and Freddy to bed, then we'll talk some more. All right?'

'Will you come with me to buy some new clothes?'

'Of course I will. And go with you to a good hairdresser. But I still think you should talk to Harry.'

'You haven't said once that I could be mistaken,' Prue accused.

'That's why I think you should talk to Harry,' Amy said swiftly.

She could not make herself say there was nothing to worry about. Yet she hoped that Harry, given sufficient warning, might do just that. How is this going to end? she wondered. She felt some gratification at knowing that now Harry would have to do something. She wondered what it would be. Would he play safe? Concentrate on reassuring Prue that all was well? Or admit to loving Amy, his bit on the side who had been his lover for more than fifteen years.

'Freddy,' she said when she had seen Prue off, 'I have to go out, only for half an hour. Stay with Margaret, will you? Read her a story. Then, when I get back, I'll get us some chips for a treat. All right?'

Amy caught the bus that passed Prue and Harry's house, sitting against the window on the right hand side to peer anxiously through the rain. She wanted to see Harry before Prue spoke to him, give him a chance to prepare. If his car was outside his house she was too late. The rain made it difficult to see, she was not sure. She sat in an agony of suspense until the bus reached The Drovers, and she got out. Harry had gone back to spending a couple of hours there each night, before going home.

She went into the bar and saw him straight away. 'Oh, Harry,' she whispered, 'I've had the most awful hour imaginable.' She told him about Prue's visit and at once he stood up.

'I'll go home straight away,' he said. Then he changed his mind. 'That is, after you've had a drink. You look as if you need one.'

'What are we going to do?' she asked.

'I'm leaving her, Amy. It's time I faced up to the fact that my life is less than full and happy. Look at me now; spending time in here, rather than go home. It's madness. I've been a fool to go on like this for so long. I love you, Amy. I want to spend my time with you. We'll be married. I'll give Freddy my name.'

'Margaret too?'

'Of course Margaret too. She's yours, and you are all my family. Oh, Amy why have we wasted all these years?'

They went to the store-room near one of his building sites and made love. Ignoring the discomfort, and dirt, they both undressed and gave themselves in a celebration of the freedom to come. Then he drove her home.

Amy bought the chips she had promised Freddy and Margaret and woke them to the fun of midnight feast. 'Not quite midnight,' she said excitedly, 'but we can pretend.'

She lay awake for most of the night, dreaming of the future that was rosy at last. Forgetting the twice Harry had let her down, convinced that this time, he would be strong.

Harry drove the short distance home full of excitement. I'm like a sixteen year old on his first date, he thought, his eyes shining, his face wearing a wide smile. A new life is opening up for me, a life with Amy and the kids. It would take time of course but he and Amy would legally adopt Freddy and Margaret. Freddy would have his father's name at last. Freddy, his son, who was already planning to join the firm. Harry Beynon and Son. His smile widened.

It would be hard for Prue of course. He didn't relish telling her. But it wasn't as if she ever loved me, he excused his forthcoming conduct easily. She just likes having someone to cook and clean for. I'll buy her a house; I can easily afford it. That will make her happy. She'll probably move away somewhere, perhaps to the sea. Yes, give her a house and she'll be happy. It's more than she'd have had if she hadn't married me. He parked the car and went in.

He went into the kitchen, where his meal was neatly set out. The cruet in the centre of the table, a serviette across his side-plate. He did not say anything until he had eaten. Prue, as usual, did not acknowledge his arrival except by placing the beautifully presented meal in front of him. Soon, he thought happily, I won't be eating alone. Amy's lovely face will be opposite me, chatting, making me feel wanted and alive.

'That was good, as usual,' he said.

Prue only nodded. Accepting praise was as difficult as giving it.

'Sorry about the other night,' Harry said, wondering how to bring the conversation around to his plans. He couldn't say it straight out, he had to work his way up slowly. Prue went on piling up plates and saucepans, waiting for him to say something more.

'The truth is, I'd had a damned awful day. I lost over ninety pounds on a man who had some work done, then vanished. The house had been sold and I can't find out where he is.'

'Would that be Bert Harris?' she asked. 'I did leave a note warning you that he was slow paying and suspicious in his excuses.' Harry noticed the sharpness of her voice more strongly tonight. Oh to be free of you, he sighed.

'Should have taken more notice of you. There were several other things too. I was angry when I came in. Shouldn't have taken it out on you though. Sorry about that.'

'Was it something about the Luther Collins' account?' she asked quietly.

'No. Why?'

'Well, I can't find any references to him paying you, and the amount of goods listed as being used was far too small for the work you did. A fiddle, was it?'

'Where have you been looking?' A niggle of fear began to stifle the happiness of a few moments ago. 'Muddled you are. Got the wrong information altogether I bet.'

'It's what I wanted to discuss with you the night you came in – all upset. I opened the other filing cabinet, the one you usually keep locked. The extra books were a bit of a puzzle at first.'

Harry stared at her. Any thoughts of leaving her and going to Amy would have to be shelved. He was confused. Could she have known what he was planning to tell her? Was she prepared to squash his dream of a new life without her? It would have to be delayed, no doubt about that. He hoped Amy would wait until he saw her. Hoped she wouldn't allow her excitement to loosen her tongue. Not now.

Chapter Eleven

It was Saturday morning and Prue made a cup of tea for Freddy, who was busy hoeing between the shrubs near the gate. Taking her own, she went to stand at the landing window where she could watch him working, and at the same time, look for Phil Davies the postman.

As she sipped her tea she saw Phil arriving at the houses beyond the church. He called at Evie and Timothy's then he disappeared.

'Just the same as last week,' she muttered in satisfaction. Her cup of tea was finished and still he had not appeared. He should have been at the row of cottages where he lived with his wife and four children, ages ago. Thirty minutes passed, and Prue kept checking her watch, tutting occasionally as she stared down through the village main road.

When her watch showed that forty minutes had passed since his last appearance she saw him, bag on his shoulder, pushing his red bike, coming out from the side of the church. She frowned. Where had he been? And, much more interesting, what had he been doing?

Prue spent a lot of time at the window. She watched what went on, who went where, and reported her observations to those who lacked such a well-placed window. She watched Phil continue his round, and glanced at her watch again. It was the same every Saturday. Next week she would call on Netta Cartwright, ask about Fay and Johnny and time her visit with care.

Taking her cup downstairs, she began to prepare the

vegetables for the evening meal. Harry had been late most evenings, stopping for a drink on the way home. But today he had promised to come home early. She sighed. When he did come straight home he spent the evening reading, listening to the wireless, never spending time talking to her. But it was a step in the right direction, she decided. And the fact that he came home early when she particularly asked was proof that there had been nothing in her suspicions about another woman.

She didn't regret buying the new clothes though. I didn't hurt to make him notice her. She had been too long in the same rut. She had even lightened her hair a little. Men noticed these things, she consoled herself, even if they didn't make any comment.

She finished peeling the potatoes for the evening meal, washed the cup and saucer that Freddy had left on the door-step as well as her own, and peeling off the rubber gloves, she touched up her makeup. The cherry lipstick Amy had persuaded her to buy was rather pretty, once you got used to the brightness. She checked her appearance in the mirror. Yes, just a touch more rouge.

She wondered how to spend her day. There were a few more phone calls to make, but that wasn't enough to fill the afternoon. The house was immaculate as always, and there wasn't anything to do in the garden, Freddy was a hard working boy who earned his money for the few hours he spent outside. She watched Freddy for a moment. Admiring the strength of him, the adult way he walked, and set about his work. Strong, and muscular, polite and very handsome. Why hadn't she been able to produce a son like Freddy?

She put on her old leather gloves and gave the brass pokers an extra polish. Looking around for something else to do, she decided to wash Harry's shirts. Seeing washing blowing on the line always gave her pleasure.

She put some Oxydol powder in the boiler and put the white shirts in to boil, after making sure the back and front studs were out and safely in the stud box beside Harry's bed. While the washing boiled, she mixed the starch for the collars, and the bowl of blue for the final rinse.

The shirts needed about ten minutes; leaving time to ring Evie.

'I saw your mother coming home last night, Evelyn, dear,' she said in a sympathetic voice. 'I'm so sorry for the trouble you have with her. Talking to some tramp she was.' The reaction to her words shocked her.

'My mother was with Timothy and myself last evening,' Evie snapped. 'In fact, she's still here.' As Prue began to splutter an apology, Evie went on, 'You, Prue Beynon, are a nosy, interfering busybody! You get your pleasures in life from evil gossip! Look to your own before you say any more about mine. Understand that, do you?'

The phone slammed down, but not before Prue heard the unmistakeable laughter of Nelly Luke. Prue took out a duster and began to polish the table angrily. How dare Evelyn speak to me like that! She's only been back in the village five minutes, and there she was calling me a liar! And she had seen Nelly with a man. Strolling up the lane with him and those filthy dogs. How could she have been mistaken? The words with which Evie had ended her outburst came back to her then. And making remarks about her sister. Amy was past the stage when people gossiped about her. Or – and the thought came as a hammer blow – or was it not Amy she meant, but Harry?

'Harry,' she whispered. 'Harry *is* carrying on, and –' this worst of all, 'and someone else knows.'

She sat for a while to allow the trembling to cease, then began to make her plans. First, she went into his office and taking out his files, began to make careful notes in her small, neat handwriting.

Evie put down the phone and she too was trembling. Furiously angry with Prue and with herself. I sounded just like Nelly, she thought, humiliation draining her face of its colour. She walked back to the kitchen where Nelly was washing up the breakfast things.

'All these dishes, Evie,' Nelly protested amiably. 'Don't 'alf make work for yerself. You're like my Mrs French. Now there's a woman fer dishes! Dish fer jam, an' pickles an' everythin'. Even the little scrap of cheese 'as to come out of its paper and go on a dish. Ration's so small it 'ardly seems worth the trouble.'

'I like things nice, mother.' Evie's voice was quiet; she was still conscious of the way she had shouted at Prue.

'I like things nice, Evie, but by nice, *I* mean comfy an' easy. Evie,' she blurted out, 'I want to go 'ome.'

'We've talked about it and you are staying here. Finding you out last night with a man who is obviously a tramp –'

'George is all right. Kind to me, 'e was. Generous.'

'I'd never have a moment's peace,' Evie finished. 'We're concerned for you and –'

'Concerned! You're afraid one of Timmy's fine friends'll see me with a bottle of gin in one 'and a wrap of fish an' chips in the other, dancin' in the street and singin' rude songs! I'm 'appy with me life, Evie. Very 'appy.'

'All right!' Evie's voice rose again as she glared at her mother. 'So we do dread people seeing you in your old coat and those filthy dogs pulling you along.'

'They ain't filthy.'

'They're filthy, and so is that cottage of yours. There's no running water except for the tap in the lane, there's no proper toilet –'

'They ain't filthy! An' I got the woods, miles of woods. That's more 'ealthy than doin' it indoors!'

'Mother!'

'Talkin' about runnin' water, I backed an 'orse called that once. Or was it Waterfall –?'

'That's another thing. Your gambling.'

'No 'arm in a flutter. Oh, Evie . . .' Nelly threw the tea towel down onto the enamel draining board. 'It's no use. Can't yer see it ain't no use? I've bin 'ere less than a day an' I'm that miserable. Let me go 'ome. I promise I'll stay away from town.' Then she added in a low mutter, her head down, 'I only went 'cos you made me so flippin' miserable.'

'You can go back at the weekend. We'll come with you and sort out things ready to be taken to the rubbish tip. That is final.'

'I like me own place an' me dogs. I like searchin' fer firewood an' comin' 'ome to a roarin' fire an' the kettle singin' a welcome.' She suddenly shouted in alarm. 'An' me chickens! Me chickens! I'll 'ave to go quick an' feed me chickens! You wouldn't like me 'ad up fer cruelty would yer? Look good in the papers, that would.'

'I'd forgotten those.'

'I'll go now. Come on, boys.' The dogs barked excitedly as she wiped her hands on her skirt and looked for their leads.

'Wait until lunchtime. Timothy will go with you after lunch.'

'No need. Come on Spotty an' Bobby. We're goin' 'ome.'

Nelly walked slowly up the lane, savouring the fresh sweet air. 'Smells better than Evie's, don't it?' she said to the dogs and they pulled and strained up the slight hill pleading to be released. She untied the ropes and they jumped into the field, their long tails wagging in appreciation of the freedom after being so long confined.

At the top of the field, at the edge of the wood, rabbits sat and stared briefly at the invaders before showing their white scuts and disappearing into the trees and down into the safety of their burrows.

As she turned the corner, Nelly stopped. She saw smoke coming from her chimney. That was odd, and as she drew nearer she saw that her door stood wide open too. From the empty space where the gate had once stood, she called,

' 'Ello? Anybody there?' A figure stepped into the doorway and waved a welcome. ' 'Ello George,' she smiled.

'I thought you'd never get back,' he laughed. 'And me with a meal waiting for you.'

'Mmmm.' Nelly sniffed appreciatively. 'Rabbit stew I bet yer. Smashin', George. Smells like a feast.' She patted the dogs who had greeted the tramp without the usual preliminary barking and signs of disapproval. 'What a welcome 'ome, eh boys?' She chuckled and added, 'Thought I counted a couple fewer rabbits in the field just now!'

They ate the stew, with the dogs enjoying their platefuls beside them and Nelly studied the tramp curiously. He had on a neatly ironed shirt, and as before, his shoes were shining like new.

'You look spankin' smart, George. 'Ow do yer keep so tidy, bein' on the move all the time?' she asked.

'I'm afraid I took advantage of your kindness, Nelly. Last night, when you left with Evie, I hesitated about staying, but when I walked down the path and looked inside, the temptation was too much. I came in, and the kettle was full of hot water and I just managed to save the fire. The bowl was easy to find so I washed myself, then, remembering where the tap was, as I've used it a few times before, I boiled more water and washed all my clothes.'

Nelly burst out laughing. 'Cor, wouldn't that 'ave been a shock fer you if I'd 'ave come back last night!' The gales of laughter increased as she added, 'An' what if my Evie 'ad come with me! Locked me up fer good then, she would 'ave.'

When George had gone, Nelly felt sad, but cheered up at the thought of telling Netta Cartwright about her adventures.

'Come on, boys,' she said later that day. 'Let's go an' see if Netta's in. I want to find out 'ow things are with young Johnny as well.'

Several times over the next few days Nelly saw the tramp. Once, she was close enough to talk, but he only waved and walked away. She shrugged. If he ever wanted to talk, he knew where she was. Twice, she came home from Mrs French's to find a pile of wood, chopped and stacked, covered with an old door to keep it dry. She smiled with pleasure. There was enough now to see her through the winter if she didn't start on it until Christmas, she judged.

She left a cake out for him twice, but each time it was still there after two days. She was curious about him, wondered where he was, but she didn't brood on the mystery. Something kept him from a normal life, she mused, even if he did keep his shoes polished.

She remembered how neatly he had ironed his shirt and decided she ought not to be quite so careless about what she wore. Perhaps if she spent a little more time ironing her dresses, Evie might be less embarrassed. She took out the two flat irons and placed them to face the fire. With a thickly folded cloth to protect her hands from the hot metal, she patiently pressed her navy dress.

Changing irons regularly, taking the hot one from the fire and replacing the cooled one, and kicking off her shoes half way through, she finished the boring task and was pleased with the result. If George can look tidy, then there's no excuse fer me, she decided.

The following Saturday, Prue suddenly felt embarrassed at the length of time she had been standing watching Freddy digging out the dead wallflowers and tulip bulbs and planting the bed anew. She decided she would go a little earlier than planned to Netta Cartwright's and perhaps have a cup of coffee there.

When she knocked on the door of the cottage, she did not expect to be kept waiting. She had telephoned after all, to say she was coming to have a word about the sewing bee. At her second knock, a deal louder than the first, it was Johnny who opened the door.

'Hello, Mrs Beynon. Mam won't be long. Putting clothes on the line she is. Come in.'

'Oh.' Prue looked decidedly put out. 'I did tell her I intended to call.'

Johnny swallowed the temptation to say that most people didn't tell them they were calling, but asked if it was convenient. He gestured towards the front room and Prue sat hesitantly on the edge of an old leather armchair with flattened velvet cushions.

Netta came in, her arms full of white, sweet-smelling washing. She was a small, plump woman, rosy cheeked and very pretty. 'Sorry about that, Mrs Beynon,' she said, her Welshness very pronounced. 'It was too good a day to waste. The last is out now, drying lovely it is. Best day for washing for ages yes, indeed.'

'Yes, well, as long as you're ready now,' Prue said with a frown. 'I have things to do.'

'Don't let us keep you then,' Johnny said with a smile. 'Call another day, when *Mam* isn't so busy. She has a lot to do too.'

Prue stood up and looked out of the window towards the church, hoping for a glimpse of the postman's red bike before she replied, 'Yes, with Fay as well to look after and wash and cook for.' She looked pointedly at the expensive and lacy underwear among the washing, that certainly did not belong to Johnny's mother. 'How is Fay?' she asked, 'better now?'

'She's fine, thank you,' Johnny said sharply.

'Very happy they are the pair of them.' Netta smiled at her son fondly. 'Two love-birds they are for sure.'

'Oh, I wondered, seeing her wandering around the lanes on her own late at night, and early mornings. And meeting that tramp fellow, I wondered –'

'What tramp fellow would that be then?' Netta asked softly, with a glance at Johnny.

'I've seen her with him a couple of times and I wondered if she was trying to help the poor man. I know how compassionate these young people are, but with no thought for what people will think.'

'Been looking out of your spy-hole again, Mrs Beynon?' Johnny asked. He ignored a warning gesture from his mother, begging him to be quiet. 'See too much altogether you do, Mrs Beynon. There's no tramp, or any other man in Fay's life except me. Right?'

Prue was surprised at the violence showing on his face.

'Why did you come? To talk about the charity work was it?' Netta's voice asked. 'Like a cup of tea? Johnny bach, go and make a cup of tea for our visitor, will you? There's a good boy.' She ushered him into the kitchen. 'Now, dear,' she said to Prue, 'what about the new project? Squares for blankets, wasn't it?'

'I came to ask if Fay would like to join. I could take her along and introduce her. But after that outburst –'

'Introduce her? To who? Lived here all her life Fay has. Knows everyone.' Her quiet voice sounded surprised.

'I thought she might be a bit shy and be glad of someone to begin with.'

'Our Fay, shy? Never. Sells hats she does; you need a lot of confidence to sell hats.'

'Well,' Prue moved away from the window, 'tell her I called and I'm sorry to have missed her. If she would like to come with me and meet some of my friends, tell her to telephone me.'

'Very well, but I don't think she will, she works a long day you see.'

'If she ever needs a friend, someone to talk to, seeing that she's so lonely, tell her I am always available.'

'Get enough gossip as it is, you do,' Johnny said, coming in with a tray of tea and biscuits. 'And my wife is not lonely.'

'Hush, Johnny,' his mother admonished in a voice that was little more than a whisper. She looked apologetically at her visitor, her brown eyes rolling in the small round rosy face. 'Children,' she tutted. 'Get you hung they would.'

'I – wouldn't know.'

'There's rude you were, Johnny,' his mother scolded when Prue had gone.

'Deserved that and more. D'you know what she's been saying about Phil Davies next door?' Johnny said angrily. 'She's noticed through that window of hers that he goes to the row of houses next to the church, then doesn't get to her house until half an hour later. Spread rumours she has, that Phil is visiting some woman.'

'Well, so he is. Old Mrs Thomas! He gets her coal in and chops sticks.'

'That's not what Prue Beynon, nosy old bugger, has been suggesting!'

Fay was still not back when he set off for the late shift, and he left her a note, propped on her pillow, telling her he loved her, and with it, a small posy of flowers he had picked.

His first route brought him past the village and as he looked up, as he often did, to the landing window of Prue's house, he saw her face. He stopped the bus, tooted on his horn and waved wildly at her. Then had the satisfaction of seeing the curtains snap shut. He laughed, but there was little humour in it; the stories she spread were likely to be very *un*-funny if they were believed.

Fay ate the meal her mother-in-law had prepared when she arrived home, then went straight to her room. 'I think I'll go to bed early tonight,' she said, and yawned to give credence to the announcement. 'I'm so tired, there's so much driving on this rain too, and on top of the actual visits to shops, I've been driving around, searching the area for new prospects, for small villages where sometimes there's a row of good shops. It's very tiring, trying to oust my opposition and introduce my lines.'

'I couldn't do it for a million,' Netta smiled. 'Go on, it's past eight and you've been out since seven this morning. Work too hard you do, I've said as much to Johnny. Go on up and I'll make you a cup of cocoa in a little while, when you're settled.'

Fay washed herself, and came into the living room, wearing a pink nightdress and a matching dressing gown.

'There's lovely you look, Fay,' Netta said. 'If that's how you look when you're tired –' she laughed. 'Go on, I'll bring your drink.' She hugged the girl and kissed her cheek. 'Lucky boy my Johnny, and he knows it.'

When the cocoa, to which Netta had added some fresh cream, had arrived and been drunk, Fay lay in the quiet room for a couple of hours. She listened to all the usual noises of the household: the slow footsteps climbing the stairs, the last light switch being clicked, the last bed-spring twanging out its protest. When everything was still, she got up and dressed and went out.

The sky was still holding on to the last of the light, but rain was falling, and she hoped that most houses would have their curtains drawn against the dull, dark evening.

She slipped over the fence and through the straggle of trees at the foot of the hill, then climbed up through the closer, thicker trees, passing to the east of Nelly's cottage and on to where the castle ruins lay shrouded in the semi-dark mists, mysterious and unwelcoming.

She almost turned back; the place was eerie, with rain darkening the colours of the stones and making strange sounds as it trickled through the openings and down secret gullys and dripped, unseen, into pools in the rocks.

A long, deep breath and she walked to the old kitchens, where she intended to wait for Alan. She knew, from her many visits that it was usually at the weekends he slept there. The dry bracken and the old blanket were not to be seen at other times.

She shivered with the cold as the dampness of the rock seeped into her back. Tucking her coat more firmly around her she sat watching the doorway. Tonight she was determined to wait until she saw him and had spoken to him. She had to know why he was here, like a wraith, instead of coming home. Tension kept her wide awake. It was difficult even to relax as she waited. Nothing broke the silence of the ancient place.

The rain fell relentlessly and she tensed herself even tighter, trying to hear over the shushing of its blanketing sound, for the first hint of Alan's arrival.

When the swishing of feet through grass reached her ears she was petrified. What if it wasn't the man she expected? In those moments she thought of the people murdered by Christie, and of the Towpath murders which had filled the papers for weeks. She remembered all the horror stories she had read as a child and the countless men who wandered lonely places seeking a dry place to sleep.

The darkness which had seemed absolute when she had first entered the kitchens had lightened slightly as her eyes became accustomed to the light, and now, the darkness changed again as a figure filled the doorway, blocking the faint light that still came from the sky. She gave a gasp of fear. If only it was Alan, she thought, her hands on her furiously beating heart.

'Alan?' The name was a prayer. 'Alan? Is it you?'

'No,' said a voice she knew well. 'It's me, Johnny.'

'Johnny?' Fay's brain, numbed by the fear of the possibilities of the figure in the doorway, refused to accept his presence.

'Yes. Johnny, your husband who loves you. I've come to take you home. No point in waiting here for a man who can't come. Dead he is, love. But you and me, we're alive and I'm glad of it. Come on, my lovely, frozen you'll be, sitting there.'

Johnny did not use the torch in his hand, but found her, knowing exactly where she would be, although he was blind in the dark, unknown place. He put his arms around her, held her tight to stop the shivering that wracked her body. He kissed her hair, her eyes, her lips, but she did not respond. In his arms she felt like a stone statue.

'Alan's alive,' she whispered. 'I've seen him, spoken to him.'

'No, love. Seen a man wandering about the village, but he isn't Alan. Probably that tramp that Nelly was accused of having a riotous time with. He's often about here, see him now and then from my bus, walking about, lonely and homeless. Glad it isn't like that for us. Got each other we have. Never no need to be lonely, you nor me.' He tried to help her up. 'Come home, lovely, home with your Johnny.'

'Johnny, I'm not crazy.'

'Far from it! Anyone who says different and I'll sock 'em.'

'He is alive. He sleeps here, at weekends. I came to wait just so I can talk to him; find out why he hasn't come home.'

'No, love. If it was Alan, he couldn't have stayed away from someone as lovely as you. Never.'

'I want to wait. Will you wait with me?'

'All right, if that's the only way you'll be convinced. But if it is that tramp of Nelly's, there's an 'ell of a shock we'll give him, poor dab.' He put his jacket down for her to sit on, and wrapped his arms around her and together, they waited.

'Johnny,' Fay whispered after a while. 'Why did you come? How did you know where to find me? Why weren't you working?'

'Stopped the bus and called in to see if you were home. Left it on the main road I did, dreading to be seen and reported by the nosy old bugger in the window. But I had to see you, I knew you were upset. Seen you walking through the field many times. There's a lot I see from my bus. People don't think it's got eyes. Better than the nosy old bugger's window it is.' He kissed her gently. 'I guessed where you were, and why.' He held her more tightly. 'Went back to the depot and reported sick after I found the bed empty. Sleep now love, I'll wake you when I hear him coming.'

'Johnny, you're so good to me.'

'Don't be daft, girl. I love you, don't I? Love isn't only for the good times, now is it?'

'Have there been any, Johnny?'

'Yes. And there'll be plenty more once we have sorted this. A partnership we are. Damn, there's nothing we can't settle, you and me together.'

She relaxed and rested her head on his shoulder. He held her more tightly and felt her body soften into sleep. There was a frown on his face as he sat there in the almost total blackness, seeing only the faint shape of the entrance. He promised her they would sort this out, but he wondered secretly if they ever would.

He turned his head and kissed her sweet-smelling hair. Was his lovely Fay unbalanced? It seemed crazy to believe that a man like Alan would not return to tell his family and his fiancée that he was alive. It must be someone who only looked like him. That would be more likely. After eight years she could easily be mistaken. Fay couldn't have been driven to insanity by believing she was married to the wrong man, she couldn't. He shifted slightly to make himself more comfortable, and sat, staring at the doorway, waiting for the dawn. He kissed her again. Whatever happened, she belonged to him now and he would never let her go. Never.

Unseen by either of them, Alan crept towards the castle ruin, a sixth sense warning him of danger. He slipped through the tumble of stones and edged his way towards the kitchen. There, he slid his eyes around the thick wood of the doorpost, where once a heavy oaken door had hung and, in the blackness, gradually made out the uneven shapes in the corner. Slowly he moved away until the night swallowed him up, and the grasses sprang back to hide the signs of his passing.

Amy put a notice on her shop door to the effect that she would be late opening after lunch, and ran for the bus into Swansea. Harry and she had agreed not to risk meeting during the day, when his car would be obvious, but today he had said it was important.

'If anyone sees you, we'll have met by accident and I'm giving my sister-in-law a lift home. That's fair enough, isn't it?' he had said.

She sat on the side of the bus furthest away from Prue's house, bought a ticket for the town, then alighted a mile past The Drovers. But the public house was not her destination. An empty house stood back from the road, and ladders and bags of cement and piles of sand and gravel were evidence of the presence of workmen.

Harry's car was parked in the driveway and she walked past it and went inside the house. She wore a tapestry cape which was very long, and this, plus a scarf worn over her hair was, she hoped sufficient disguise for other than the closest of scrutinies.

'Harry?' she called, and he came out of one of the rooms

which gave a view of the distant road. She threw off her cloak and went into his open arms.

'Amy, what do you think of this?' He gestured widely, his arms encompassing all the rooms visible through the open doors.

'All this space,' she said in awe as he showed her around. 'Compared with the top half of a small cottage, like I have to share with two kids, it's a palace.' She went from room to room, admiring the views of the green hills from the back of the house. At the side a small stream wandered through the garden, before the fields rose up to steep fields where sheep grazed. 'It's heaven,' she said.

'I've bought it.'

'You and Prue are moving? But she won't like this, it's too far from the village. She likes to know what's going on.'

'Not for Prue. For you, and later on, for me.'

'Harry.' Strangely her only emotions were fear and guilt. 'How can we explain to Margaret and Freddy? What would people think if you bought me a house?'

'Amy,' Harry laughed. 'You have two children and no husband. What can they say about you that they haven't said loudly and repeatedly before?'

'Telling Prue you wanted a divorce was somehow clean and straight. But to give me this and still pretend we aren't lovers, it – it would be impossible.' She kissed him and added, 'How we've kept it a secret all these years I'll never know.'

'We haven't,' Harry replied. 'Nelly knows and I'm sure she isn't the only one.'

'But wouldn't your business suffer if people began to talk?'

'It's only for a little while longer. I don't want to tell Prue until I can get rid of the evidence she found. A bit of fiddling. She spotted it and I think she would report me if she had the chance.'

'Her own husband?' Then she smiled. 'No, I don't blame her really. I'd do worse if you were mine and someone tried to take you away from me.'

'Not a chance. And as for losing business, I'm a damned good builder and people put that first, even in small villages where approval is as important as a good breakfast. Aren't you pleased?' He frowned anxiously. 'I thought you would be . . . Amy, you do love me? It wasn't all talk? I mean, after all this time, you haven't changed your mind, have you?'

'Harry. It's what I've always dreamed about. But now I'm faced with telling my sister that I'm taking her husband from her. The reality is frightening and –' she held him close – 'Get the books sorted, let's tell her soon. I can't go through weeks and weeks of having it on my mind.'

'I could take a risk and tell her tonight. Trust her not to use what she knows about my "extra business deals". But I can't protect you from her anger and her wrath. You'll have to take it and take it. Prue isn't the type to accept this easily. The embarrassment will be what she hates most. I wish I could save her that, but I can't move away; my work is here, your shop is here. The kids are settled and it would be a great upheaval for them. It's one versus the four of us I'm afraid.'

'Perhaps Prue will leave if we give her time. I think she would prefer that.'

'I'll ring you tonight, when I've told her,' he said.

'Give her time,' Amy said softly. 'It's a terrible thing we're doing to her.'

'I know. But I can't live the rest of my life half alive. I want you, Amy. My constant regret is that I didn't have the courage years ago, when you asked me.'

'Perhaps the baby would still have died. I tell myself that it wasn't the stuff you made me take that killed him, but I wouldn't have felt so alone and bereft of any comfort. It's over now, only revived at all because Nelly found the death certificate.'

'From now on, we'll look ahead at all the good years, not back. That way we won't waste any more of our lives.'

'Are you expecting any of the workmen today?' she asked suddenly.

'Yes, in an hour or so. Why?'

She took his hand and led him to the staircase. 'Then

there's time to christen a bedroom or two.' She went slowly up the stairs, shedding clothes as she went.

Harry drove her towards Swansea and waited with her until the bus came. 'I'll ring you,' he said, and drove off, leaving her to get on the bus alone. She found a seat, but dreams about living in the beautiful house with Harry were constantly punctuated by stabs of guilt.

She reached the shop to find Prue waiting for her. Amy gasped. Could she and Harry have been seen? She said nothing, waiting for Prue to ask where she had been, but she only bought the items she needed and went home.

The phone went late in the afternoon and again she felt the surge of fear and shame for what she and Harry were going to do. But it was Mrs French; would she deliver a loaf of bread. Amy said Margaret would bring it after school. Her hand trembled as she replaced the phone.

Chapter Twelve

Nelly was late finishing at Mrs French's that day. It was one of the times when there were several extra jobs to be done. The curtains were washed and ironed and re-hung and Nelly cleaned the windows and washed down the cream paintwork ready for them. They had eaten a snack lunch and worked until the children came out of school, and Amy's daughter arrived with the extra loaf of bread.

'Come in, dearie,' Nelly said as the girl hesitated at the back door. 'Mrs French'll want to pay you for certain. Mrs French!' she yelled at the top of her voice as the girl stepped inside. 'Go on, pretend you're a caller an' wait for 'er in the front room.' Nelly coaxed and pushed Margaret into the comfortably furnished lounge with its fat armchairs and the grand piano. 'Mrs French won't be long. Sit down, why don't yer?' She winked and left her.

Margaret stood uneasily looking around her for a few moments, then the piano drew her and she stepped over to it, staring at its keyboard. Giving a surreptitious look to see that the hall was empty, and listening for the continuing sound of the vacuum cleaner from upstairs, she was emboldened to try a few notes. She became less aware of where she was as she picked out a tune and experimented with combinations of sounds.

Mrs French watched her unseen for a while, then moved over and said, 'You have a good ear, Margaret. Have you had any lessons?'

The girl jumped and looked ready to run, but Mrs French's hand held her and the woman smiled. 'Don't run away. I don't mind you trying the piano. Do you have music lessons?' she repeated.

'No, Mam says there's no room for a piano above the shop.'

Mrs French drew up a chair and sitting beside her, showed Margaret the notes, naming them and encouraging her to play. 'Come over on Saturday mornings, while your brother is working for Mrs Beynon, I'll teach you a few simple tunes. Would you like that?'

Margaret's eyes lit up, their deep brown depths glowing with pleasure. 'Could I, Mrs French? Really? I'll ask Mam, but I'm sure she won't mind.'

'I'll ring and ask for you, shall I? Perhaps you'd like to stay for a while now?' She didn't wait for a reply, but picked up the phone.

When Margaret left, Nelly was polishing in the hall. The young girl was flushed with the thrill of discovery. The piano spoke to her; she had been given a magic key so she could begin to unravel its mysteries. She chatted happily to Nelly about what she had learnt, and of the promise of Mrs French to teach her more. Nelly nodded knowledgeably.

'Likes music Mrs French does. 'Er 'usband ran music shops; 'er daughter still does. Alan played beautiful, pity 'e was killed. Yes, I expect she'd enjoy teachin' yer.'

In the window, far above them, Prue was watching them and was struck for the first time of the similarity between her niece Margaret, and the daughter of Mrs French, now grown up and moved away. There was the same rich auburn hair and dark brown eyes. She watched them walk away, then went downstairs to look through the carefully filled photograph albums.

She found what she was looking for and went across to Mrs French. So excited was she at what she discovered, she did not wait to phone first, but ran across and knocked on the door.

'So sorry to bother you, Monica; but do you have the number of the bank in Greenfield Street? I seem to have mislaid my telephone book.'

Monica French looked at her visitor doubtfully. Prue was not the type to mislay anything. The book, she was certain, was in its allotted place on the hall table. She wondered what the real reason for Prue's visit might be.

'Do come in, Prue. I'll have it in my book. Trouble, is there?'

'No, just a slight discrepancy in Harry's figures. I like to have everything correct.' She took the number that Monica gave her and went towards the door. As she passed the table in the hall, something fell and Monica bent to retrieve it.

'Prue, you've dropped something –' she stared at the photograph. 'It's my daughter, Rosemary. Why were you carrying that?'

'Oh, er, I, I was looking at it, after seeing young Margaret, my niece. So alike, I thought, and I took the photograph out to compare. Isn't it amazing? Those lovely eyes, so dark, just like Rosemary and her father. And the hair. She's a pretty girl, isn't she, like your daughter is.' She laughed deprecatingly. 'Lucky you aren't the suspicious type, or you wonder about the mystery of Margaret's father.' Smiling, Prue let herself out, leaving Monica to stare at the photograph.

Nelly came in from the hall and took it from her.

'I 'eard enough of that to know what she's tryin' to do, dearie. Ignore 'er, the nosy old cow!'

'Nelly!'

'Well, she is! Always on at someone's reputation she is. Let Johnny 'ear about this an' 'e'll ring 'er scraggy neck. 'Ates Prue Beynon 'e does.' She looked at the photograph and went silent. The likeness was uncanny. 'Nothing like Margaret!' she said emphatically. She stuffed the photograph into a kitchen drawer, slammed it shut and dusted her hands, then pulled on her coat and picked up her large leather-cloth bag. 'Got to go now, dearie. Don't think no more about it.' She left, promising to come back the following day to 'finish off', and untied the dogs. When she glanced back into the kitchen, Mrs French was holding the photograph and staring into space, her face white.

Nelly knew it was none of her business, but she told Johnny when she called there later that evening to listen to *Educating Archie* on the radio. He was just leaving for work, a split shift, he expained. His comment, when she told him about the photograph was curious.

'Where can I borrow a set of ladders?' he asked.

Harry went home and rather than try to find the right moment, went straight to the kitchen, where Prue was putting the finishing touches to his dinner. She was wearing a new dress. Pale blue with a pocket edge and a belt of crochet. Her small mouth was adorned with pink lipstick.

'Prue,' he said, and something in his voice made her stop what she was doing, and look at him. She usually did not react to his arrival other than to do what was necessary to his meal, but now she waited for him to speak.

'There's no easy way to say this,' he said, meeting her gaze. 'I'm going to leave you.'

'What?' She sat down so suddenly that at any other time it would have been comic. 'You're out of your mind! Why?'

'I don't love you.'

'So? You never have. But that hasn't stopped me being a good wife. You haven't any complaints.' There was a slight emphasis on the word *you*. That, and the coldness in her voice and the calmness in the way she answered him, chilled his blood. 'Have you?'

'I love someone else.'

'That won't last. Good housekeeping and good food will.'

'Sorry Prue. I know this is a shock, but it isn't the sort of thing I can hint about, build up to, or rehearse. I want to move out. The house is yours to keep or to sell. I'll make any other arrangements that are reasonable.'

To his surprise, Prue stood up and walked from the room.

'Prue, we have to discuss it.' He began to follow her, wondering what she was going to do, but she went into the office and came out almost immediately with her arms full of ledgers.

'Discussion is it? I'll begin the discussion, shall I?' she

said, and threw down a large accounts book filled with her neat writing. 'Start with this, shall we? Let's discuss this. It's my version of your double book-keeping.'

'What are you on about?' He picked it up and his face drained of colour. Every job he had done in the past two years was entered, both in the way he had set them out for the taxman, and showing his true profits. A list of items, received but not paid for through the usual invoices was also included. Goods he and some lorry-drivers had made deals on. Cheating the firms who supplied him out of hundreds of pounds. 'Prue. What is this?'

'If you want to know, then do what you say, leave me, I think the police would find these – concoctions, this – fiction – quite fascinating. Don't you?'

It was Harry's turn to sit down suddenly. 'You mean you'd show these to the tax office? If I leave you, you'll use blackmail to stop me?'

'If you left me, I wouldn't be devastated,' she said, bitterness making her voice harsh. 'But I would feel foolish. I can't bear to feel foolish.'

'That's something you've inflicted on plenty of others. Spreading untrue or half-true stories. It didn't bother you when others were made to look foolish, or stupid, or embarrassed.'

'They deserved it. I don't.'

'I – I don't know what to say to you.'

'You don't have to say anything to *me*. Go and explain to *her*, whoever she is.' She pushed him. 'Better go now hadn't you? Your bit of fluff, or whatever they call it these days, will be waiting with bated breath to hear your news. Tell her now, don't keep her waiting!' She picked up the telephone and handed it to him, her eyes like ice.

He stumbled from the house and walked along the road, unseeing, unhearing, oblivious of the traffic danger as he crossed the road and went through the village passing Amy's shop without a glance. After more than two hours he became aware that his legs were aching and he searched his pockets to see how much money he had on him. Satisfied he had sufficient, he went into the first pub he saw and got solitarily, quietly and awesomely drunk.

When he tried to stand and failed, he asked the landlord to call a taxi and book him into an hotel.

Prue sat for a long time after Harry had left, wondering how to deal with the next few days. She had not really expected it, had not really believed Harry was carrying on. She went hot at the thought of others guessing. Someone must have seen them together. Her lack of popularity would have made that an irresistible item for gossip.

She doubted that Harry would stay out all night, so she did not bolt the doors as she usually did, but just locked them. After turning off all the lights she went upstairs. It was late. She had sat for hours, tense and waiting for his return. Sleep was nowhere near but she did not now, want to be up when Harry came back. Best to carry on as normal.

Sleep would not come. She was so distressed. In the bathroom cupboard were some sleeping tablets. She went down and made a cup of Ovaltine, hurriedly washing up the saucepan and whisk when she had finished.

She took off the new blue dress and threw it on the floor with an angry gesture. Harry had not even noticed. She felt humiliation as she thought of the way he had said, 'Prue', when he came home. She had turned, expecting him to say, 'you look nice,' and instead, he said he was leaving her. The way she had turned expectantly seemed now to have been embarrassing. She had looked a fool, begging for the crumbs of affection from him.

Unable to leave it in a crumpled heap, although she knew she would never wear it again, she picked it up and slipped it onto a hanger. She would give it to Nelly. Let her sell it. She would give her all the clothes she had bought to give herself a new image. Let Nelly sell them all and get drunk. It would serve Evelyn right for the way she had spoken to her!

The tablets did their work and although her mind tumbled with thoughts of where the events of the past hours might take her, soon, she slept.

She woke to a feeling of confusion. It was pitch black yet she felt as if it were time to get up. It must be at least seven o'clock. Even with a sleeping tablet she never woke later than seven. She reached out for the clock and tried to read its dial. Then she sat up and switching on the bedside light, saw that it was indeed after seven.

She frowned. The clock must be wrong. Stepping out of bed into her slippers, she reached for her dressing gown. Even in her puzzlement she stopped to do up each button and to fasten the belt firmly around her waist. She opened the curtains and could see nothing. She went into the next room, calling Harry's name as she went. The landing curtains were pulled open but they too failed to give any light. The reason for the darkness was apparent but she did not want to believe it. Someone had painted over all the windows in the house with black paint.

She ran to open her front door. Daylight streamed in and across the cardinal red tiles was written, NOSY OLD BUGGER. The paint was not dry, and before she telephoned the police, she scraped it off.

Amy watched as Victor Honeyman carried in the last of the boxes. She had recognised him as soon as the lorry stopped outside. He had danced with her at the Coronation party. She flirted with him a little, persuading him that she was too weak and helpless to stack the heavy boxes, and he had grinned and put them in the place she requested, with ease.

'Can't have a pretty little thing like you straining herself, can we?' he said as he piled the last box on a high shelf. 'Call me when you want them lifted down again, anytime,' he said, 'day or night, mind.'

Amy laughed, signed for the goods and waved him off. From his cab, he called, 'What about another night of dancing, you and me?'

The phone went and she shouted, 'One of these days, perhaps,' and ran back to the shop.

It was Harry. He explained briefly what had happened between himself and Prue.

'Where are you?' Amy asked.

'At an hotel. I haven't been home yet. Got a terrible headache.'

'Darling, what can we do?'

'Nothing for the moment. Just remember I love you and I'll find a way round this. But, Amy, we'll have to be more careful. If she can do this to me, she's capable of doing something equally nasty to you if she finds out it's you I'm in love with.'

'Not meet for a while you mean?'

'I have to see you. But we'll be more cautious, or one day she'll put two and two together and things will be impossible.'

Amy replaced the receiver and she was trembling. Her emotions were mixed. She felt guilt, and dismay, but mostly she felt anger, against her sister, and Harry, and herself for allowing this to happen. Yet, she thought, there was no way of stopping it.

She and Harry had been lovers for years. Since before he went into the R.A.F. They had quarrelled a lot, and it was after one of their fights that she had discovered she was pregnant with Freddy and gone back to tell him. He had been horrified. He didn't want to know anything about it. He had thrust some pound notes into her hand and told her to do what was necessary.

Later he had put a note through her door, with the address of someone who would 'help'. The next day she had left home and gone to live in Yorkshire. When she eventually returned, war had begun and Harry had married Prue. It was not long before she and Harry were lovers again and he had failed her once more.

She automatically got Margaret ready for school and helped Freddy with a last minute homework test. Then she opened the shop. Her first customer was Nelly, gleeful with some news to impart.

' 'eard, 'ave yer?' she said as she pushed open the door. 'Your sister's winders. Painted all over they was, all of them. What a laugh. Teach 'er to be so nosy.' She covered her mouth with an open hand like a child will, and said apologetically, 'Sorry, dearie; I know she's yer sister, but she does deserve it.'

'What happened?' Amy asked, going outside to have a look.

'Seems she woke this mornin' an' thought it was still the middle of the night. Then she found that someone 'ad gone there durin' the night an' painted black over every winder in the 'ouse. There was a message on the porch too, the paper-boy saw it. Nosy Old Bugger, it said, but she washed it off before she called the police.'

'What did Harry say?' Amy asked. She could admit she knew he had not been there. Then a thought struck her. Surely Harry hadn't –? No, of course not!

' 'Arry wasn't there, an' 'e 'asn't turned up. Off early she said, but she would, wouldn't she?' Nelly looked quizzically at Amy. 'Better be careful 'e 'ad. I've always thought she could be a nasty bit of work, that sister of yours.'

Amy looked at the crinkled face and the bright brown eyes. There was little that missed her notice, she thought, but fortunately she lacked the malice of Prue. She guessed she was being given a warning. 'Here you are, Nelly; I've found a couple of tins of pork sausages. Packed in fat they are. Have one. You'll enjoy them. No charge, they've been here for ages,' she smiled.

'Oo, ta ever so!'

'Nelly!' Amy added in exasperation. 'Stop that dog piddling on my floor!'

Amy went to find a cloth and some disinfectant to wipe up after the dogs and when she came back, Nelly was still standing on the steps.

'I can see my Mrs French comin',' she explained. 'Might just as well wait. She locks up tight when she goes out so I won't be able to get in and start me work.'

Mrs French was dressed in a black suit with a small red hat on her head. A red handbag swung on her arm and her shoes and gloves were black. Nelly thought it amazing that people went to so much trouble to dress up when they were only walking a few yards. But she admitted that her Mrs French was a lady and always looked the part.

'Take the key and make a start, would you, Nelly?' Mrs French said. 'I would like a word with Amy.'

Nelly took the key and, stuffing the tin of sausages into her shopping bag, gave Amy and Mrs French a cheery wave, went across the road and past the end of her lane to start her morning's work.

Amy stood waiting for Mrs French to speak, wondering what would happen next. She must ring Prue and commiserate with her, although she agreed with Nelly that the attack was well deserved, and did have its funny side. Prue was a gossip, which made it all the more surprising that she had not realised about Amy and Harry.

Mrs French was fumbling in her black handbag, and produced a black and white photograph. She hesitated, then showed it to Amy. 'It's a picture of my daughter, aged eight, the same age as your Margaret,' was all she said. Amy stared at the picture but said nothing.

'There is a remarkable resemblance, don't you think? It was Prue who pointed it out. So similar in appearance and colouring, and Margaret also happens to be muscially talented.' Amy glanced at the woman and saw a nervous tic in her pale cheek. She said nothing but continued to stare at the photograph in her hand.

'Freddy too?' Mrs French asked in her gentle, modulated voice.

You'd think she was asking about the weather, Amy thought. In answer to Mrs French's question she shook her head.

'This has been quite a morning,' she said at last, handing back the photograph. 'I wish I could go back to bed and start it all over again.'

Customers came and went, and still she and Mrs French held the silence on their explanations and questions. Where do I begin? Amy wondered. Her hands were clumsy, she fumbled as she opened paper bags, dropped things and spilt change, and caught her fingers in the till and she didn't know where to find things on her familiar shelves.

'Will you have a cup of tea?' she asked when there was a longer than usual lull in the stream of customers. 'I could do with one, couldn't you?'

She went into the store-room at the back, where a water-heater gave facilities for making tea. Her hands shook uncontrollably. This was a day for facing her past all right. Something she had lived with for years was about to come out in the open. Glancing at the calm, strained face of Mrs French standing in front of her wearing a black suit and a red hat, she felt vulnerable and quite alone. She handed a cup to the older woman, taking in the expression on her face and realising with some surprise that she was feeling the same. In her misery, she had avoided the idea that Mrs French was facing something pretty devastating too.

Discarding all the lies she had been preparing, all the outrage she had been about to portray instead, Amy said with honesty,

'You're right in what you think. Margaret is Richard's child. He was my lover for a while, but you were always his love. I hoped you would never notice how like him Margaret was becoming. I – I should have gone away.'

'It's obvious now, but I doubt if I would have noticed, without your sister having the pleasure of pointing it out.'

'It wasn't you who – no, that isn't in your nature.'

'Painted her windows? Not in my capabilities either; but you know, for the first time ever, I revelled in someone else's misfortune.'

The two women sat discussing their involvement with the same man as calmly as though they were talking about complete strangers. They spoke of him with affection, his kindness and consideration remembered, his gentlemanly standards, even in this, a retreat from those standards. Mrs French had already suffered the worst of the shock and dismay alone before she came. And Amy was almost relieved that the secret was out. It was becoming more and more difficult to hide as Margaret grew up.

'You'll still let Margaret come for music lessons?' Mrs

French asked. 'I won't do or say anything to suggest she is more than a very able pupil.'

'Of course.'

When Mrs French had gone, Amy locked the shop door for an hour and cried. She cried for Richard, and for Richard's wife. For Harry and herself, and the mess her life had once more become.

Then she bathed and put on one of her prettiest dresses, a tight-waisted floral print with a full, swinging skirt, and a low, square neckline. She made up her face and added a pair of her longest and most sparkling earrings with a matching necklace and she was ready to face whatever else the day held.

Prue was in a rage and she cleared through the wardrobe taking all the new clothes she had bought and threw them into a pile on the kitchen table. 'Waste of good money,' she muttered. 'Rubbish, most of it!' That it was expensive rubbish seemed worse. She went outside and, seeing Nelly wandering up the road towards Mrs French's back gate, she called impatiently. 'Here, you, come here a moment.'

Nelly walked towards her, her face breaking out into a wide grin as she glanced up at the windows with their covering of paint. 'Thought the blackout finished years ago!' She laughed her harsh laugh.

Prue went inside and came out with her arms full of the clothes, some with labels still attached. 'Take this lot. You could do with something decent. Show your daughter up disgracefully you do. Take them and tidy yourself up a bit.'

Nelly was affronted. She staggered back with the force of the clothes Prue thrust at her. 'What d'you mean, tidy meself up? What's it got to do with you, eh? Bleedin' cheek! 'Ere, take yer rubbish back and stick it up yer arse!' She threw the clothes at Prue and they spread themselves in a drunken heap over the hedge and the gate that Prue slammed shut. The house door slammed as well, and Nelly picked up a few clods of earth and pelted them at the door shouting more insults.

'What's going on here then?' Nelly turned and with a last clod in her hands, saw P.C. Harris walking towards her. 'She's a cheeky cow. That's what's wrong!' Defiantly she threw the missile and glared up at him. 'What's it to you?'

'Know anything about these windows?' he asked.

'Yeh. Someone painted 'em!'

'Any idea who?'

' 'Ow many people live in this village?'

P.C. Harris thought for a moment then said, 'About three hundred.'

'That's 'ow many could 'ave done it!' Nelly walked off with her nose in the air, leaving the constable hesitating about what to do about the clothes spread over the hedge. He stepped towards Prue's gate then changed his mind and walked away, after scribbling something in his notebook.

When Nelly finished her work for Mrs French, which she did in record time out of pure anger, she saw the clothes were still there, sprawled like fancy scarecrows across the hedge.

'Pity to waste 'em,' she muttered, and mouthing a few more insults at Prue's door, collected them over her arm and staggered home.

Evie was waiting for her and Nelly imagined the air bristling around her when she saw the expression on her daughter's face. ' 'Ello, Evie,' she said warily. 'Come fer a cuppa, 'ave yer?'

'I've had a visit from the police and a phone call from Mrs Beynon.'

'Fancy. Tell yer about the thoughtful person 'oo painted 'er winders, did she? Public spirited I calls that, nosy old cow that she is.'

'She said you insulted her and threw stones at her house.'

Nelly shook her head sadly. 'Mistake that was. I threw 'em at 'er door. Should 'ave opened up a few winders for 'er, shouldn't I?'

'Mother, I've been to see the doctor and he's coming to see you with some people from the welfare. Timothy and I will be taking steps to have you taken away from this place and put where you will be safe from any more trouble.'

Nelly stared at her daughter for a long time. 'Ow did I manage to 'ave a daughter like you?' she said sadly. Without another word she pushed the door wider and went inside. She began to revive the fire and once it was brighter, she swivelled the kettle over onto the heat and when she went outside again, Evie had gone.

Chapter Thirteen

Alan was sleeping. His sleep was far from peaceful; he struggled against unseen enemies, and cried out and panted as if unable to find enough air to breathe. He was living again the horror of that night when he was buried alive in the building where he and five others were standing, watching for the approach of the enemy.

The night had been full of noise; gun-fire, the distant sounds of traffic and bombs too, but none near them. The town in which they were situated was placed at the junction of two main roads, and it was Alan's job to report any movement along it.

They were all tired, and too jumpy to sleep. Knowing the war must end soon made them irritated to be holed up miles from the rest of the battalion, guarding a completely empty and demolished town. There were only rats, cats and a couple of dogs to keep them company, they had not seen any other human beings for a week.

But Alan was alert and watchful. He knew the importance of their task, understood that his neglect could cost the lives of others. His eyes ceaselessly swept the horizon, barely visible, and every shape became familiar to him. Again and again they moved around his view, every shadow memorised. He was ready to warn the rest if anything changed and revealed a movement of any kind.

When the time came to change guard, Alan went down thankfully into the cellars of the once grand building to try and sleep. It must have been at the precise moment when he ceased to watch and before the other began that the tank rolled into view and fired. The misfortunes of war, he remembered thinking.

The bombardment began without more than a flash of the huge gun to warn them. The cry of the guards was lost in the explosions and the tumbling bricks and stone. Alan's mind, as everything became black, was full of anger with himself. He knew he should have killed those dogs. Anyone seeing them walk to the front porch and wag their tails expectantly, would know there was someone there. Alan knew he had failed his men.

When they found him he was unconscious and his right arm was shattered. His face was covered in dirt-encrusted blood and he could not see. When the medical orderly cleaned his face, the sight returned and Alan looked up to see walls falling on him again and again.

The dream was always the same. He saw the walls bending, cracking and falling, he heard the rumble as the building roared its final agony and the sound invaded his brain, became louder and louder as he tried to escape from it. He felt the agony of his torn face, and the wrench of his arm behind pulled from its socket and the snapping of his bones, and he blacked out.

Each time he woke from the nightmare and the panic had faded, he felt the same disappointment, that he had lived it again, and again failed to act fast enough to avoid it.

He had not been able to sleep easily in a house since. During the week while he was at work, he spent the nights between Monday and Friday in a chair, sitting beside an open window, dozing fitfully, afraid to sleep and wake others with his horrors. On Friday evening he had always come to the woods above his old home and slept under the stars, or in the half-open kitchens in the castle ruin. He could relax and know he would disturb no one. Since Fay and Johnny waiting for him that night, he had avoided the castle and found instead a sheep fold, where an old tarpaulin across the corner gave him all the protection from the weather he needed.

Now, in the sheep-fold on the Welsh hills, far from the

destroyed house in Germany, he opened his eyes. Then he jerked upright, leapt to his feet, prepared to run. Sitting opposite him was Fay.

'You know you've spoilt things now you've found me,' he said bitterly. 'Now I'll have to break the connection, and it's all I have.' He turned and glared at her. 'Can't you understand –' He stopped. How could she? How would he explain that everyone had to have a reason for staying somewhere. There had to be something, however small, that made this place or that place better than anywhere else.

For him, it was the memories of a happy childhood. He relived the days which, looking back, seemed to be filled with sunshine and blue skies. When he was away from here, he could dream of coming home and belonging. If this was forbidden to him, where else could he go? No home, and not even the dream of one, there would be nothing for him, anywhere.

'Come home, Alan. Come with me now and see your mother.'

'No. Best she thinks I'm dead. The years have softened the pain and I'd only bring her more.'

'She would rather you alive, no matter what pain you give her. Your father died six years ago and your sister Rosemary lives in Cardiff. She's very lonely.'

'What about me?' he shouted. Then more quietly, 'She's better off not knowing. I stopped being Alan French years ago. I took a new name, and invented a past to prevent anyone knowing I had survived. Mother is happier accepting my death.'

'How can you say that? How can you decide for her?'

'I have tried you know – tried to go back. On the day of the Coronation party – I did intend talking to you, but I lost my nerve.'

'So that bunch of flowers in red, white and blue, it was a message?'

'There was too much to explain. So much had happened things I don't understand myself. And if I did come back

I would have to alter everything in my life. I don't think I can ever face that. All the upheaval.'

'You'd have people who love you to help. You'd be coming home, Alan.'

He crouched and prepared to run and Fay gently touched his arm.

'There's too much to tell. Too much to explain.'

'Try,' she pleaded. 'To begin is the hardest part.'

'If I'd come back when I escaped from that hospital – I was in there for two years you know. If I'd tried then, there wouldn't have been much to tell. But now – it's hopeless.'

'But don't you see,' Fay coaxed, 'that if you wait a few more years, you'll know that now would have been possible. Time passes and you're getting nowhere.' She put a hand on his face, moved to kiss him, and he jumped up and tried to run. He was immensely strong. She held on to him and he rained blows on her hands, trying to break her grip. She kept saying, 'Alan, Alan, Alan,' loudly, then more quietly as he calmed again until the name was no more than a whisper.

'I told them I didn't remember who I was, you know.'

'But you do know. You're Alan French and your mother lives less than half an hour from here. Come back, Alan.'

'You haven't told her?'

'I tried,' she admitted, 'but she wouldn't believe me.'

'Promise me you won't tell her.'

'No, I won't promise that. If you won't go home, come back with me. I live –'

'I know where you live. You married Johnny Cartwright.'

'Johnny knows you're alive, at least he believed me when I said I'd seen you.'

'I know. I saw him the night you were waiting for me.'

'You came?'

'I came. That's why I had to find somewhere else. I don't want to make changes. I'm so tired. It's so much effort to re-plan.'

'Nelly knows too.'

For the first time he smiled. 'Yes. Nelly knows. But sh

won't try and interfere. She'll leave me to live the way I've chosen.'

'Come and see her. Talk to us, then the first steps will have been taken,' Fay pleaded.

'I have to go now. I usually walk through the fields around the town to where I live. It passes the day.'

'At least tell me where I can reach you. Please, Alan, don't just walk away.'

'It's best.' He stared at her and she tried to see past the distortion of his scar and the confused and unhappy frown to the young man she had loved.

'Selfish now aren't you? You never used to be. Your mother has no one. She needs you.'

'It's best I leave things as they are.'

She watched as he picked up his brown coat, snatched it away when she tried to help him, and tied the belt tightly around his small waist. He looked small and unable to cope. She was bursting with the longing to help him, but knew that this time at least, she could not.

'Perhaps there'll come a time when I can tell you, but don't try to find me. If you do I'll have to start all over again. Leave everything and start all over again.' He looked at her intently, willing her to understand. 'Don't do that to me, Fay.'

'All right.' She leaned forward and this time he allowed her to kiss him, a mere touch; strangers with a secret.

'Leave a message if you want anything,' she said.

'Goodbye.' He turned, raised his left hand in a casual wave and walked swiftly away, the limp barely noticeable. Fay wondered how much pain even that simple pride cost him.

As soon as he was out of her sight, Alan slowed his pace to ease the pain in his hip. It had been crushed when the building collapsed and walking was painful still. Fay's pleading echoed in his mind. Could he go back? Tears glistened as he dreamed of waking in his own room, with his mother bringing in a cup of tea. For a while he leaned against a tree and wallowed in the joy of it. But it was no more than wishful thinking.

How could he begin to explain? If he could just walk in and

sit down and have his mother accept his presence there as normal he would go back now. But she would expect to be told all of what had happened to him. For without being told, how could she begin to understand?

His thoughts were all of his mother. Fay had no part of his life any more. Only his mother would be able to accept him without conditions and promises. But was Fay his *way* back? If she could persuade his mother to meet him and not question him –? He began to walk again, thinking of the possibilities, a new lightness in his eyes.

He was parallel to the main road, and below him but out of sight, traffic moved at intervals. A lorry changed gear as it climbed the hill and then rumbled at a faster rate down an incline. The sound was loud and grew to a roar and Alan was back again in the house with the bricks falling and filling his brain with noise and terror and guilt. He staggered to rest on a stone wall, his hands stifling the screams. How could he *ever* go back?

Fay sank to the ground and sat for a long time, staring after him and wondering what she should do. His mothe ought to be told, but was it Fay's responsibility to tell her? And would Mrs French believe her? She needed someone to talk to. Not Johnny. He was understanding and kind, bu he couldn't help her in this. That was hoping for too much

She strolled back home and slipped into the still quie house and made a cup of tea. The stairs creaked and Johnny came and sat beside her.

'Did you find him?' he asked, staring at her, demandin the truth. When she gave an almost imperceptible nod, h added more quietly. 'What shall we do now, love?'

Fay looked at him, at the quiet strength of him and wa grateful for the 'we'.

'Nothing until he's ready to face us,' she said, taking hi hand. 'Then we'll do whatever he wants.'

Since Prue had threatened Harry with exposure over hi illegal dealings, Amy and Harry had not met. Regular con versations on the phone were their only contacts, but eac felt the need to talk, to meet, and touch, and be reassured of the other's love. When Freddy and Margaret wanted to go to the pictures in town, Amy realised it was their opportunity.

'Can Oliver come with us as well?' Margaret asked. 'He wants to see it as well. Loves cowboy films he does.'

'I'll ask his mother,' Amy promised. 'Mr Chartridge will probably take you into town and I'll meet you to come home.'

There was an outburst of protest at her words.

'Mam, going in on the bus and finding our own way home is part of the fun!' Margaret insisted.

'If she isn't, I certainly am!' Freddy said. 'I've been dozens of times on my own to town. Go on, Mam, don't be a spoil-sport.'

'I'll ask what Oliver's parents think, and I'll see,' Amy said.

'Good!' Margaret danced around the small living room. 'When Mam says she'll see, it always means yes!'

'I meant I'll *see*.' Amy laughed. 'Nothing more!'

Running the village shop meant that Amy had allowed her children more responsibility and at an earlier age than most. Freddy had been forced to grow up quickly as he had to assist his mother and become the man of the house while still a child. He had often been sent into town on errands for Amy and accepted the early adulthood easily.

Margaret had remained more of a child. Partly because Amy clung to her childhood, not wanting to waste the precious years as she felt she had with Freddy, and partly because Margaret herself was less mature than her brother.

But even Margaret had to go into town without her sometime soon. The alternative, as Freddy was quick to point out, was them spending most of their time in the room above the shop, and not going to any of the places other children went.

Amy agreed to their going and after a discussion with them and with Evie, persuaded them that Wednesday was the best day for their jaunt. She gave them extra money for a snack in town to add to the adventure.

Once it was arranged, Amy rang Harry.

'Meet me at the house,' he said. 'The workmen have almost finished. I'll make sure we aren't interrupted.'

'I'll go via town as before,' Amy said. 'No point taking any chances. If anyone from the village is on the bus, I'll go to The Drovers.'

Wednesday was hot. Few people came into the shop and Amy thankfully tidied the cheese board and the bacon away before one o'clock and was able to get away as one o'clock chimed on her mantelpiece clock. She caught the bus and with no one she knew on it she alighted at the lane leading to the newly repaired house.

The day was perfect, the trees barely moving in the still, sunny countryside. Birds sang and added music to the air. Harry was standing in the doorway, his arms open for her. She dreamed of this as a preview to many future days.

She was thankful of the coolness of the house after the stuffiness of the bus and the pressing heat of the sun as she had walked up the lane and along the driveway. In fact she shivered in the sudden chill of the long-empty building.

The lounge was at the back of the house, overlooking a wilderness that would one day be a garden. There were french windows opening out onto a small paved area. But it faced north and even on such a warm day the room was cool. It was a surprise and a pleasure to see a fire burning palely in the grate. Harry had gathered some discarded pieces of wood from the new skirting boards and the replaced windows and lit it to warm the cold walls.

A blanket had been brought from the car and laid across the hearth and they sat on it and ate the simple picnic Harry had brought, and pretended that their lives held no problems. That the future did not mean secret meetings and lies but an open relationship that was perfect, with everyone happy, no one hurt. Then the fire went out, storm clouds darkened the room, rain began to fall and they had to go back to the real world and its problems.

They had intended to each make their way home separately. Amy going into town, then, after a few items of shopping, back again on the bus, but it was raining heavily

Thunder and lightning snarled across the sky and Amy was worried about Margaret and Freddy.

'I'll drive you,' Harry said. 'No one will see us in this. We'll pick up the kids from the bus stop.' He looked at the thin, summer dress she wore. 'You can't stand waiting for a bus in that. It isn't much of a chance; come on.' He ran to open the van door and she got in. He drove to town and saw the children easily, huddled in a corner, at the bus stop.

Oliver was thrilled with the added excitement of riding home in the van. The two younger ones chatted happily, telling Amy and Harry of the film they had seen, and the icecream they had bought and eaten, standing in the rain.

Harry stopped first at Oliver's house and waited as he ran in, then drove a little further to the shop and helped Amy and Freddy and Margaret out. He held Amy's hand a moment, and whispered, 'I love you, Amy,' then he went home, to Prue and his other life.

In the shop the following day, Nelly was listening to Oliver telling of his adventures. 'Pelting down it was, Gran, I'm sure the rain was bouncing back up as fast as it usually comes down! Then Mr Beynon and Mrs Prichard came past in a van and we all climbed into the back and had a ride home. You'd have enjoyed it too, Gran.'

Prue was in the shop and she exchanged a glance with her sister. Amy guessed that Harry had not mentioned the lift home. She smiled brightly at Prue. 'I think they enjoyed the ride in the old van more than the films they saw! Just like kids. Buy them a beautiful present and they play with the box.'

'I didn't know Harry gave you a lift as well, Amy,' Prue said. 'I thought the children went on their own.'

'We did, we did,' Oliver said excitedly.

Nelly smiled at the way he chatted so easily. So different from the shy boy he had been when he arrived. He'll soon be a real chatterbox, she thought fondly. Because she was concentrating on the way Oliver was telling about his adventure, she was not really listening to the other conversations. When she did, she heard alarm bells ringing.

'Where did you meet Harry then?' Prue asked.

'He drove past me as I was running for the bus. It was pelting with rain. He stopped and gave me a lift and when I told him about the kids being in town, he went to find them too. Good like that, your Harry. Near Boots, it was I think,' Amy added to make the lie more convincing.

'But Harry was in Cardiff. How could he be passing Boots?'

Amy shrugged. 'I don't know. I didn't ask him where he'd been. Too glad to see him I was.'

'Harry wouldn't let her walk in all that rain, them bein' related an' all,' Nelly said. 'Only natural, 'im givin' 'er a lift, ain't it? What's to wonder about that, eh? Nothin' odd about Harry givin' 'is sister-in-law a lift that I can see.' Nelly felt the air crackle and she knew she had said too much. She had over-explained, and revealed the fact that an explanation was necessary.

She smiled at Prue nervously, and avoided looking at Amy as she sidled out of the shop. 'See yer tomorrow,' she said to Oliver. 'Glad you 'ad a good time, dearie.' She blew out her breath in a long sigh of pent-up dismay when she stepped outside the shop. She didn't quite know how, but she had made things worse for Amy and Harry, whose secret she had kept for months.

Prue waited until the shop was empty, then asked slowly, 'How long, Amy? How long have you and my husband been lovers?'

Amy laughed and tried to bluff, but saw it was useless.

'Talk to Harry,' she said.

'How long?'

'I – I can't say. You'll have to talk to Harry,' Amy said more firmly.

'I think you had better come to the house this evening. We have to discuss this, all of us.'

'I can't. I don't want the children involved in this.'

'You should have thought of them before embarking on this sordid affair.' Prue glared, her eyes slightly reddened with incipient tears. 'But then, you never did think before you acted, did you, Amy?'

Amy watched her go, wondering what would happen next. Would Harry stand by all he had promised her? Now the secret was out, there was no need to delay. They could arrange a divorce and start their long awaited life together. The thought gave her less than the joy she had dreamed of, behind it all was the memory of the times when Harry had backed away from the final commitment, and had chosen to leave her.

Prue's eyes were bright as she walked, head down, across the road and home. Her mouth was trembling as she asked herself, why? What had she done to force Harry to find someone else? And suddenly it was Amy's fault.

Amy had always been – *loose*. She had come back from Yorkshire with Freddy, a little boy who she said was adopted. Amy, who had to have a man, even if he belonged to someone else. Freddy's father was probably a married man; that was why she had been forced to lie about him. Amy was responsible. Amy had stolen Harry from her own sister. Prue managed to close her door and lock it, before beginning to cry.

For the rest of the day and the whole of Friday, Prue said nothing. Harry and Amy were on edge, waiting to hear what she would say, wondering what she would do, but nothing happened. Amy waited for Harry to say or do something, but Harry could not bring himself to open the dreaded discussion. He believed Prue capable of sending him to prison, so he waited and said nothing. He went home as usual, and as usual his meal was produced and placed before him without a word. He spent his evenings in his office, and went to bed in the spare room and nothing was said.

Prue was trying to decide on the best way to punish them. She did not want Harry to go to prison. If he had understood her better, he would have known she would not be able to face the shame. No, better think of a private punishment. On Saturday morning, it came to her.

'I won't be coming any more on Saturdays, Auntie

Prue,' Freddy told her. 'I'm starting work for Uncle Harry.'

'Perhaps you are, perhaps you aren't,' Prue said.

The boy looked startled. 'Why?' he asked. 'Something wrong?'

'There might be. If I'm displeased with you, you won't start. There are plenty of young boys only too anxious to get the job.'

'But I want it. Uncle Harry promised me –' Freddy looked at her and frowned. 'What is it, Auntie Prue? Haven't upset you, have I? Left something not properly done?'

'There's a curtain rail I want fixing in the spare bedroom.' She went to the stairs, and kicking off his heavy, mud-caked shoes, Freddy followed.

'Sure, I'll do that for you. Uncle Harry showed me once how to fix screws in the wall and –' He stopped, puzzled when Prue closed the door and began to un-button her dress.

The buttons went from the neck to the hem and underneath she was wearing a slip, and a bra, in pink satin. Slipping the straps from her shoulders she wriggled and allowed them to fall. The French knickers bought to please Harry, needed only the opening of a button and they too joined the rest of her clothes.

Shock registered on Freddy's face and he did not move. Prue saw sweat burst out on his face, the blue eyes widen and show a large amount of white. She tried to smile but there was a throb in her cheek as a nervous tic developed. Then Freddy smiled too and she knew it was going to be all right.

She opened her arms to him and he stepped towards her with a gasp. Speechless, he began to groan his pleasure and the sound was enough for Prue. Inexpert as she was, and clumsy in her attempts to give him what he wanted, to the completely innocent boy, her movements were electric. He was ready for her, wanting her, desiring her and making her feel like a woman again. Wrapped in the pleasure of it she forgot for a moment who he was and what she was doing.

Afterwards, she sat on the side of the bed and watched Freddy dress. He stood facing away from her confused and alarmed by what had happened. He bent down, hunching his broad shoulders, and she watched with guilty pleasure as the muscles in his strong thighs moved. His buttocks were small and the only part that made him seem younger than the man he was.

She was confused as she sat, wrapped in a dressing gown, modesty quickly returning, and waiting for Freddy to fix his jacket. She hadn't thought it through; what should she say? They both waited for the other to speak. Slowly he raised his eyes to her face. 'Auntie Prue –' he began painfully. Compassion came then and she stood and hugged him, stroked his hair.

This time he did not hold her like a lover, but hid his head low on her shoulder. She patted his broad back and whispered, 'Next Saturday, as usual, Freddy?'

He kissed her awkwardly and stumbled from the room. Outside the house, he ran, past his house, on along the road leading to town, until he couldn't take another step; then he sat at the side of the road for a long time just watching the traffic. Being young, it was hunger that finally persuaded him to go home.

Prue washed her body in the bathroom, puritanical disgust returning. She re-made the bed on which Harry usually slept but did not change the sheets. Part of the revenge was using Harry's bed for the seduction of his mistress's son. She lay on her own bed and slept.

Prue woke with a wonderful feeling of well-being, and her resolution that it would be the first and last time faded. Her longing for Freddy's loving increased as the days went by and Saturday seemed a long time coming. She watched from the window anxiously, afraid he would not arrive, but he came, and after a wave towards the window where she stood, he began his work. With hands that shook slightly, she began setting out the cups for his coffee break.

Chapter Fourteen

Nelly was playing some of her Donald Peers records when the dogs barked and warned her there was someone coming. She went up the path to greet Phil Davies, who waved a letter at her, and slipped on wet leaves and fell heavily on the rough, stone edge of the ash path. Phil dropped his bag and ran to help her up. She groaned a bit and complained of a bruised hip.

'Seems to give out now and then,' she said, as he helped her to the old wooden chair beside her door. 'Don't tell Evie that, though.'

'Not a word,' he said. 'Make you a cup of tea, shall I?'

'Yes, and bring out the cakes I got coolin' why don't yer?'

When they were settled with their drinks and the plate full of cakes, Phil passed on all the news. He rubbed his nose and hesitated before saying, 'Shouldn't say this of course, but – Johnny and Fay seem to be having a few problems. She's out walking all hours she is. I see her, getting up for work early like I do. She isn't meeting someone is she?'

'Not without Johnny knowin' about it!' Nelly snapped. 'An' I don't want you sayin' nothin' different, Phil Davies!'

'I only thought, seeing her walking about the fields last thing at night and early in the mornings like, that she must have been having rows or something. Not right, is it, for them to have to share with Johnny's family. Can't have a good row and finish with it.'

'They don't need no rows,' Nelly insisted. 'But she ain't

got enough to do even if she does work all the hours Gawd sends. Used to 'avin' an 'ouse to see to, Fay is. Finds it 'ard to sit an' do nothin' so she walks. And that's all!'

'Yes, like I said, it's living in that house with Netta and all the rest. Not right for a young couple.'

'Where did you and Catrin start then, Buckin'am Palace was it?'

'Mam's front room,' he laughed. 'Still, Fay's a bit above that now, isn't she?'

'Fay an' Johnny is all right.'

'Yes indeed. Can I have another cake then?' He took a third cake and rubbed his nose again and leaned forward.

'Funny about your Freddy; saw him coming out of Prue Beynon's on Saturday doing his boots up, he was in such a hurry to get away. Had the worst of her tongue I bet. Wouldn't like to work for that one.'

They were still sitting there when Oliver arrived.

'Heck,' Phil said, looking at his watch and taking another cake. 'Late I am. That Prue Beynon will have something to say about you and me, Nelly!' He tousled Oliver's straight hair and added, 'I've left a few cakes for you, don't worry boy.' He assured himself that Nelly was all right and climbed on his bike and set off to complete his round.

'What's the matter, Gran?' Oliver asked, hearing the enquiries from Phil.

'Nothin' to worry about. I slipped, that's all. Want a game of darts do yer?' She stood up, hiding the fact that her hip was painful, and went to fetch the darts and the board.

Finishing the cakes between throws, they played a game of three hundred and one and Nelly was lagging behind. As she threw each dart, Oliver called out how many she needed, and advised her on the double to aim for. Neither of them saw Timothy watching from the top of the path. Oliver won and they started another game. 'A short one,' Nelly pleaded, 'me leg's a bit tired.'

'Double seventeen, that's thirty-four, plus three, that's thirty-seven, and double three makes forty-three. Take forty three from seventy-four and that leaves you with thirty-one to get, Gran. Are you tired; you threw them all at the bottom of the board.'

'No I ain't,' Nelly said, glaring at him. 'An' you ain't gettin' out of this game that easy, young Ollie. I'm not beat yet!'

Oliver laughed and threw two darts.

'Good boy, Ollie. You only want a double three to win. Think you'll do it with the next dart?'

Timothy called then and Oliver threw the dart into the door, close to the three he wanted.

'Won't be a minute,' Nelly said, aiming her first dart. 'What's left fer me to get, Ollie?'

Oliver looked nervous. He shook his head. 'I'm not sure, Gran. I can't remember. You work it out.'

'Needs a double eleven, I do.' She turned to Timothy who was watching the board. 'Go on in an' make a cuppa tea, why don't yer?'

'Good idea.' Timothy disappeared into the cottage and Nelly and Oliver finished their game. 'Who won?' Timothy asked when he came out with the re-filled teapot.

' 'E did! I taught 'im the game an' now I 'aven't won a game fer weeks!'

'Your mother wants you to go shopping with her, Oliver, she's buying you some new sandals.'

'Goody!' He put out his hand for his father to take but Timothy said, 'You go on, son, I'll follow in a few minutes; your mother's waiting for you.'

When Oliver had gone, Timothy said, 'You're doing a remarkable job on Oliver, mother-in-law.'

'Go on, I only showed 'im 'ow to play darts.'

'And work out betting slips.'

'Oh Gawd. Evie knows, does she?'

'He still doesn't do very well at school. Strange isn't it? He isn't willing to write things down. Spelling terrifies him and he is so untidy because he's nervous. Arithmetic too; he shuts off when he's asked a question, but there's nothing wrong with his brain.'

'If 'e was a bit slow to start, there'd 'ave bin a lot of teasin'. Ollie's quiet too, an' they gets overlooked if the teacher ain't on the ball. Evie was like that, shy, certain she'd fail an' look stupid. 'Ates lookin' stupid, my Evie.'

'I think I've pressured him too much, to be honest,' Timothy admitted.

'Yes you 'ave!' Nelly was emphatic. 'An' Evie too. *No* doubt.'

'You would have made a good teacher, mother-in-law.'

Nelly laughed her loud laugh. 'Go on with yer! Me? Just think what they'd learn from me that would upset their mothers!'

Later that day, Oliver returned and to his delight, arrived at the same time as the tramp, who was carrying three small trout.

'What a surprise,' Nelly shouted, waving from her chair near the door. She didn't get up and Oliver asked if her leg was hurting. She shook her head and forced herself to rise.

'I wondered if you would like to go on a picnic,' the tramp said, and Oliver's eyes lit up. 'A real one, with a fire, and fish to cook on it, and a pot of tea without milk but tasting of the fire and the wood.'

They chose a spot near the stream and George showed Oliver how to wrap the fish in mud and wet newspaper, then place it on the fire to cook. Once everything was underway, Oliver and the dogs played among the trees in the warm sunshine while Nelly and George talked. Nelly's hip was aching but she tried not to show how thankful she was to find a comfortable place against a tree on a moss-covered bank, or how anxious she was about getting back up.

'There won't be nothin' like this when I go an' live with Evie,' she said, sipping the tea George handed her.

'Then don't go.'

'Seems I'll 'ave to. I ain't got one good argument left, an' the doctor's on Evie's side now. They say they'll "take steps".'

'You can't be forced to leave your home if you don't

want to, no matter what "steps" they take.'

Nelly chuckled. 'Pity I'm not a bit younger, I'd run away with you, George. That'd be a laugh, wouldn't it? Me, runnin' away from me own daughter!'

'No, Nelly; don't run away. Here is where you belong.' There was a gleam in his eyes and he rubbed his beard thoughtfully.

'Why did you run away, George?' Nelly waited, but he did not answer immediately and she regretted the question. 'Sorry. I'm a nosy parker. Shouldn't 'ave asked.'

'I don't mind telling you, but it sounds such a weak story. I was unable to cope with a problem that thousands have to face.' He smiled at her, reassuring her he did not object to her curiosity. 'I was married and I worked as a book-keeper in a small wholesalers. We lived in a flat near a small park. It was very pleasant. It was a simple life, but I asked for nothing more than to spend my life in the same way.'

'What went wrong?' Nelly coaxed.

'I was in the army for a couple of years, until I was wounded and invalided out. I went home, started work again, then, the flat was bombed and my wife was killed.'

'Oo, George, 'ow awful. My Norman was took sudden too, but 'e was took by a bus.'

'But you coped. I couldn't think straight after her death and I had no incentive to start again.'

'I 'ad Evie to care for. I was lucky.'

'Things got more and more muddled. I forgot to pay my rent then found I didn't have enough to settle the debt, and was evicted. I began sleeping rough then, as I was untidy in my apperarance and my work, I lost my job.'

'Smart an' clever chap like you could 'ave got another one?'

'I decided to walk to Cardiff and stay with a cousin until I'd sorted myself out but when I reached Cardiff, my cousin had moved. By then, sleeping out and wandering had become a way of life.'

Nelly shuddered. 'Sleepin' out an' belongin' nowhere sounds a lot worse than my life.' Then she laughed, 'but a bloomin' sight better than livin' with Evie!' She frowned at him, her head on one side as she asked, ' 'Ere, where was you wounded then?'

The tramp chuckled. 'I don't think I've known you long enough to show you my scars!'

'Don't worry, I've seen all I want to of you. Seen you bathin' in the stream, same place I use when it's very 'ot, so you ain't got many secrets!'

'Nelly!'

'Well, I expect you've watched me an' all. 'Ow else would you know the best place to bathe?' They both laughed and then, catching sight of the panting dogs and the equally hot Oliver, called to say the meal was ready.

When Oliver had been taken home, with George staying well out of sight, Nelly and George walked back home through the trees.

'Nelly, don't leave here.'

Nelly became upset. The day had been perfect, except for her injured leg. The company of both Oliver and George, the friendliness of Phil and all the others in the village, whom she called her friends.

'I'm afraid they'll win,' she said, wiping a tear from her fat cheek defiantly. 'They say I'm a drunk, an' in need of protection or somethin'. I want to argue with 'em but I don't know 'ow. I don't know the words.'

'I have an idea.' George stopped, then shook his head. 'No, I couldn't suggest it. But, it would serve them right.'

'Go on, George. Tell me.'

'All right. First you must go there and tell them they are right, that you will sell up everything and live there with them as they ask.'

'What?' Nelly put her hands on her hips and glared at him, convinced he had gone crazy. 'But I thought you said –'

The tramp laughed, his teeth white in the fading light. 'Wait 'til you hear the rest of my idea. They must give you time, say seven or eight weeks. You'll think of a reason, your garden perhaps, and selling the young chickens for the best price.'

As he continued to tell her his idea, Nelly's brown eyes grew wider and wider. When he finished, she roared with laughter. 'If that ain't justice,' she said. 'If that ain't justice.'

They went back to the house and revived the fire and sat talking and perfecting their plans.

'Nelly, be careful on that leg for a few days.'

'I never thought you'd noticed me limpin',' she smiled. 'S'nice to have someone 'oo cares.'

'Oh, I care.'

They sat for a long time, listening to records of Winifred Atwell and Donald Peers, smiling at the pleasure the day had brought. Darkness fell and Nelly lit a candle to light her way upstairs to bed, smiling contentedly.

Timothy and Oliver had been into Llangwyn to the library. Oliver was sitting in the back of his father's car, turning the pages of the book he had chosen, and through the mirror, Timothy saw him mouthing the words occasionally as he picked out those he knew.

He had been tempted to criticise the book his son had chosen, seeing it was mostly pictures, but had changed his mind. Better he enjoyed a simple book than avoided opening the covers of one more suitable for his age. He had been reminded of that by Nelly.

He parked the car and, talking to Oliver about what he had learnt from the story in his book, went into the kitchen. Evie was preparing lunch and when Oliver had gone up to his room, Timothy said, 'Nelly has had quite a lot of success with Oliver, you know. Did you realise she was helping him with his work? I didn't, until one of my teachers pointed it out.'

'Nonsense.' Evie looked outraged at the thought. 'You believe my mother – and I'd prefer you not to call her Nelly – you think *she* has succeeded in helping him to read and master arithmetic? I've spent *hours* with him, with books and without, encouraging him to read. Coaxing him, urging him to make the necessary effort. Hours!'

'We pressured him. Both of us, for different reasons. Me because of pride I suppose. I was a teacher so I had to have an above average child. You, because you were afraid he would be a poor achiever, like your mother.'

He could see she was angry. Besides the voice, which became louder, her actions increased in speed as she threw the cutlery onto the table and pushed it into place beside the plates. He was tempted not to go on, but knew that for Oliver's sake he must.

'She's helping him more than you or I could.' He put a hand on her shoulder. 'Evelyn, surely that's the important thing?'

'My mother was a poor achiever as you put it, but worse than that, she has never wanted to better herself. My father couldn't read or write. He was a casual worker who travelled the roads finding work where he could, coming home when he happened to be in the area! Of course I'm afraid. But this is rubbish. What could my mother know about helping a slow pupil? And what books does she use? I've never seen any books in her cottage except those stupid romances she gets from the library van.'

Timothy hesitated before answering, wanting to walk away and not say the words, then he said slowly, and with apparent calm, 'She uses comics, newspapers and simple stories about things he knows and understands, like the wild creatures they watch, and the chickens Oliver has seen grow from day-old chicks. And –' the final hesitation – 'and, the arithmetic comes into games they play, especially darts, and some things he's learnt from working out her betting slips.'

'Timothy!' Evie gasped. 'You can't be serious! The influence of such talk –'

Timothy turned her to face him. 'If you want Oliver to succeed, say nothing about this. Promise me. She's made reading and the rest have some relevance. To read and work out simple sums because Nelly needs his help, has made him want to learn. She's a clever old woman, whatever you think of her.'

Evie's lips tightened. 'I'll promise not to say anything about this – for a while – as long as you promise not to go back on your agreement to have her living here.'

'Evelyn, she's so happy where she is.'

'She came here this morning while you were out and she has agreed to come.'

'What did you say to persuade her? What did you threaten her with?'

'She came and said she would come to live here, she would give up her cottage and come.'

'But why?'

'She wanted a little time, about six or seven weeks, she said, to get rid of her furniture and find homes for her hens.'

'I think we're wrong to make her come.'

'She's leaving that cottage! I can't risk her going into town again and being seen staggering home with a tramp! You promise, Timothy?'

Timothy sighed. 'I'll support you as she has agreed to come, but I don't like it. And, she gave in too willingly, unless you threatened her?'

'I didn't.'

'Then perhaps she's up to something.'

Amy laughed as Victor Honeyman left the shop, carrying the last of the empty boxes he was collecting. Since they had danced together at the Coronation party, he had been more friendly, and, she suspected, would like to make the friendship grow into something more. Seeing Prue walking past, on the other side of the road, her laughter at one of Victor's silly jokes became louder, and her attitude to him, more hearty and warm.

As he was about to climb into the cab of his lorry, he changed his mind and came back to her.

'Fancy a drink, do you? Tonight? We could go into Swansea if you like, have a bit of a night out.' He winked and she shuddered inwardly. He smelt slightly of sweat and his teeth were stained with the cigarettes he constantly smoked.

'Sorry, I can't,' she smiled, ashamed at the way she had

led him on. 'It's difficult to get a baby minder for my seventeen kids,' she joked.

He shrugged away his disappointment. 'Another time, say?'

'Perhaps,' she said. She watched as he drove through the village, past the church and the school and out of sight around a bend in the road. She saw Prue, who was unable to resist a glance back to see her and she waved defiantly at the disappearing lorry.

Prue no longer shopped at Amy's store. She had sent a message with Freddy, asking for her ration books to be returned, and Amy had seen the grocer's van from Llangwyn calling each Thursday with a box of groceries for her sister. Best really, she decided. It was difficult to talk to Prue after what had happened.

She had not seen very much of Harry either, although they continued to meet each Wednesday afternoon in the almost completed house. On impulse, she rang him at his office and as usual, just hearing his voice made her long to see him and feel him holding her close.

'Harry, it's me; can you talk?' she asked.

'Amy, love. Yes, there's no one here. Nothing wrong, is there?'

'I've just seen my stony-faced sister but no, nothing's wrong, except I want to see you.'

'Prue's been very good over all this, Amy.'

Something in his voice chilled her. 'Harry, are we finished?'

'No! Meet me at The Drovers tonight, we have to make some plans.'

Relieved, Amy agreed.

Harry was waiting for her in their usual place; he stood as she entered the room and went to the bar in the next room to get her a drink. She sat there waiting for him to return, uneasy, remembering the tone of his voice when he had said, 'Prue has been very good over all this,' and wondering what he was going to say.

He seemed longer than usual getting the drink and she

felt her worry turn to anger. He had brought her here to tell her it was all over. She knew it. His face, when she had arrived showed none of the usual welcome. She stood, almost deciding to leave, now, before he came back and used the words that would destroy her, but at that moment, Harry returned.

This time he welcomed her properly. There was no one else in the small room, most people preferring the activity of the larger room with its dart board, bar skittles and the roaring fire in the big fireplace. He put down the drink and opened his arms to her.

'Amy, Amy love. It's been so long,' he said, 'I need you so much.'

They sat close together on one of the uncomfortable Welsh settles that was the only alternative to separate chairs, struggled with the sliding cushions to give them the least painful position, and talked. Mostly foolish talk at first, then gradually they began to discuss their plans.

'I've searched for the books, but Prue has hidden them well. There's only one place they can be and that is kept locked. I've tried to open it, I've tried to find the key, but it's no use.'

'Harry, Prue can't report you to the police and accuse you of fraud. She's guilty too. She does your books. Call her bluff, she can't do anything.'

He looked away from her and again she felt the cold fear. He was not going to leave Prue. She stood up, pushing away his attempts to hold her.

'You're like a child, Harry. You want your sweets and your pocket money too!'

'What d'you mean?'

'You won't leave Prue! She makes you too comfortable. She treats you too well! I've been a fool and I'm not going to fool myself any longer.' With trembling hands, she picked up her handbag and the coat she had worn around her shoulders and pushed past him to the door. 'Leave me alone. Don't speak to me again until you've spoken to Prue – about leaving her.'

'Amy, stop and listen to me. I will do something, I promise, but I need time to sort things out.'

'You're no man. How could I have been taken in for all these years. A *man* wouldn't succumb to blackmail from a woman.'

She was crying and Harry pushed past her and stood against the door, stopping her from leaving. For a moment she thought he was going to face things, promise to go at once and tell Prue he was moving out, the look on his face was so determined.

'Amy, love. You stay here and I'll go. It wouldn't be wise for people to see you with your makeup all messed up.' She swung her bag and gave a low scream of rage, but she hit only the door. Harry had gone.

The door opened again and she tensed, ready for another attempt to hit him, but it was Nelly who came in.

'What's the matter, dearie? Someone upset you, 'ave they?' Amy smiled and opening her bag, took out a ten-shilling note and asked Nelly to get them both a drink.

'It's not me, but my friend,' Amy explained later when they had both finished their third drink. She went on to explain about the mythical friend who loved a man who was not hers to love.

Nelly sympathised, then said, 'My advice to your friend, Amy love, is to enjoy herself and say, Sod 'em all!' They both laughed and did not hear the door open.

Vic Honeyman stood there, surprised at seeing Amy, he said, 'This is my lucky night. Now you can't refuse to have that drink with me.'

'Yeah,' Nelly said nudging Amy. ' 'Ave two, why don't yer?'

Nelly, who had called to buy some bottles for when George came back, left them and dragging the dogs, walked home. When Amy left, Victor Honeyman went with her.

Fay continued to leave notes for Alan, and one day there was a reply. 'Meet me at four on Wednesday,' it said, and she was overjoyed.

It was easy to re-arrange her week's schedule, and by working without lunch and cutting short some of the more garrulous customers; she was free from midday on Wednesday and walked to the sheepfold, where she guessed he would be.

'I've decided to try and return home,' he said.

'Alan! I'm so pleased. What do you want me to do? Shall I prepare your mother for your visit?'

'No. Not yet. Promise me you won't do or say anything until I'm ready.'

'I promise. But your mother, she'll be the first one you'll see?'

'I can only deal with people one at a time. Perhaps you could bring her out here? Without telling her why, then, if I find I can't face it, she won't be distressed.'

'I'll try, but I don't know whether she'll come with me. What excuse can I give her?'

'If you can't –' He turned away and Fay guessed how easily he would change his mind.

'Alan, darling, of course I can, I was thinking out loud, that's all. When shall I bring her?'

After Fay had gone, Alan strolled back to the edge of the woods, where he could look down on his old home. A great longing filled him. Fay was right, he had only to start things moving then every problem would solve itself, all the pieces of his shattered life would fall back into place. He looked at the smart houses in the area that had once been his garden, where he and Fay had played as children. The trees they had climbed were gone, replaced by the walls of the houses, the green grass hidden by concrete and black tarmac. The wild flowers had been discarded, their places taken by orderly, weed-free beds filled with carefully selected plants to give neat patterns of colour and shape.

He knew everyone who lived in the houses. He had stood at this same spot many times, during the night as well as the day, and learnt where each person had lived, had watched children come and go, had seen washing put out, and left to blow in the cleansing wind before being taken in again.

As he watched now, he saw Prue Beynon come out and look about her in an agitated manner, stopping and starting, running one way then another, as if she had suffered some terrible shock. She looked up and he knew she was looking at him. He was tempted to wave, but thought better of it.

Then Prue ran back inside and he turned his gaze to other houses, other small dramas. It was only a few minutes later that a police car arrived, followed by others, each spilling out the occupants, who scanned the fields, as they waited for instructions, until Prue came out and pointed at him, and the blue-coated group began to run up the field towards him.

Alan knew he had been careless, standing far beyond the edge of the tree-line. He moved away, steadily, unhurriedly, his limp hardly noticeable, and avoided them all with ease.

His face had not altered, but his heart was racing and he was once again back in enemy territory, where to be hunted was normal, and to be found was death. Using all his skill he hid as the men searched quite close, and with a choking panic, suddenly came out of his dream to find his hands around a sergeant's throat. He let the man fall and ran. He ran without stopping for the whole day and the night.

Fay was met by an angry Johnny when she went home after meeting Alan.

'Fay. You shouldn't have gone alone. You promised me we'd deal with this together.'

'Sorry, Johnny. I felt he wouldn't cope with more than one of us, and he said as much himself. Darling, I know I was wrong to go without you, but I really think he will soon be ready to go home.' She told him what had been said, and Johnny shook his head.

'Best you don't see him alone. We're a partnership aren't we?'

'Yes. I'm sorry.' She kissed him affectionately.

He grinned. 'Well, tell the truth, I've been doing something on my own too. I've only found out his address!'

'Johnny!'

'I suggest we go together and talk to Mrs French.'

'No, I promised Alan –'

'Promises can be broken when it's in the person's interest, love. We'll tell her all we know and go with her to find him, but,' he looked at Fay, held her firmly and added, 'But, my lovely, she will go in alone to see him, right?'

'Right. He told me he can only manage people one at a time.'

It took them a long time to persuade Mrs French and many tears were shed, but eventually she agreed. As she was locking the door, Prue Beynon came out and delayed them.

'Can't it wait until later?' Mrs French asked, as Prue began to tell her of her suspected burglary.

'No, I think you ought to be warned. There's a dangerous man loose. I found a cupboard forced and some papers missing, he obviously thought there would be money in there, and I saw this strange-looking man up on the hill, just standing there he was, staring down at me. I called the police and they're out there hunting for him still.'

'You what?' Fay lunged at the woman, hitting her furiously across the face. 'You stupid, stupid fool!'

Johnny and Mrs French held her arms and calmed her down, then Johnny explained to Prue that it was a patient, who had walked out of a nearby hospital.

'He injured one of the policemen,' Prue said. 'What would he have done to me if I hadn't called the police?'

'Then it wasn't Alan,' Fay said. 'Thank goodness for that.'

'Alan?' Prue's sharp ears had heard the whispered name. 'Alan, you say?'

'Come on,' Johnny said, taking Fay's hand and pulling her towards the car. 'We have business in town. *Private* business!' He glared at Prue. 'Right?'

Leaving Prue rubbing her bruised face and watching them curiously, the three of them drove away.

* * *

Alan was hiding in the woods above them, in a place he had prepared for the time when he needed to lay low. It was little more than a dip in the ground which he had carefully covered with branches and turfed over, so it blended perfectly with the surrounding area. Inside it were all his possessions. A few clothes, some books, a photograph of himself with his sister and his parents, now bent and cracked and very faded.

Having decided to go home, he had vacated his room, and given up his job, shutting off all the trailing existence of the past eight years and stepping out to find a place with some permanence and comfort.

Now all hope of a comeback was gone. Cut off from him in the moment when he had come out of his dream to find he had almost killed the policeman. The hunt had brought back the days of terror when he had been in enemy territory. Kill or be killed. A movement gave you one chance, to deliver the first blow, and it had better be a good one, you won't have a chance of a second; he could hear the sergeant's harsh voice insistently urging him to remember. *Kill or be killed.* In the dream, he had become again that automaton, killing before he could be killed. Now he could never go back. The nightmares were bad enough to have kept him away all these years, but Fay had convinced him that his mother could cope. But not with this.

He stayed in his hole for two days, and when he was sure the hunt for him had moved away he went out, built a bonfire and destroyed all his belongings and his clothes. Naked, he sat in the ruin of the old castle and took tablet after tablet, he had stored them during his years in the hospital for just such a time as this, when everything was beyond hope.

He heard piano music in his head and his hands moved as if on a keyboard. The music swelled in his head, and blotted out the pain. As the walls began to crash and crumble around him the music blotted out the sound and became a crescendo that was pure joy.

Chapter Fifteen

Leaves were falling and opening out the woodland, allowing the autumn sun to penetrate to the floor and encourage a late showing of grass in patches of brilliant green. The colour above changed with every day, and Nelly revelled in the beauty of the new season.

She and Oliver wandered through the trees, gathering logs for her winter store, and picked the blackberries that covered the branches of the brambles that abounded in places where few people walked. The garden looked sad, with most of the vegetables gone and the winter digging not yet done. The chickens were searching and scratching for what they could find.

In the fields behind Amy's shop they walked with carrier bags in their hands and filled them with the heads of wheat left by the harvesters. This would be a treat for the chickens when their scratching produced nothing more than the occasional worm.

Oliver often called to see Nelly before school began. Evie's household was early rising and he usually had time to spare once breakfast and dressing for school had been completed. If Evie noticed him with nothing to do, she would push a book into his hands and insist he read to her while she washed the dishes and made the beds. This morning he escaped.

The sun was already showing the promise of a pleasant day when he walked past the propped up gate and walked down the ash path. He was surprised to see the chickens still locked up, and wondered if he should open their door and allow them to scratch in the garden as usual.

The door was tightly shut too. He had never seen it other than wide open. Even if it was raining the door was not closed. Alarm filled him. Something must be wrong. He called, and knocked on the wooden door, but the only response was the wildly excited barking of the dogs. That should wake her if she's overslept, he thought, but although he waited until he had barely enough time to get to school, she did not appear.

He wondered if she had overslept because of a visit to town on the previous evening. Better not say anything to Dad, he decided, and ran off to school.

At playtime he was unable to join in the games. The offer of some cards to flick against the wall would normally have given him a lot of pleasure, but today, he shook his head and stared at the gate, wishing he were free to go and see if Nelly was all right.

'Is something the matter, Oliver?' his father asked.

'Nothing – at least –'

'Yes?' Timothy coaxed.

'It's Gran. She wasn't there when I called before school.'

'Out with the dogs?' Timothy suggested.

'The dogs were inside barking to be let out. The chickens were still locked up.'

'She must have overslept.' Timothy frowned when he thought what that might mean. 'We'll call at lunchtime, shall we? Just you and me?'

'Lunchtime's a long way off.'

'Forget about it for now, Oliver. She's all right I'm sure.'

The bell rang out to call the children into lines to return to their classrooms.

'But if she's hurt –' Oliver said, but his father had already turned away, back into the building to watch as the lines of his pupils walked in an orderly fashion back to their lessons.

Oliver moved to the end of his line and when the teacher had disappeared leaving the last few to come in unchaperoned, he ran across the wide playground, through the gate, along the road and up the lane to Nelly's cottage. This time he pushed and pushed at the door and finally opened it wide enough to slide in and let the frantic dogs out.

'Gran? Gran. Are you there?'

The room was dark after the sunlight and the curtains were drawn and there was no flicker from the fire. There was no sound except the ticking of the clock on the mantelpiece. Oliver was frightened and wanted to run. 'Gran?' he called again, but this time his voice was a whisper.

He pushed the door wider and climbed onto Nelly's big armchair to pull back the curtains. Then he saw her. She was lying at the foot of the curved staircase, and as he watched, she moved and turned her head towards him. He was still standing on the armchair and for a moment he did not move.

'What you gawpin' at?' Nelly said. 'Ain't yer never seen a Gran flopped on the floor before? Make me a cuppa tea why don't yer? But first, I think we'd better try an' get me up.'

'What happened?'

'Fell on these bleedin' stairs, that's what!'

'Shall I fetch Mother?'

'Not bloody likely! 'Ave me put away she would, given a chance like this. No, pass me a nice fat cushion.' She pushed it against the wall between her leg and the first stair and sighed contentedly. 'There, that's better. Soon be able to get up. Let me chickens out, will yer?'

Slowly she began to rise, first onto the lowest stair, then onto a chair brought by an anxious Oliver.

'There, see? I'll soon be walkin' about as if nothin's 'appened. Got a bit cold down there, though. See if the fire'll revive with a bit of coaxin' with some sticks, will yer?'

Oliver soon had the fire burning brightly and a kettle singing with the promise of a pot of tea. Nelly found she could move about by resting her painful leg on a chair, using it as a sort of crutch. She made tea and they were sipping it, chatting happily when Nelly heard the dogs growl. Oliver looked out of the small, deep-set window and said,

'Oh heck, it's Dad.'

It was only then Nelly realised he should have been at school. 'You bin mitchin' then, young Ollie?' When he nodded, she asked, 'On account of me?' He nodded again as Timothy entered, followed by the fussing dogs.

'Oliver!'

'What a marvellous boy 'e is!' Nelly said quickly. 'Knew I was in trouble and even broke school rules to come an' find out what was wrong. There's bravery for yer. You must be ever so proud of 'im, Timmy.'

The words about to fall from Timothy's lips fumbled and instead, he asked, 'Are you all right, mother-in-law?'

'Yes, thanks to your carin' son I am. Fell I did and no, I wasn't drunk! Fell on them stairs when me leg sor' of gave out.'

'Shall I send for the doctor?'

'Gawd 'elp us, what for? Put me in bed 'e would. People dies in bed! I'll get something for the bruises, that's all I need; don't want to worry no doctor.' She laughed away the idea.

'Are you sure?'

' 'Ere it's about dinner time, ain't it? Let Ollie – I mean Oliver, stay an' 'ave a bite with me. Right as rain I'll be then. Honest.' She smiled her crooked smile and nodded to encourage him to agree.

'Be sure you aren't late, Oliver,' Timothy warned, 'and we'll say no more about this.' He picked up the battered clock from the mantelpiece and carefully put it to the correct time.

Nelly looked at the small boy, who always seemed smaller in the presence of his father. If only Timothy could bend a little and be a dad sometimes, she thought sadly, instead of always being a headmaster.

'Ollie,' she whispered urgently when Timothy had gone. 'Will you do something for me? Secret? I want to send a message to George; you know, the tramp.'

'Why? How?'

'I 'ates admittin' it, but I'm goin' to need a bit of 'elp fer a while. I want you to write a short message for me an' send it to the *Daily Mirror*. George 'as promised to look in there every day, and 'e'll come as soon as 'e can when 'e reads it.'

Oliver looked upset. 'I can't, Gran. You *know* I can't,' he added accusingly.

'This ain't an occasion fer words like can't. Look at me 'ands. All swollen where I was lyin' on 'em. Ollie, I'm dependin' on yer.' Nelly pretended not to see the frantic shaking of his head. 'There's a pen and a bottle of ink in the table drawer. Come on, Ollie, we mustn't miss the midday post.'

'I can't!'

'But you'll try, won't yer. Good boy you are Ollie, no-one never 'ad a better grandson.'

After a few false starts, the letter was written and the postal order which Nelly had bought in readiness was filled in. Proudly, Oliver walked down the lane and posted it in the box outside Amy's shop. Then he went back to school to tell his story to his curious friends.

The tramp arrived a few days later, and Nelly pointed to the saucepan on the fire. 'Just in time you are, George. There's a pot of soup made with an 'ambone Amy brought for me.' She smiled at him, her dark brown eyes glowing with pleasure. 'Nice to see yer, George. I'm glad you could come. So quick an' all. Young Oliver's been lookin' after me, but I'm glad *you've* come.'

Nelly was sitting in her armchair, covered with a warm, Welsh plaid blanket sent to her by Mrs French. She had a pile of books and magazines beside her and her records were within easy reach. She smiled and showed her crooked teeth and the expression on her sun-weathered face was almost wicked, her eyes crinkled with a suggestion that whatever life threw at her, she would always see the joke.

The tramp laughed with delight at seeing her again.

Oliver came after school and was delighted to see George. He jumped up and down, asked dozens of questions about what George had been doing since he last called. Nelly was reminded again of how different the boy was when he was not in his parents' company. With the finest of intentions, he was being smothered.

'So it was you who wrote the letter to the *Mirror*?' George said. 'Well done.'

'I had to. Gran's hand was swollen and stiff.'

'I got it stuck under meself when I fell an' it got a bit squashed.'

'I have a present for you, Oliver, for being so kind to your Gran.' George took a package from his bag and handed it to Oliver, who opened it with haste.

'Gosh, thanks. A proper fountain pen and a propelling pencil. Thanks! None of the boys in school have these!' He looked anxiously at Nelly. 'Gran, can I talk about George being here? I mean, to Mother and Dad.'

'Course, Ollie. You'll want to tell them where you got the pen an' pencil set. It's no secret, but don't say nothin' about 'is stayin' 'ere, not for a week. All right?'

'What's happening next week then?'

'Well, your Mum wants me to go an' live with you all.'

Oliver looked thoughtful. 'I'd love you to live with us, so I can talk to you whenever I want to. But I wouldn't like not being able to come here. Couldn't George live here? Then we could both come and see him? Gran! Why not?'

George and Nelly laughed.

' 'Ow's that fer an idea, eh, George?' Nelly said and for once they did not include Oliver in the joke.

The shop door opened and a voice called, 'Where d'you want these boxes of apples, lady?'

Amy looked up prepared to argue.

'I haven't ordered any – Oh, hello, Vic. What are you doing here on a Wednesday?'

'I wondered if you were free to meet me tonight, for a drink, or a meal if you like?'

'I'm going into Cardiff,' she explained. 'I don't know what time I'll be back.'

'Pity it isn't on Friday, I could give you a lift.'

'No need; I have a lift.'

'Harry Beynon, is it?'

'What business is it of yours?' she demanded.

'Got me the sack he did, your brother in law. Persuaded me to add a few items to the lorry when I loaded up his order. Copper tube and plaster board, then let me down when I was caught.'

'You stole from your boss and you say it was Harry's fault?'

'Persuaded me he did. Promised to pay and say he'd asked for the extra and let me out of it. But he didn't.'

Amy was quiet, as Vic went on explaining how and what goods had been stolen. So these were some of the papers that Prue had threatened him with. What else was Harry besides a thief? She ushered Vic Honeyman out and closed the shop.

'A coward. That's what,' she muttered as she went upstairs to get ready to meet him.

Harry had to attend a meeting in Cardiff at the Park Hotel, and Amy sat in the Sophia Gardens reading a book until he had finished. They went for an early meal and as they ate, Amy mentioned Victor Honeyman.

'I saw a man who claims you got him the sack,' she said. 'We had a drink together at The Drovers and he took me home after.'

Harry looked at her, his laughing eyes bearing a glint of something other than his usual good humour.

'Don't try blackmail to persuade me to talk to Prue. I'll tell her our plans when I think the time is right.'

'Harry! What an awful thing to say! He took me home after buying me a drink. That's all!' She waited until she felt calmer then asked. 'Did you? Get him the sack?'

'I used the money to buy the house for us. He was caught but it was a risk he took. There's nothing noble about owning up when there's no need. I haven't bought anything from that builder's merchants since though.'

'Harry, now Freddy's working for you, you wouldn't involve him in anything - shady - would you?'

'No. He's my son, isn't he? I'll look after him, don't you worry. Getting on well he is; understands a lot of the business already. Sharp. More a man than a boy, for all he's not yet sixteen.'

Something of the day had gone sour for Amy. She knew from his expression when she raised the subject that their relationship was doomed to continue in the same semi-secret way into the forseeable future. Could she accept that? Spend even more years going nowhere?

She had always known Harry was weak. She had been let down by him, badly. Once when they were young and before he was ready for marriage, he had refused to admit the baby she carried was his, had tut-tutted with the rest of the village when she came home some time later with Freddy, whom he now proudly called his son.

Her eyes glazed over as she thought of the second child, who she had nursed for those few hours before he had died. That was when their relationship had been renewed after he had married Prue. As before, he could not face the embarrassment and had let her cope with it alone. The attempted abortion had not succeeded and in the months before the baby was born she did not see him. At the time of the baby's death he had sent a bunch of flowers, without even a card to say who they were from.

Now he talked of blackmail. How easy it would have been for her then. She looked at him, finishing his meal, a smile of contentment on his face as he thought of his son, now working in the firm; a son who did not bear his name.

'I want to go home.'

'But I thought we'd go and see a play, or a film?'

'Take me home.'

'What have I said now?' He was slightly exasperated. 'Don't spoil the day out.'

'You've said nothing. What makes you think I'll spoil your day? Nothing upsets me. I'm Amy, that "good sort", remember?' She stood up and collected her coat from the stand and without waiting for Harry, left the restaurant.

She walked up the street fast, crossing the road heedless

of traffic and not knowing where she was going. She went into a cinema, seeking solitary darkness, and sat in a cocoon of isolation in an empty row not seeing the screen, only aware of the loneliness without Harry.

She had been here before, in this deep dark misery, wondering if she should finally end the affair with him. But other than moving right away, starting again somewhere without any friends, it was impossible. Knowing his faults brought anger, but the anger was with herself for not being strong enough to break away. And she called Harry weak. How she wished she could face never seeing him again. What could she do to motivate herself to blot him out of her life? 'Till death us do part' didn't have to be said in front of a parson. So were they tied for the rest of their days to this half life? On the screen two lovers kissed as all their troubles were ended, and some of the watchers, stood up and left. Without waiting for the main film, Amy stood and shuffled out after them.

Harry searched the streets for an hour, then went back to where he had parked the car. He waited there for another hour then, leaving a note for her on the windscreen went for a drink. He came back after a further two hours to find the note in the gutter and his car missing.

Amy. She's done it again! he thought. He checked to see he had enough money for the fare and walked to the railway station. He had twenty minutes to wait for the Swansea train and as it was getting cold, he went into the waiting room. Amy stared at him with complete disbelief when he opened the door.

'Harry! How did you find me?'

'Where's the car?' he demanded.

'Car? I don't know. I can't remember where we parked. I've been in a cinema for ages. Can't you find the car either?'

'It's been stolen. I thought you –'

Suddenly they were laughing and hugging and all that mattered was being together. Damn the future, Amy thought, it's today that's real.

They went back to Swansea on the train, after reporting the loss of the car, then by bus to Llangwyn. Pooling their remaining money, they decided to have a taxi for the last part of their journey.

'You get out at the beginning of the houses, Amy love,' Harry said. 'I'll go on right to my door; that way we're less likely to be seen.'

'There won't be many people about now,' Amy pointed out. 'They'll all be indoors listening to the radio.'

But as Amy walked parallel to the church and the school and was about to turn into the lane behind the shop, she noticed that the village street was far from empty. Groups of people were gathered around the houses, and several policemen were among them. She went in to see the children, then phoned Evie to find out what had happened.

Harry's taxi drew up near Mrs French's house and he saw that all the neighbours were outside open doors, standing in groups, waiting. An ambulance drove along the main road and as Prue was nowhere to be seen, he walked back to the road to see what was happening.

The ambulance stopped at the end of Nelly's lane, and several policemen stood near it.

'What's happening then?' he asked. 'Someone ill?'

'Found a body, up by the castle ruin. Don't know who he is; young chap, but not from here,' Constable Harris told him.

'Thank goodness,' Harry said. 'Thought it might have been old Nelly.' He stood with the policemen and waited while the stretcher was taken up and the men returned with their sad load. He looked at the scarred face of the young man but no recognition came. Gradually, the street cleared, lights went out and Harry at last saw Prue, who had been with Evie and Timothy, and who had also looked into the dead face.

'Fancy, a sudden death in the village,' Harry said. 'Never been known.'

'It was the criminal who attacked that policeman, the one I reported as a suspicious vagrant,' Prue told him. She explained what had happened and he let her talk. That way she was less likely to ask where he had been, although the car theft gave him an excellent story.

When they reached home, Prue did not go inside, she stood talking to the neighbours for a while, then noticed that Monica French had not been told. She knocked on her door to spread the interesting news.

The incident of the dead man was not high on Harry's mind the following day. He was thinking of Freddy, and the way he had taken to the business. Even if he and Amy did not get together he would have Freddy and, with or without his name, Freddy was still his son. The thought pleased him more and more. If he did leave Prue and go to live with Amy, his son might despise him for the years he had not owned him. His explanations of loyalty might not sound very noble when compared with his lack of loyalty to Amy and Freddy.

He would be foolish to risk it. Prue was not a loving wife and they had not been very successful at attempts to make their relationship more close. Prue was undemonstrative and tightened up rather than relaxed at his shows of affection. But she was a good wife in every other respect. With Amy as his mistress, life was good.

He had already started proceedings to make the house over to her. That would please her and she would not press so hard for him to leave Prue, for a while at least. The house was almost ready for occupation. Soon, he would hand her the deeds and she would be able to move in. The rooms above the shop could be let, she would have a small income from them, yes, she would see the sense of letting things continue as they were. They would both be better off.

His mind made up, he rang the solicitor and told him to make haste with the transfer of ownership then went home to talk to Prue. Best to set her mind at rest as soon as possible. He looked at his watch. Freddy had gone to collect some plumbing fittings, but he would be back soon and it wouldn't hurt to leave the phone unattended for a while. He locked the door and using one of the firm's lorries, drove home.

He was surprised to see the carrier bike outside his house. Then he smiled. Since Prue had stopped shopping at Amy's, she often rang to ask him to bring something home. She must have missed him and asked young Freddy. As he parked the lorry in the confined space of the close, he saw he was correct, Freddy emerged from the house and waved before getting on his bike. Harry hailed him and ran to talk to him.

Freddy was very flushed, the redness reaching high into the roots of his brown hair, he refused to meet Harry's gaze.

'Hello, Uncle Harry, I've been –'

Harry waved away his explanation. 'Don't worry, I bet you've been shopping for Auntie Prue, right? She's always asking me to bring something from the shops, and now she's got you at it.' He patted the strong shoulder and smiled at his son. He thought again of how big and mature he was. A moustache, unshaped, but dark and thick, grew on his upper lip, making Freddy look far older than his years. His body was powerfully built, his arms filling the sleeves of the old coat he wore to work. Harry thought he would give him an advance on his wages and ask Amy to buy him a new coat. He couldn't have his son looking anything but smart. He'd pay for dressing, as his mother would have said.

Freddy rode off and Harry walked into the house. Prue was in the kitchen, she was polishing the brass, the pokers and other fireside ornaments on the table which was spread with newspaper. She too looked slightly flushed and she did not look up when he entered. That was not unusual, and Harry smiled and said, 'So you're using Freddy as an errand boy, are you?' He was smiling, but the smile slid from his face when Prue said angrily, 'I don't want him to come here again. He's Amy's son and I want nothing to do with any of them.'

Harry stared at her; at the fingers rubbing furiously at the brass, at the gloved hands, so clearly showing her anger.

'What's happened?' he asked, dreading her reply. Had she found out he was Freddy's father? That must be it. He didn't know what to say, whether to deny it, bluff it out, or own up and tell her of his decision to stay with her, to make a success of their marriage and never see Amy again. He realised he did not know how she would react to either response. Married for all these years and he did not know her at all.

'Freddy's a fine boy,' he began, trying desperately to think. 'Strong and very useful in the firm. He's going to be a real asset. He's so mature and grown-up. You'd never think he's only sixteen.'

'I want you to sack him.' Prue still had not looked up from her furious rubbing. The brass seemed to be taking all her attention, yet Harry recognised the tension in her voice and knew something had angered her. She must know.

'You know. Who told you?'

She looked up then and stared at him. She did not speak, but waited for him to continue. Cleverly she waited, knowing he would not be able to stand the silence. He would have to say more and she would find out easier than by asking her own questions, what he had not wanted her to know. She was not worried, a sense of excitement filled her. Watching him and feeling the guilt flowing from him, she allowed her own guilt, and the sensations of the recent love-making fade.

'You know,' he repeated. Prue waited. 'About Freddy.' Then Prue had to speak, Harry had turned away, presuming she knew all, he was not going to enlarge on the brief words.

'You'd better tell me.'

'All right, so Freddy is my son. It's a miracle you haven't worked it out before. What are you going to do about it? Don't do anything hasty, Prue, let's talk about it. I don't want to lose you. Yes,' he went on quickly. 'I've finished with Amy. It's all over. I want to stay with you, and Freddy will stay in the firm. He's a fine boy, Prue. My son. I know I should have told you years ago, but –'

He stared in horror at Prue, who was reaching for the brass pokers on the table.

'No, Prue. Don't be stupid. It's not that important. Prue –!' His voice was cut off as the heavy poker hit him on the side of his head and made him stagger.

Prue felt sick. She was still unwashed from Freddy's love-making and she felt unclean. Amy's son, a fine revenge for stealing her husband. But Harry's son. She felt clouds fill her brain, shutting out the unbelievable. Blocking the shame and guilt and humility. *Harry's fault. Harry's fault. Harry's fault.* Each time the words issued from her tight lips, she hit him. He stood up once, and seemed to be coming for her, his eyes glazed, his face blue. She struck him again and again, hate pouring from her. He tottered, then fell towards her. Prue tried to move away, to escape from his final embrace, but she fell beneath him. Her head snapped back hard against the grate and she lay still.

Chapter Sixteen

Nelly's leg was still painful, but she insisted on going to Mrs French's the morning following the discovery of Alan's body. She knew that Mrs French would probably not be there, but also knew where to find a key. She felt the sadness of Alan's tragic ending both for Fay, who had tried to help him, and for his mother, who had not known of his survival until it was too late.

'Pity it 'ad to be Prue Beynon what told 'er,' she grumbled to the dogs as they walked up to Mrs French's back door. 'She's bound to 'ave embellished the story. No doubt about that.'

As she was unlocking the back door, she heard shouts and unable to resist, it being Prue's house from where the sounds came, she quickly tied up the dogs, threw down the key and ran to see what was happening.

Prue and Harry were fighting. She could see through the open back door that Harry seemed to be having the worst of it, as Prue was armed with a poker and he had nothing but his bare hands. Nelly hesitated on the doorstep and was about to shout and distract them from attacking each other, when Harry fell. A last blow aimed by Prue fell against his head and then she disappeared beneath him, her shouts cut short and leaving a horrible, eerie silence after the row.

Nelly went inside hesitantly, calling Prue then Harry. Both lay still. 'Oh, my Gawd!' Nelly ran back to Mrs French's to telephone for the police and an ambulance. She looked at where she had thrown down the key but could not see it.

She was crying, saying, 'Oh my Gawd!' over and over but failed to find the key. In her panic she had not thought to use Prue's phone. She thought of it now, and ran back, but not to the back door. Her legs were like lead and she knew she would have difficulty walking past those prostrate bodies. She stretched up and looked through the window, foolishly hoping she had imagined it all.

Prue was slowly rising, having pushed Harry's heavy body away. Mesmerised, Nelly watched as Prue sat for a moment, taking in the situation, then got a cloth from the sink and begin to wipe the blood from the grate near where her head had landed. The fire was lit, and she removed the working gloves she was wearing and put them into the flames. She did not look at the small side window where Nelly still watched.

Walking stiffly, Prue walked to the drawer near the sink and took out a clean pair of working gloves. She put them on and, lifting a poker, walked into the hallway and out of Nelly's sight. There, she opened the door of Harry's office and began throwing out the contents of the desk drawers. She smashed at the metal cabinet with the poker, before throwing it down in a corner.

There was a cash box in the top drawer of the cabinet, and she took this and scattered the contents over the carpet, as if it had been dropped in haste. Two pound notes and a ten shilling note she kicked out into the hallway. She stood for a moment, then went back into the kitchen, where Nelly's eyes still peered over the sill of the window.

Prue's small apron was spotted with blood and she removed it and almost fed it to the flames, then changed her mind and put it back on. She pushed the fire to make sure all the dusters had disappeared and added wood to conceal their ashes.

The cloth with which the blood had been wiped up was also burnt, and Prue's face, as she watched the fire take it, slowly at first, then as the flames touched the Brasso-soaked gloves, in a sudden rush, was like a picture from a horror story. Eyes bright, her skin a strange reddish brown, tinged with blue and green as the flames were reflected. Nelly moved away from the window, unsure what to do next.

After a long, timeless wait, she heard Prue's voice. She was obviously calling the police. Her voice was high-pitched.

'I've been beaten, I think my husband's dead,' Nelly heard her say. Then she screamed, and Nelly hurriedly stepped into the shrubs and worked her way around until she was back inside Mrs French's garden.

She sat on the back step for an age, and then the police arrived. There were policemen everywhere, and someone came and asked if she had seen or heard anyone running away, she answered with complete honesty, 'No, I ain't. Locked meself out and can't find the key. Waitin' 'ere for Mrs French.'

The police searched the garden, tried all the doors and windows, found the missing key and followed Nelly in. When they were satisfied she was alone they left, promising to come and talk to her again later.

She tried to do her work, but wondering what she should do and shaking with the horror of it, she spent more time sitting, staring into space than working. She left a note of apology for Mrs French, let herself out and went to tell Amy what had happened.

Nelly sat silently watching Amy. She had broken the news as gently as she could, but when she had said the unbelievable words, 'Harry is dead, dearie,' all the life seemed to drain from Amy's face. She was looking at Nelly, then at the door and back to Nelly as if waiting for someone else to arrive and tell her it was not true, that there had been some stupid mistake.

'Good sort, 'Arry Beynon,' Nelly said softly. 'I mean a *really* good sort. Not – well, you know what I mean – 'e took everyone for themselves and never wanted to change people. He always treated me proper, 'e did. Sorry 'e's gone I am, real sorry.'

'You knew about us, didn't you, Nelly?' Amy said at last.

'Yes I knew that you and 'e were, well, you know. That's

why I wanted to tell you, before Prue comes across, to give yer time to settle yerself.'

'Thanks.' Amy stood up and blew her nose then added.

'What happened? Tell me again.'

'All I know is that 'Arry an' Prue were hit by burglars. That's what the police said. Don't know nothing else yet. Make us a cup of tea, why don't yer?'

Having said nothing to the police about seeing Prue and Harry fighting, Nelly was committed to the lie. She couldn't go and tell them she *had* been there, and had seen them hitting each other, not now. Anyway she was not too clear about what happened even though she had looked through the door at that unfortunate moment.

Every time she closed her eyes she saw Prue's face, and her arm holding aloft that brass poker. The shock had numbed Nelly's brain and she couldn't think straight for the moments following; even now she was still confused.

The police had not pressed her, but had accepted what she had told them, that she had been sitting on Mrs French's doorstep and had seen nor heard nothing. She had seen Prue strike Harry, but what had happened before that? She would never know. Perhaps Harry had hit out at Prue? She was enough to make anybody mad, with her disapproval and her rigid ways, but Harry had treated her bad, having an affair with her sister. No, she'd done the right thing to say nothing. Let the police sort it out. Half of a story could get an innocent woman hanged.

'Here you are, Nelly. A cup of tea with something in it to warm us.'

There was a knock at the door and Nelly took the opportunity to slip away.

'Come an' 'ave a chat, why don't yer?' she said as Amy unlocked the shop door to let her out and P.C. Harris in. Nelly couldn't look into his face. Lying to the police was a worrying thought, but admitting it and telling him what she had seen was even more frightening. She hurried back over the road and up the lane home.

She built up the fire and turned the swivel to put the

black, sooty kettle over the heat. She huddled close to the fire and began to feel afraid. What if someone had seen her stretching up and looking through Prue's window afterwards? Could she still say she had been sitting on the steps and had seen nothing?

She looked around her at the familiar room. Six years ago she had kept another secret from the authorities and now she wondered if her luck would hold a second time.

Footsteps crunched down the path and she clasped a hand to her chest. She glanced towards the open door and, expecting to see the dark uniform of Constable Harris, gave a huge sigh of relief when she saw it was Johnny.

'Heard the news then?' he asked, reaching for a cup from the shelf in the corner. 'It makes you wonder what'll happen next. Don't they say important things happen in threes?'

'Oo, don't!' Nelly shuddered and Johnny looked surprised.

'Come on, Nelly, don't take notice of me, only joking. What else could happen?' He took the filled cup and raised it in salute, 'Here's to you, Nelly.' She didn't raise her cup to his as she usually did in their silly game and Johnny frowned again. 'There is something bothering you. What is it? Not upset about poor Harry, are you? Sorry I am, but he wasn't a close friend. Pity it wasn't Prue, that's all I think!'

'If I tell you something, young Johnny, will you promise to keep it to yerself?'

'Of course.'

'Remember when I come 'ere, in 1940 it was, my Evie had been here a year, and I thought to meself, what am I doing up in London bein' bombed while she's down 'ere safe? So I evacuated meself and came down to join 'er.'

'Very sensible too.'

'I 'ad to find somewhere to live. This cottage was a bit of a mess, but old Mr Gregory, remember 'im? Well he let me 'ave it for four shillings a week.'

'It was a mess all right. You worked hard getting it clean and comfortable.'

‘Yes, well; when old Mr Gregory died, there was no one to pay the rent to, so I sort of said nothing. I didn’t go to see anyone about it, I just kept putting the rent away each week and hoping no one would come and tell me the place wasn’t mine no longer.’

‘I remember when Mr Gregory died there was no one to even attend his funeral. Mam went and you went. But apart from the vicar, there was no one. I should forget it, Nelly. If anyone asks for the deeds, tell them they got lost, eaten by mice, thrown out by mistake. There’ll be no one to ask about him. Forget it, make us another cup of tea.’

Nelly visibly brightened. ‘You sure, Johnny?’

‘Never more certain. This house is yours. Forget you ever worried about it. And as for the rent, well I’d spend it, get yourself something really nice with it.’ He thought for a moment, ‘If you like, Nelly, I’ll go and see a solicitor and ask him, no names, like, and see what he thinks.’

‘Thanks, Johnny. ’Ere, what about a drop of something in this to warm us, eh? One of Amy’s specials.’

Bracing herself for abuse and possible rejection, Amy went to see her sister. Prue opened the door, and, seeing who it was, closed it again. Amy tried several times that day and in the days that followed, but her sister refused to see her.

Amy was not allowed the luxury of grief. She had only to show regret at losing a brother-in-law. Prue was his wife. Mistresses had no rights, not even to show their anguish and sorrow. Only to Nelly could she show how devastated she was.

The police were still searching for the burglar who had attacked Prue and killed Harry and Prue was constantly questioned. Amy knew this from Constable Harris; her sister told her nothing. Then, one day, just before that set for the funeral, Prue arrived as Amy was closing the door of the shop. Amy invited her upstairs.

Amy looked at her sister and felt worried for her. She wished she would break out of the tight, cold shell she was inhabiting. Surely it would be better for her to grieve and cry? Or at least shout and rage against Harry's death? Keeping her emotions so firmly in check was not good, even for someone as unemotional as Prue. It did not occur to Amy to wonder if Prue was in fact holding nothing back, that there was no loss to cry and rage over. That Harry's death was no more than a satisfying end to an impossible situation.

Amy made a tray of tea and put biscuits on a plate, but Prue refused any refreshment.

'I saw the solicitor again yesterday,' she said when Amy was settled with a cup of tea. 'What he told me might be of interest to you.'

'Oh?' Amy searched Prue's face for a clue to what was about to come. There was none.

'Apparently, Harry had bought a house for you and your children.'

'I – yes – that is he did tell me –'

'He died before he signed the papers.' There was still no change in Prue's expression. 'So I told the solicitor not to proceed with the transfer of ownership.'

Amy put down her cup with a shaking hand. She looked at her sister and waited, knowing there would be more.

'The solicitor said that as it was obviously Harry's wish to provide for you and your children, I was honour bound to make the gift. I said not. I know Harry was Freddy's father, he told me the day he was killed. But all I'm prepared to do is keep Freddy on in the firm, give him a reasonable wage. That's all.'

She walked down the stairs and the only sign that she was other than calm, was the loud slamming of the door as she left.

Freddy saw Prue leave and came out from where he had been hiding. Since the day of the tragedy he had not seen her. The double shock of almost being found in her bed, then learning of Harry's murder had terrified him. He had been questioned by the police and could tell them nothing, but he waited with dread, expecting another visit.

He put his cycle away in the shed behind the shop, threw his fishing rods and the box of tackle in beside it, and went upstairs. Amy was washing up a few cups and she looked drawn and pale. It was not a good time to worry her, he could see that, but he had to get things settled.

'Hello, Mam. I've been fishing.'

'Any luck, love?' she asked, trying to force enthusiasm into her voice.

'I've been into town as well. Swansea in fact.'

'Fishing in the Tawe river?'

He did not reply and she turned and saw at once that today's shocks were not over. 'What is it, Freddy?'

'Mam, I'm going into the army.'

'You're what? But you have a job with –' She hesitated before adding, '– with Uncle Harry's firm. Auntie Prue has just been here to tell me it's still all right.'

'No, Mam. I'm not staying here. I'll help you in the shop for a while, until I'm old enough and things are settled. There's plenty of jobs you need doing. Then I'm off.' He took off his shoes and searched near the fender for his slippers. 'It's best, Mam. I can't work for Auntie Prue.'

Amy mashed the boiled potatoes fiercely and doled them out on three plates with baked beans and slices of spam, but she was unable to eat. She left Freddy, and putting Margaret's on top of a saucepan of boiling water to stay warm, she went out.

She wandered up the lane to Nelly's cottage. She wasn't really aware of where she was going, but seeing the open door and light of the oil lamp glowing out onto the path, she went through the gateway.

'Amy love. Come on in. This is George, don't take any notice of 'im, a good friend of mine, George is. Cuppa tea?'

Amy sat on the settee near the window and George smiled apologetically.

'If you and Nelly want to talk, would you like me to go?' he asked in his carefully modulated voice.

'No, don't disturb yourself on my account. No, I'm just

feeling a bit low and thought I'd come and be cheered up by Nelly.'

'Very good at that, Nelly is,' George said with a smile. He stood up and handed her the cup of tea that Nelly had poured.

'Still upset at – you know – what 'appened?' Nelly asked. 'Shock like that'll take some gettin' over.'

'I've lost everything, Nelly.' Amy began to sob and at once Nelly stood up and put an arm around her. George reached into his pocket and brought out a spotlessly clean handkerchief which he pressed into her hand.

'I'll go for a walk,' he said. 'I'll be back later.' He went to the door and closing it as much as the old wood allowed, set off up the cinder path.

'Prue's won,' Amy said as the tears subsided. 'I've lost everything.'

'What you talkin' about?'

'Freddy is leaving. He's going to join the army. Margaret is having music lessons from Mrs French, she's been over there all day. Harry is dead. The house he was buying for me, that would have been a proper home for us has gone to Prue.' She explained about the house, described it and told Nelly of how the solicitor's plea had been ignored. 'I know it's hers by right, I wasn't married to Harry, and I doubt if he would ever have left her for me, no matter how often he swore he would, but I did want that house.'

Nelly looked thoughtful, then searched for paper and pen and ink.

'Amy, will yer leave me for a while. I 'ave to get something written down on paper. Somethin' to upset that sister of yours.'

'Sorry, Nelly, I shouldn't have come here worrying you.' Amy stood up to go.

'Glad you did. It ain't often that I can do something useful, but today I think I can.'

An hour later, armed with a note of all she could remember about the moment of Harry Beynon's death, Nelly called on Prue. She had defied the authorities twice – didn't Johnny say everything went in threes?

* * *

'And that's what I'll swear to when I talk to the police,' she said, when Prue had read the pages of writing. 'No matter about them bein' mad with me fer not sayin' nothin' before. They can put it down to me bein' a bit soft if they like.'

'I'll go to the solicitor first thing in the morning,' Prue said. 'If I can be sure this is the last I'll hear of this.'

'The village wouldn't sleep if it came out we 'ad a murderess in our midst. No, it's best we keep some things to ourselves. Just as long as I 'ears from Amy that the –' she brought the words out slowly, '– the deeds of transfer of ownership, have been signed.'

'It was an accident.'

'Well, we'll say I believe you, or I wouldn't cover it up, no matter what it cost.' Satisfied with her work, humming cheerfully, Nelly went home.

The news made Amy more cheerful and she was singing when Victor Honeyman came with a delivery of groceries.

'You seem happy, Amy? Got something to celebrate?'

'In a way. Something terrible happened, then it got a bit better.'

'What on earth you talking about?'

'Too difficult to explain. Just say that life seems a bit better than this time yesterday. I've been left a house in someone's will.'

'That's a good excuse for a celebration. Meet me tonight and we'll have a great time. Dancing to start with? What d'you say?'

For a moment Amy was inclined to refuse; then she thought, what have I got to lose? It might stop some of the wagging tongues if she had another boyfriend.

'Why not?' she said. 'Call for me will you?'

'Well, I finish work in town, it's best if you meet me there, save time, see.'

Pushing her home-made cart along the road, Nelly shouted at the two dogs. They were tied to the handles of what had started life as a wooden crate, and now, with the addition of a set of pram wheels, made a useful handcart. Although they appeared to be helping tow it, in fact they pulled it to one side and her arms ached with the effort of straightening it. Struggling to keep it on course, she managed to turn it into Gypsy Lane.

Past The Close, where Prue and Mrs French lived, and where curtains were still closed in mourning, and into the narrow land called Gypsy Lane because it was where a family of gypsies camped every winter, she pushed the bouncing cart. There at last she could release the lively dogs and take a more leisurely pace.

'Go on, Bobby an' Spotty, 'ave a good run before we gets to the farm.'

She was going to collect a small sack of potatoes, which Mr Leighton had promised to let her have cheap. 'I'll 'ave to fix the brake on when we come back down,' she shouted to the dogs, 'or we'll cross that road at the bottom like a bleedin' racin' car!'

The sack was tied on and she set off again, leaning on the cart, glad of the support to ease her hip. She reached the bottom of the lane without mishap and it was as she passed the entrance to The Close that it became difficult to hold. Faster and faster it went, the dogs, once more tied to the handle adding to its speed. Nelly gave a shout, seeing Victor Honeyman and Amy standing outside the shop.

'Help! Save me spuds!' she shouted, and the two people ran across the road. They brought the runaway cart to a halt and laughed at Nelly's puffing thanks.

'Don't thank us,' Victor Honeyman said. 'You gave us a good laugh. Just what Amy needed, that was.' He winked at Amy and added, 'More of the same tonight, eh?'

Nelly frowned as he climbed into the cab of his lorry.

'None of my business, Amy, but you don't want to get mixed up with no more married men, do yer?'

'Married?'

'Yes, I called on his wife when I was collecting fer the Coronation party. Nice little woman she is.'

Amy ran across the road and caught Vic just as he was pulling away.

'Hey, you! Forget it! Clear off and don't come around here again. I don't want any woman coming complaining that I've stolen her husband! Damn cheek! Go home after work, where you belong!'

Nelly noticed tears in Amy's eyes and couldn't resist adding, 'Yes, sod off and don't come back!'

Behind her, coming out of Netta Cartwright's Evie gave a groan of dismay.

The talk in the village gradually subsided. Once the two funerals were over, people settled down to the usual routine. Police still appeared but their enquiries lessened. The murder of Harry Beynon helped Mrs French in a way, by taking some of the attention from Alan's strange reappearance and lonely death.

Nelly's plans for moving in with Evie and Timothy went on through all the upheavals and on the day she had specified, her daughter and son-in-law stood at their window waiting for her to arrive. Evie showed her tension in irritation. Timothy was sad at the success of Evie's persuasion. He knew it was not the best arrangement for Nelly, to take her from her cottage.

'I should have been told about her falling,' Evie said. 'She should have been brought here, to me.'

'She didn't want to come. She's coming today, so please, Evie, don't start complaining about it.' He patted her shoulder to take the sting out of the words.

'You should have insisted on fetching her. Where is she?'

'Nelly didn't want to be fetched. It's bound to be difficult for her to leave her home. She'll want to say goodbye to it in her own way. Evie, I still doubt if we're doing the right thing.'

'We can't let her wander the lanes drinking the proceeds of her clothing sales! I'll hate it too; she isn't easy. But I must have her where I can watch her, make sure she doesn't do anything embarrassing.'

There was a knock at the door and they both jumped.

'That will be Nelly now.' Timothy held Evie's arms. 'Please, love, treat her as a welcome guest. Allow her time to accept her new life. She is your mother, and you owe it to her to try.'

Evie kissed him and nodded. 'I will try. I've had my own way over this and it's up to me to prove it was the right thing for us all.'

There was a second knock, louder and more insistent than the first and Evie smiled. 'Perhaps she's anxious to come here after all, though why she doesn't walk straight in I can't imagine.' She was still smiling as she opened the door. Timothy was beside her and they both gasped in surprise to see Nelly, dressed in the pink dress and wearing a navy velour hat with flowers decorating the brim, with a matching flower in her buttonhole. George was standing proudly beside her, also sporting a large buttonhole.

' 'Ello, Evie, meet yer new Dad. George an' me got married this morning.'

Evie and Timothy stood with mouths wide open as Nelly pushed past them and went into the hall.

'Which bedroom we goin' ter 'ave then?' she asked. 'I 'ope it ain't got a single bed. George ain't fat, but I'm definitely on the plump side.' She laughed her noisy laugh and George joined in. The other two just stared.

'Nelly,' Timothy said. 'You should have told Evelyn what you were planning. She *is* your daughter.'

Evie looked stiff enough to snap as she asked, 'I suppose you really *are* married?'

George struggled to pull some papers from his inside pocket.

'If I can just get my wallet out – ah. There it is, look, our marriage certificate.'

'This is a terrible shock, mother,' Evie said, still holding onto the door, which was wide open.

'Surprise, dearie, not shock. Just think, you won't 'ave to worry about me no more. I'll never be lonely, you can go out on your social whirls an' we'll be 'ere, lookin' after

Ollie and the 'ouse for yer. It'll be just like our own 'ome, won't it, George?'

George smiled and in his careful diction, said, 'Of course, it isn't the same as starting out in a place of our own. Living with relations isn't the best way to start –'

'Have you actually sold all your things?' Evie asked feebly, closing the door and leaning against it.

'Every stick, just like you told me to, Evie,' Nelly lied cheerfully. 'An' that Mr Evans, what's caretaker at your school, 'e's 'avin' me chickens and me dogs. Says we can go over an' see them any time. We thought we'd go over of a Sunday, didn't we, George?'

There was a brief silence, Evie and Timothy exchanging worried glances, then Oliver's voice, calling excitedly as he came through the kitchen made them all look up. Evie was still slumped against the front door.

'Mother? Has she arrived? Has Gran come yet, Mum?'

'Mother!' Evie automatically corrected. 'Yes, she is here.'

'Hello, Gran. Hello, George.' He was laughing excitedly.

'Go to your room for a while, Oliver,' Evie instructed firmly. 'We have something to discuss.'

'But – aren't you going to tell me?'

'Tell you what?' Evie snapped.

'Gran?' Oliver looked at Nelly, then handed her an envelope. 'This is for you.' He looked from one to another, a frown on his young face, as Nelly opened the envelope.

'It's a card. Happy wedding day! Ollie! That's lovely! Look, George. But, how did you know?'

Oliver laughed, dancing about in his delight. 'You left the certificate on the table and I read it!'

Nelly and George congratulated him.

'Well I never did. Just shows 'ow 'andy it is to be able to read proper, don't it?' Nelly said proudly.

'What are we going to do?' Evie whispered to Timothy.

'Let them go home, dear. It's best.'

The day was very hot, as if the summer had decided to give a final fling before accepting that autumn had come. Nelly and George began to walk slowly home. Nelly was carrying two cards. One made by Oliver and the other, signed by Johnny and Fay, their witnesses. On the card, Johnny had written, 'Good luck in your *very own home*.' The words were underlined. He had obviously checked and was reassuring her that all was well and the cottage was hers.

Johnny and Fay were waiting as they climbed the lane and came in sight of the smoke rising from the chimney. He felt a bit guilty about telling Nelly the cottage was hers. But when he had spoken to the solicitor, the complications were so frightening, he decided it best to forget it. Fight it when and if it happened. No one had come to claim it in six years, there was little chance of anyone coming now.

'Welcome back, you two,' he shouted. 'Fay and I have brought everything back, even the dogs.' He took Fay's hand. 'We'll be off now. See you later.'

'The plan worked a treat,' Nelly shouted as the young couple began to walk away from them. 'Thanks fer yer 'elp.' She laughed as the dogs bounded to greet her.

George opened the door. 'What a day. Wasn't that a surprise, young Oliver making us a card?'

'Yes,' Nelly laughed. 'A Happy *Weeding* day!'

'You'll be left in peace now, but don't do anything they can complain of, just in case.'

'I'll save up for a night out fer you when you come back again. Nothin' wrong with goin' out with me legal 'usband. 'Ere, fancy you bein' an 'Enry. Put you down fer a George any day I would.'

George had set potatoes to bake in the ashes under the fire. 'We'll sit outside and eat, shall we? It's still warm.'

'It was fun, you buyin' me a button'ole an' all. I'm ever so grateful, George.'

'Nonsense. I enjoyed it too.'

'No, really, an' if you ever want to come 'ere, in the winter per'aps, I'd be glad. It's bin nice 'avin' someone as easy to talk to as you about.'

George looked uncomfortable. 'I – er –'

Nelly laughed her loud laugh. 'Don't worry, I'm not

tryin' to persuade yer. I've 'ad a taste of people makin' plans for me, so I know. But, if ever you need a place –'

'I'll be back from time to time. Perhaps, one day, when I'm sure I won't spoil things for you.' He smiled then said more briskly, 'I'll stay for the weekend if you don't mind. There are a few things I want to do before I go. I'll fix the gate back on for a start. Then I'll chop some more firewood,' he patted her arm affectionately, 'and then I'll be off.'

Nelly nodded. 'That kettle's singin' so if you'll make a cuppa, I'll find the plates for the spuds.' They sat near the door, the dogs waiting hopefully for scraps, and Nelly's mmm's and ahh's as she ate were echoed by George. It grew quite dark before they moved.

More compulsive fiction from Headline:

MALCOLM ROSS

A rich West Country saga
in the bestselling tradition of POLDARK

On a Far Wild Shore

Young, beautiful and newly widowed, Elizabeth Troy travels to her late husband's Cornish home hoping to find comfort in its fertile hills and valleys. But she is shocked to discover the vast, decaying acreage of Pallas is now solely her responsibility – a legacy as unexpected as it is unwelcome.

Elizabeth's plans for her inheritance provoke the bitter hostility of her sister-in-law, Morwenna, whose word has been law at Pallas for thirty years. To bring the troubled estate back to prosperity Elizabeth must look for help elsewhere. And there are many very willing to be more than a friend to the widow – David Troy, a poor relation whose sober exterior hides some disturbing secrets; Courtenay Rodda, the sensual newspaper proprietor; and James Troy, the rich and worldly wise American cousin who begins a thrilling but dangerous liaison with Elizabeth . . .

'The book is beautifully written, the characters depicted with a passionate realism that held me entranced. I simply loved it!' Patricia Wendorf, bestselling author of *Larksleve*.

FICTION 0-7472-3001-3 £2.95

More compulsive fiction from Headline:

HARRY BOWLING

Conner Street's War

Behind the grimy wharves of London's docklands lies Conner Street, where women stand gossiping in doorways, small boys play marbles on the cobbles and the dockers pop down the 'Eagle' for a quick pint. Corner shops nestle beside tiny terraced houses and two minutes away is the Tower Road market where, it's said, if you can't buy something then it's not made.

Children swap cigarette cards while the wardens hand out gas masks. And when the wail of the air raid siren splits the night all of Conner Street rushes out to the shelter . . . silly Bobbie – a bit slow since his father beat him round the head once too often; Patrick Flannagan, the genial Irishman who likes a drop and Stanley Nathan the grocer who falls for pretty Julie Brett, little guessing her dark past. Meanwhile, down the 'Eagle', Florrie the landlady tempts innocent Albert Conlin behind the blackout curtains with disastrous consequences . . .

FICTION/GENERAL 0 7472 3063 3 £2.50

More compulsive fiction from Headline

Reflections IN BLACK GLASS

MARY MELWOOD

Bella Dashby owns land and marries land. To her it is more important than people. "It's only land that lasts," she says, "and the only way we'll last is when we're buried in it."

Archie and Cyrus Millander are half-brothers, owners of Painsmort, a prosperous farm in Nottinghamshire. Cyrus, who marries Bella, is as hungry for land as she, and they devote their lives to enlarging their estate. But for gentle, warm-hearted Archie, happiness is life with Clio and their children, and his mystical attachment to Black Glass, a scrap of marshland he believes is his birthright.

When he loses this with the rest of his inheritance, Archie is forced to accept charity from Bella and Cyrus. Infected by the belief that only the ownership of land confers prestige and dignity, Clio lets disappointment and envy sour her life, tainting her feelings even for Archie and their children. But the full force of her bitterness is turned towards Bella, who seems to possess everything that Clio desires.

"A fine study in compassionate observation." Irish Times
"The story . . . has a satisfying realism about its telling."
Irish Independent

FICTION/GENERAL 0 7472 3120 6 £2.99